continued . . .

"Extraordinary . . . powerful."   —*Library Journal*

"Gripping reading."   —*Pen & Dagger*

"Powerful . . . Without polemic, Harris gives us survivors, women who find strength alone and together, to stop the violence and rebuild their lives. *A Secret Rage* is a very special, very real statement as well as an excellent novel of suspense."   —*Wilson Library Journal*

PRAISE FOR
Sweet and Deadly

"A first-rate mystery with special character . . . As convincing as it is surprising in the final revelation."
—*The Washington Post*

"Harris writes neatly and with assurance, and she avoids the goo that makes equivalent books so sticky."
—*The New York Times Book Review*

"Packs a perennial punch. It offers a rarity in popular fiction: an unromanticized portrait of a Southern Girl."
—*The Philadelphia Inquirer*

A Secret Rage

CHARLAINE HARRIS

BERKLEY PRIME CRIME, NEW YORK

THE BERKLEY PUBLISHING GROUP
Published by the Penguin Group
Penguin Group (USA) Inc.
375 Hudson Street, New York, New York 10014, USA
Penguin Group (Canada), 90 Eglinton Avenue East, Suite 700, Toronto, Ontario M4P 2Y3, Canada
(a division of Pearson Penguin Canada Inc.)
Penguin Books Ltd., 80 Strand, London WC2R 0RL, England
Penguin Group Ireland, 25 St. Stephen's Green, Dublin 2, Ireland (a division of Penguin Books Ltd.)
Penguin Group (Australia), 250 Camberwell Road, Camberwell, Victoria 3124, Australia
(a division of Pearson Australia Group Pty. Ltd.)
Penguin Books India Pvt. Ltd., 11 Community Centre, Panchsheel Park, New Delhi—110 017, India
Penguin Group (NZ), 67 Apollo Drive, Rosedale, North Shore 0745, Auckland, New Zealand
(a division of Pearson New Zealand Ltd.)
Penguin Books (South Africa) (Pty.) Ltd., 24 Sturdee Avenue, Rosebank, Johannesburg 2196,
South Africa

Penguin Books Ltd., Registered Offices: 80 Strand, London WC2R 0RL, England

This is a work of fiction. Names, characters, places, and incidents either are the product of the author's imagination or are used fictitiously, and any resemblance to actual persons, living or dead, business establishments, events, or locales is entirely coincidental. The publisher does not have any control over and does not assume any responsibility for author or third-party websites or their content.

A SECRET RAGE

A Berkley Prime Crime Book / published by arrangement with the author

PRINTING HISTORY
Houghton Mifflin hardcover edition / January 1984
Ballantine mass-market edition / July 1985
Berkley Prime Crime mass-market edition / August 2007

Copyright © 1984 by Charlaine Harris Schulz.
Excerpt from *An Ice Cold Grave* © 2007 by Charlaine Harris, Inc.
Cover art by Diane Fenster.
Cover design by Judith Lagerman.
Interior text design by Kristin del Rosario.

ISBN: 978-0-425-21453-4

BERKLEY® PRIME CRIME
Berkley Prime Crime Books are published by The Berkley Publishing Group,
a division of Penguin Group (USA) Inc.,
375 Hudson Street, New York, New York 10014.
The name BERKLEY PRIME CRIME and the BERKLEY PRIME CRIME design
are trademarks belonging to Penguin Group (USA) Inc.

PRINTED IN THE UNITED STATES OF AMERICA

10 9 8 7 6 5 4 3 2

For Donna

It looked as if a night of dark intent
Was coming, and not only a night, an age.
Someone had better be prepared for rage.

—ROBERT FROST

Chapter 1

TRAFFIC NOISES AND STINGING SMOGGY AIR AND men brushing against me. I marched through the stream of the city, looking purposeful, not meeting glances, in the style I had learned kept me safest.

Two blocks to go until I reached my apartment, two blocks to go until I could drop my street mask. I was wondering if I had any wine in my refrigerator when I saw the crowd gathered in front of my building. I was too angry to work my way to the back entrance, too anxious to reach my own place and indulge in some heavy self-pity. I waded through the crowd until I reached its center hollow containing the snag around which the debris had accumulated.

She was gray-haired and gray-faced. Her blood was still fluid and bright on the filthy sidewalk beneath her head. I had never seen a dead woman before.

"Miss Callahan!" a voice said at my elbow. My doorman was quivering with excitement.

"What happened, Jesus?" I asked. I tried not to look, but I caught myself flicking sideways glances at the dead woman.

"Kid grab her purse, threw her off balance, she hit the sidewalk, *thunk!*" Jesus' English was not perfect, but it was graphic.

"You call the police?"

"Sure. They be here in a minute. Ambulance, too. I saw the whole thing, I was a witness!" Then Jesus' face altered from sheer excitement to dismay. He had suddenly realized the inconvenience of involvement.

"Can you get me in the building?"

"Oh, sure, Miss Callahan."

Jesus gave value for his Christmas tip. He waded into the crowd, elbows flying: a little tug pulling a much loftier ship into harbor. I was at least six inches taller than my doorman, but my fighting spirit was diminished by the day I'd had.

I reinforced Jesus' Christmas when I was safely inside the lobby doors, then began the stairs at a fast clip. I heard the sirens coming near, drowning out Jesus' voluble thanks.

I always took the stairs instead of the elevator, for the benefit of my leg muscles; but I regretted it by the time I reached my apartment. Reaction hit as I fished my keys from my purse. I worked the keys in the locks with clumsy fingers. Once inside, and after relocking, I pulled my hat off and felt my hair tumble down my back. I'd just jammed it on any which way at my agent's office; I'd been too upset to put it on properly. I took off my dark glasses (more protective camouflage) and headed for the refrigerator. Even my own apartment—everything in it beautiful to me, chosen with love, arranged with care—didn't give me any comfort today.

The afternoon was overcast, so my living room was dark. I didn't switch on any lights. The gloom suited my mood, and the wine suited my gloom.

I thought I would drink a glass, brood, and maybe cry a little; but my dark side drew me into my bedroom, to the waiting mirror. I sat on the stool before my so-aptly-named vanity. There I did switch on the lights. I took a second swallow of wine and then gave myself up to the mirror.

It was the same face.

Sometimes I didn't even feel I owned it. It had been grafted onto me. I lived behind it, and it earned my living. I took care of it; it took care of me.

My agent had just told me that it wasn't going to take care of me anymore. People were tired of it. There were newer, fresher faces.

But the face was still beautiful. I touched it with respect. Straight nose, high broad cheekbones, blue eyes, beautiful skin. Carefully drawn lips. Neat chin. Blonde hair to frame the whole assemblage.

And people were tired of this?

Yes, according to my agent.

"I swanny, Nellie Jean, some people shore are finicky," I told my mirror. Then I turned away from it and buried my face in my hands.

At twenty-seven, I was overexposed and going down the other side of the hill. And I was lucky I'd lasted the years I had, my agent had told me today, shaking an elegant copper fingernail under my nose for emphasis.

"If you didn't have some brains, you wouldn't have lasted this long. Quit while you're ahead. I'm your friend." ("Right, sure, uh-huh," I muttered through my fingers now.) "Otherwise, I'd let you drag on and on and get every little cent I could. I'm doing you a favor, Nickie."

I swung back around and stared into that mirror for five minutes. And I made myself admit she had been my friend and had done me a favor.

I was sick of my own vanity and how easily it could be wounded. It was what came of living off my face.

"You have other irons in the fire, Nickie," my agent's voice retold me in my head. "You're burned out on this business yourself; I know. I can tell. The camera can tell. And you can't tell me you love the camera like you used to."

Before I turned from that mirror, I made myself admit that everything she had said was true.

So that was that.

I switched on a lamp in the living room and put on my

reading glasses. I turned to my solace in times of great trouble—Jane Austen. I could open any chapter of any book of Jane's and immediately feel more peaceful. Tonight, Jane worked almost as well as she usually did; but I had to put a box of tissues on the table beside the lamp. I caught myself wandering, thinking bitterly that at least the woman on the sidewalk had no more woes; and I slapped my cheek in rebuke. Melodramatic, foolish.

I buried myself in the troubles of Miss Elinor Dashwood, until I felt able to sleep.

BY NEXT MORNING MY COMMON SENSE HAD raised its head. I woke up with a mild hangover from crying, set the coffeepot to perking, and did my exercises while I waited for it to finish. Since I was no longer a model, I treated myself to butter on my toast. I riffled idly through the morning paper to find a mention of the woman on the sidewalk, and found she had rated one brief paragraph. I wasn't surprised.

Since I'd had more unbooked days in the past year than I'd cared to notice, I was accustomed to free time. But now that I knew that part of my life was over, I felt jangly, at loose ends. The once-weekly cleaning woman had done her job while I was gone the day before, so I hadn't even straightening up to do. I scanned the titles in my bookshelves, trying to find something worth rereading; I had to save Jane for crises. Nothing seemed to strike a chord.

It occurred to me that I could try reworking one of my own novels again, but I felt too drained to be creative in a major way. My eyes roamed around the room for something that looked fruitful. The only item that held instant appeal was the blank notepad I kept by the telephone.

I love to make lists.

A grocery list? Not sufficiently enterprising. After a thoughtful moment, I decided that this morning was a prime time to Count My Blessings. I sharpened a pencil and set to.

1. Nice apartment, good location; but lease due to be renewed

2. Money in the bank, money invested, and a smart (and reasonably honest) financial counselor

3. Two brilliant novels that have been unaccountably rejected by dimwitted publishers

4. Friends. My agent, a couple of other models, a photographer or two, and some bona fide beautiful people whom I suspected would prove to be in the fair-weather category—and, of course, Mimi

5. Furniture and books

6. Jewelry

7. Clothes

8. Brains, undisciplined

I hesitated. I wanted to make as long a list as possible, but I really couldn't include my mother among my assets. And the only male-female relationship I had going was casual to the point of boredom. I finally settled on:

9. Southern background

10. Fair education, as far as it went

Surely there was something else? But after a moment's brooding I couldn't come up with anything.

The list as it stood wasn't bad, however. I could be proud of achieving financial security at twenty-seven, right? Modeling had been good to me, if not good for me.

The phone interrupted my pleasant contemplation of my bank account. I reached for it absently, my pencil still tapping the list, itching to write "11."

"Nick?" The voice had the remote buzz of long distance.

"Mimi? It *is* Mimi!" I said delightedly. "Hey, I was just thinking about you."

"It's me all right. Hey, honey, how are you?"

"Mimi, I'm so glad to hear your voice. Just talk for a while, and let me hear that accent." Sometimes I felt I lived in a land of squawking blue jays. The sound of home gave my ears a rest.

"Well, I called to talk, so I might as well. Listen, Richard left me and divorced me. I mean, we're divorced."

"Whoosh." I made a hit-in-the-pit-of-the-stomach sound, an exact evocation of what I felt. "Okay," I said after a second. "I've absorbed that."

"Good," she said, and started crying. "I haven't. After one of those painting trips of his, he came home for one day, and he said—while I was changing the sheets, can you believe that?—he said, 'You know, Mimi dear, this just isn't working out for us, is it? If you aren't petty enough to contest it, I think I'll go to Mexico or somewhere and get a quickie divorce.' "

"Just like that?" I asked weakly.

"Nickie, I assure you. Just like that."

"Has he come back to Knolls?"

"Oh no." The temperature of Mimi's voice dropped to freezing. "He's in Albuquerque. Since he needed some of the stuff he left, he wrote me. He's living with a *fantastic* woman who makes her own jewelry. She's never in her life cut her hair. She can," Mimi said venomously, "*sit* on it."

My nose wrinkled. "Good God, Mimi. That alone should tell you something about Richard. Never cut her hair? Yuck."

"You won the bet," Mimi said.

"What? What bet?"

"Remember the bet you had with Grandmama?"

"Oh. Oh, hell. How'd you know about that?"

"She told me while she was in the hospital. She was sort of weak and wandery towards the end, you know, but she still thought that was real funny. She told me that even if I got divorced right away, she owed you five dollars because

Richard and I had stayed married more than two years. She told me to be sure I gave you your money."

I entertained myself with a pleasant fantasy of stringing Richard up by his—toes. If he'd had the sensitivity of a table, he'd have realized he was dealing Mimi a blow on top of an unhealed wound. Celeste, Mimi's grandmother, had died only five months ago. I'd been very fond of Celeste; she had been my substitute grandmother, since all my grandparents were dead. Mimi had been especially close to Celeste.

"Well, I guess I'll be all right," Mimi was saying unconvincingly. "I just wanted to call you to cry on your shoulder. I expect I didn't love him anyway. He was really awful selfish. But good-looking, wasn't he? Oh, Nick, I feel so durn old! I've been married and divorced twice now, and I'm only twenty-seven."

I was feeling pretty old myself, so I couldn't whip up the energy to give Mimi a pep talk.

"I've wailed enough now. How are you?" Mimi asked. "Tell me you're raking in money from modeling, and some big publisher gave you a huge advance for your book, and you're dating a beautiful man who's single and rich and good in bed."

"Ho ho ho," I said nastily. "I'm washed up as a model; my agent dumped me yesterday. I have writer's block, following rejection by three major publishers. The only man pursuing me with any enthusiasm is my landlord, because he wants me to renew my lease."

Thoughtful silence.

"Hmmm. Were you serious, in your last letter, about wanting to go back to finish college?"

"I've thought about it," I admitted cautiously. "Why?"

"Then why don't you come live with me and finish school at Houghton?"

I pantomimed amazement for my own benefit, staring at the receiver and holding it away. Then I pressed it close to my ear again, lit a cigarette, and quit fooling. "Are you serious? You're serious."

"I mean it," Mimi said. "I'm selling my house. I can't stand to live in it anymore, after two bad marriages. I'm moving into Grandmother's house, she left it to me. I had planned on selling it, but I just haven't been able to bring myself to actually list it with a realtor. Then I thought yesterday, 'Aha! I'll just move into it myself!' I'll be a lot closer to campus, and I've always loved that house."

"Me too," I said, and the memories began to crowd in. The high ceilings, the large rooms . . .

"—but you know, it's real big. We wouldn't fall all over each other, and you could go to Houghton. I have furniture and you have furniture and we ought to be able to fill up the house between us."

"What happened to all Celeste's furniture?"

"Oh, she left different pieces to different people: the great-aunts, Cully, Mama, and Daddy. After all, I got the house. Can I have the top story? I've lived in a ranch style so long. I want to be up in the treetops and climb stairs."

"You can have whatever you want; it's your house," I said unguardedly.

"Yahoo!"

What had I done? I couldn't possibly . . . I opened my mouth to retract, but then I snapped it shut. I pinched myself. I listened to Mimi's beautiful southern voice running on and on. I ached to see her. I imagined hearing only that accent around me—no more squawking blue jays. I thought of the old woman dead on the sidewalk. I imagined walking down the street *unafraid*. I remembered my agent's copper fingernail waving in my face. I thought of the heap of typing paper lying pristine in my top desk drawer, and I wondered if the discipline of study and the stimulation of reading other writers would give my writing a better chance of success. I thought of clean air, and space, and jonquils, and Mimi's laughter. Knolls, Tennessee.

I'd been desperately homesick, and I hadn't known it until this moment.

"Do you really mean it?" Mimi was asking anxiously.

"Why not?" I said, after one more second's hesitation.

"Oh, when? When?" she asked jubilantly.

"Let me get to work on it." I ripped the list of my assets off the pad; it had lost its interest. I began a new one: lease, movers, Con Ed, Bell, post office. The pad was filling up even as I spoke.

Over all those miles, Mimi said accusingly, "Nickie! Quit making one of your lists and give me a time estimate! I have to move my own stuff, too!"

"I'll call you back tomorrow," I promised. "Can I have that bedroom by the stairs?"

"You can have any room in the house."

When I hung up, I was tingling with excitement. Out of New York. A complete change. I took a moment of peace before the scurry began, to think of how I would arrange my furniture in my bedroom-to-be—the big one off the hall on the ground floor. It was difficult to visualize it empty.

When Mimi and I had spent the night with Grandmother Celeste, we had always had that bedroom off the hall. We'd slept in a beautiful four-poster. Every night we'd crawled into that bed we'd felt like princesses; safe and beautiful and destined for everlasting fame. In the summer, we'd switch on the fan and watch it circle against the ceiling. In the winter, there was a beautiful old hand-stitched quilt that Celeste's mother had made . . . Even as we grew older we still felt the same about that bed.

All those years and seasons.

We had met, Mimi and I, when we were fourteen—thrown together as terrified roommates at Miss Beacham's Academy for Girls in Memphis. I was from a small town in northern Mississippi. As our yearbook put it, Mimi "hailed" from Knolls, Tennessee, east of Memphis. Her christened name was Miriam Celeste Houghton, which I decided was beautiful and romantic. I disliked my own, Nichola Lynn Callahan; I thought it sounded like my parents had wanted a boy.

Mimi Houghton had Background. In Knolls, there was a Houghton Street, a Houghton Library, and of course,

Houghton College. Fortunately, I didn't know any of this until Mimi and I were already close friends.

Mimi had come to Miss Beacham's because her mother, Elaine, had gone to school there. I had been sent by my father, to keep me away from my mother, who was becoming an alcoholic.

I don't know if Father was right to send me away or not. My mother's drinking began to increase after I left home, as if my presence had been holding her in check. But I guess she would have accelerated her drinking in time anyway. I try not to criticize Father in hindsight. He meant to protect me from ugliness. Then, too, the fights between Mother and me outweighed the pleasure he got from my company when I was home. He was a plain and straightforward man. He didn't understand that the bitter scenes did not happen because I didn't love my mother but because I did love her.

I suppose Mimi had explained my situation to her parents, Elaine and Don. They always made me welcome.

As my home gradually became a place to fear, a haunted house, I began to see my parents for only a couple of days each short vacation, maybe a couple of weeks during the long summer breaks. After my duty times at home, my father would drive me to Mimi's. At first we were close on those drives; but as time passed, a silence fell between us. We couldn't talk about the thing that most concerned us. He dreaded what he would find when he returned home. His hours at his law office lengthened and lengthened. He became well-to-do and far too busy. He probably suspected the condition of his heart, but he never mentioned it to me or my mother. Aside from making a will, he didn't prepare for the cataclysm at all.

When I was a senior at Miss Beacham's, my father died of a heart attack in his office. Six months later, my mother remarried. The tragedies were too close. I didn't absorb either of them for years.

I went home once following my mother's remarriage. I hoped she needed me despite her new husband, Jay

Chalmers. The second day I was home, my mother left to attend some bridge-club function. Thank God the builder had installed sturdy doors with sturdy locks. I had to stay in the bathroom for two hours, until Jay passed out. (He drank, too.) It was mostly dirty talk, and a clumsy attempt to kiss me; but quite enough, from an older man, to terrify a seventeen-year-old. Though he hadn't managed to lay a finger on me, I felt dirty and guilty; I was very young. That evening, I packed my bags and made Mother take me to the bus station. I trumped up a story about having forgotten some school committee meeting for which I had to return early. When Mimi came back from her own weekend at home, I told her what had happened. Then I threw up.

I'd always planned on going to Houghton College with Mimi. Since the college had been founded by her great-grandfather, naturally she had been enrolled from birth. But Mother and Jay were spending Mother's portion of what my father had left as if there were no tomorrow; and since I wouldn't inherit my share till I became twenty-one, I had no money of my own yet. His own shame and guilt having crystallized into hostility, Jay told me there just wasn't enough for Houghton's steep tuition. So I enrolled in an obscure, cheaper college, living carefully and earning a little extra from modeling for department stores and regional magazine ads, as I'd begun doing at Miss Beacham's.

One of the store buyers casually remarked that I should go to New York and try my hand at professional modeling. The idea took hold. I needed a change, and at that point college meant very little to me. I was about to turn twenty-one; and I'd be receiving a small steady income from investments my father had made in my name, plus a moderate lump sum.

I vividly remember calling Mimi in her dorm room at Houghton to tell her about my resolution. She was stunned by my courage. I was, too. It was the bravado of sheer ignorance. Even now, it seems amazing to me that the city didn't chew me up and spit me out.

For the first two months, my heart was constantly in my

mouth. Where I came from, New York qualified as a synonym for hell. It had the glamour of hell, though. Inadequately armed with a little money and a short list of names, I scuttled through the streets of the Big City.

Luckily for me, two of those names on my list paid off. A former fraternity brother of my father's helped me find a place to live, fed me some meals and some invaluable advice, and withdrew his hands when I shook my head. A connection of the buyer's steered me to a reputable agency who liked my looks.

And I caught on. Within a year, I was able to move out of the hole I'd been sharing with three other women, into my own place. I slowly acquired the most beautiful furniture and rugs I could afford: that was very important to me. I bought books. I began to write a little myself. I imagine I was trying to refute the "beautiful but dumb" image that clings to models.

That year was a golden year. I was given up utterly to the mirror.

Toward the end of that year, which had been a big one for Mimi too, I returned to Knolls for her first wedding. The groom was a down-home good ol' boy she'd met at Houghton.

In a moment of absolute insanity, I picked an outrageous dress to wear to the rehearsal dinner. I was far too full of myself as a glamorous model. That dress was the most serious social mistake I had ever made.

I brazened it out, though I almost began screaming the fifth time I heard Mimi's mother murmur, "Well, you know, she *is* a New York model." (Elaine was defending Mimi, not me.) I realized that for years I would be "that friend of Mimi's who wore that dress to Mimi's rehearsal dinner." I knew my home ground.

I drank too much that night, rare for me with Mother's example before my eyes. And I alternated sulking with self-reproach all the way back to New York.

At Mimi's second wedding—the good ol' boy had lasted eight months, Mimi's mother talked the marriage to death—I wore a completely proper, even severe, outfit. Even after the passage of two years, I wasn't *about* to forget my lesson. It did help a lot; I read that in the approving smiles and extra pats on the shoulder, the little nods the ladies gave each other. But my redemption had less exposure than my damnation, since this was a much smaller wedding, of course. It was "solemnized" in the living room of Celeste's big house.

Since Mimi was coming down the stairs alone, having vetoed attendants altogether, I sat with Celeste. We skirted our fears for Mimi (we didn't like Richard, we had decided after a little conference) by laying bets on how long the marriage would last. Celeste bet on Richard's doing something unforgivable in the first two years. I laid my money on Mimi's pride and gave it three.

The marriage dragged on for almost four years; and when Richard decamped to Albuquerque, Celeste posthumously owed me five dollars.

Chapter 2

As a child, I'd always imagined that the Memphis airport looked like champagne glasses cast in concrete. I still thought of it that way, though I was now far more familiar with champagne glasses.

It was a pleasure to be in it again, a delight to see Mimi waiting for me as I emerged from the gate. We held each other tight with a pure joy I had almost forgotten.

When I stepped out of the terminal, I knew I was home. There'd been tinges of fall in New York. It was hot as hell, full summer, in Memphis. I began sweating as we loaded my bags into the trunk of Mimi's Chevrolet. The sweat became the signal of homecoming. I took a deep lungful of the heavy humid air that clings to the skin like a soggy body stocking.

After the initial shrieking and hugging and inquiries about my trip, Mimi and I were a little shy with each other. To get past the inevitable period of adjustment to each other's physical presence, Mimi told me about the changes in Memphis. The Peabody Hotel had been re-opened. The population had grown. The crime rate was up. Elvis Presley's death had gradually made Whitehaven, suburban site of Gracelands, a traffic nightmare and a tourist trap. But Memphis would always be dear to us from our years at Miss Beacham's.

"And Knolls?" I asked. "How many Seven-Elevens now?"

"One bona fide and two imitations. Quickie Snackie Pickies, or Stomp 'n Grabs, or some such abominations," Mimi said sadly. "And a Burger King, and a Hardee's, and two McDonald's—I guess because of the college. But they can't come close to the campus," she said in clear triumph. "It's all residential for blocks. Zoned, by God! Signed, sealed, and delivered!"

Getting Knolls zoned had been Mimi's latest battle. No one had ever seen the need before.

"Maybe a little inconvenient for students without a car," I suggested, pokerfaced.

"Tough luck," said Mimi callously, scanning her entrance to the expressway with care. And quite rightly: Memphis drivers tend to have very individual styles.

She expanded on the zoning battle when we were safely heading east. The whole brouhaha had been set off—the gauntlet flung down—when Mimi had discovered a restaurant owner was trying to buy one of the very few rundown houses close to Houghton College, with the vile purpose of converting it into a so-called student hangout.

"With an *amusement arcade*," Mimi told me grimly.

When I laughed, she stared at me indignantly before she began laughing too. At that moment, I felt we'd never been apart.

Mimi is a sort of hybrid, like a lot of young southern women. Like me. She is part carefully bred elitist, though she tries very hard not to be, and she is also a partisan who believes fervently that women are equal to (or better than) men in most ways. The clash and combination of these two parts of Mimi have produced an unpredictable woman. I never knew which half would win out in any given internal argument between the two parts of my friend. I only knew that the partisan side had an awful habit of vanishing when Mimi cared for a man. Mimi was always the most traditional bride and wife imaginable. Blushes, deference, hot suppers every night. In one of my stupider moments, between husbands one and two, I had—gently, I thought—pointed this out to Mimi. It took her three weeks to forgive me.

"Did my furniture get here okay, really?"

"Very few scratches," she reassured me. "One broken bowl, one dented tray. Duly entered on the little form. They like to have never found the house, though. The driver told me that everyone he asked kept telling him it was 'just down the street a little bit, look for the big magnolia.' He'd never seen a magnolia, can you believe it? I went on and arranged all the furniture, so you'll just have to tell me if it doesn't suit you."

"I imagine it will." The thrill of saying "I imagine" again! And Mimi had actually said, "They like to have never." I couldn't stand it, I was so happy. Superficial, I know, but signs I was home.

I took a deep breath. "How are you all doing?" I asked proudly.

Everyone in New York had felt obliged to say that to me. They had completely misunderstood the term, always using it as singular. I'd corrected people at first, until I found they thought that was even funnier. After a few such laugh fiestas, I had omitted it from my conversation consciously.

"We're all fine," Mimi answered casually. "Daddy had a summer cold last month, but he's okay now. Mama's joined the DAR, which I should've expected, I guess . . . at least it keeps her busy and out of my hair. And Cully's settled in okay. All he could find was a weentsy garage apartment, but he flat refused to move in with our parents. Which was smart of him."

My smug contentment vanished. "Cully?" I said stiffly. "Settled in where?"

"In Knolls."

"You didn't tell me."

"Well, with all my own news, I guess I just forgot. He's been back about a month now, I think." Her voice was overly casual.

With an effort, I closed my lips on more questions. I would find out about Cully later. It was ridiculous of me to react so strongly.

Now, I wanted to look out the windows at the fields rolling by; cotton and soybeans. Some rice—that was a new development. I soaked up the sights like a sponge: the chickens loose in the yards of the tenant houses, the earthen sidewalks lined with Coke bottles or tire halves, the horizon unbounded by concrete and brick, the late-summer limpness of the foliage.

We whizzed by a grove of pecan trees that abutted a beautiful house. Its front yard would have contained my apartment building.

The landscape grew more and more familiar. I grew easier with every mile. Every sentence began, "Oh, there's . . . !" The John Deere place, the bait shop, the wonderfully named Maubob Motel (Maureen and Bob Pitts, proprietors), Grandma's Sizzlin' Steaks, Grace Funeral Home . . .

By the time we were into Knolls, any doubts I had had were gone. When we pulled into the driveway of Celeste's old home, our new home, I had put them behind me, along with New York City.

"A GIRL GOT RAPED HERE THIS SUMMER," MIMI said suddenly.

I looked over at her. I had been stroking the cats in perfect peace. She was sprinkling oregano into the pot of sauce bubbling on the stove.

"Here?" I was surprised.

"Yes, here. On the campus."

Since Mimi was a Houghton, no doubt the location of the attack seemed almost as deplorable to her as the fact that it had happened.

"At night?" I saw a snag on my index fingernail and rummaged in my purse for a file.

"Yes, of course." It was Mimi's turn to sound surprised. Knolls might endure the shame of an occasional rape, but certainly not in *broad daylight*, I gathered.

"White girl?" And I pinched myself, hard. I'd fallen right into the same old pattern. The first question, always the first question, when anything had happened to anyone, be it wreck, kidnapping, assault, sudden death, or a win in a sweepstakes: *Are they white? Is she black?*

"Yeah. A freshman student named Heidi Edmonds. She wanted to get in a few courses before the fall semester began." After tasting the sauce, Mimi added a pinch of salt.

"I don't know why a crime always seems so much more evil if the victim is virtuous," she said thoughtfully, "but it does, doesn't it? Heidi was everything in her high school, Nickie. Valedictorian, Honor Society, National Merit Scholar. The kind of student we love to get. Since I'm on the admissions board, I'd seen her application. And I'd met her at one of those punch-and-cookies receptions."

So Mimi knew the girl. Heidi Edmonds's little tragedy began to have flesh. I shifted on the breakfast-nook bench to make more room for the cats; Attila and Mao praised me with purrs for my intelligence. Mimi, finally satisfied with the meat sauce, turned and propped one hip against the stove.

"It's so good just to see you sitting there," she said.

"It can't look as good as it feels."

But the warm moment passed when Mimi's face tensed again. She really wanted to finish her story. "She was on that sidewalk that meanders through the gardens. It goes indirectly from the library to the women's dorm area—you remember? It's been years since you were on campus; I keep forgetting."

I did remember, vaguely. I nodded.

"Then of course you remember how tall those camellias are? They're old as the hills, and just huge, and they grow on both sides of the sidewalk there. She had a big armful of books, because she'd been studying at the library until it was about to close; nine or thereabouts. It hadn't been dark that long—you know how long it takes to get dark in the summer. But it was dark."

It was dark outside now at half past seven, with the season coming to a close. The secret night outside the bay window suddenly made me anxious. I got up to close the three sets of blinds covering the sections of the window. I didn't want to hear any more. But Mimi, I decided, would think I was selfish and callous if I cut her off.

She had always been a good storyteller. Her thin hands and dark eyes worked together to illustrate her narrative.

"... he was in the camellias, or just beyond. He came through the bushes and grabbed her from behind. She dropped all her books and papers, naturally. That's how they found her—a couple looking for a place to smooch. They wondered why there were books all over the sidewalk."

"She was *dead*?" I thought of gray hair and red blood against a dirty sidewalk. The woman had not crossed my mind since Mimi's phone call. I felt goose bumps tighten the skin of my arms.

"No, no. Unconscious. Evidently, when he grabbed her, she fell and hit her head on the concrete. He'd dragged her off the sidewalk into the dark. And raped her. And slapped her around a little bit." Mimi's voice had gotten crisper and crisper, as it does when she's talking about difficult things. "Maybe—I think—he was trying to bring her to, so she wouldn't miss anything. Her face was pretty badly bruised."

The muscles of my own face tightened and pinched. Beaten in the face. What if someone had done that to me in New York, when I was just starting out?

"I went to see her in the hospital—representing the college, you know. The dean of women was out of town. Jeff Simmons—you won't remember him, he's the college president now—he kept saying that since I'm a woman, it would be better for me to go than him." Besides pity and anger, Mimi's mouth showed a certain distaste. "A dirty job he just dumped on me."

I made a face, to show I'd registered the cowardice of Jeff Simmons. Yet I thought that he might have been right.

I started to ask Mimi what had happened to Heidi Edmonds afterward; if the police had been kind to her, and so on. I was curious, finally. But alerted by the hiss of the boiling water, Mimi had turned back to the stove to break up the vermicelli.

"To tell the truth," she said over her shoulder, "I kind of wondered if her folks would sue the college for negligence."

"Did they?"

Mimi dropped in a handful of pasta. "Never even mentioned it," she answered absently. "Her father turned out to be a minister. I've gone over and over it, the whole incident, trying to see how Houghton could have prevented what happened. But I swear I just can't think of anything we could've done, Nick. The sidewalk was well lit. The actual distance the girl had to walk wasn't that far. And she could've called one of the security guards to walk her back to the dorm. That's in the brochure for freshman women. Not that I think any of them have ever done that, because this has always been such a quiet town. But it is possible to have an escort if you want one."

I mentally filed that fact. I would begin attending Houghton in a few days. Maybe I would be working late at the library some nights.

I had to ask one last question. "She couldn't identify the guy?"

"She never saw his face," Mimi answered tersely.

The goose bumps spread to my chest. Celeste would have said someone was walking on my grave. I lifted the orange tabby, Attila, and hugged him for the comfort of his warm fur. He wriggled indignantly out of my arms and stalked to the kitchen door, loudly requesting that Mimi let him out.

And I watched Mimi double-lock the door behind the cat's retreating tail.

That one small act told me how much Mimi had taken

to heart what had occurred in the late-summer darkness on Houghton campus. I could not remember a house in Knolls ever being locked, all the years I'd visited Mimi.

WE TALKED HALF THE NIGHT. WE'D FAITHFULLY written and called each other during all the years of separation; but even communication as constant as ours didn't equal face-to-face conversation.

Mimi rehashed Richard's defection. I decided that though she was sincerely grieved, mostly her pride had suffered. Mimi had always been the leaver, not the left, even when she'd had to scramble to get out the door first.

And naturally, I in turn rehashed the mortification of being an old face after a few years in the limelight; though I'd never exactly been a top model, I'd had my share of magazine covers.

Well, a few, anyway.

The second novel I'd shakily put together in my steadily increasing leisure time had actually gotten a very long letter of rejection from one publisher. As I explained to Mimi what a good sign that was, and she grew excited about that rejection, I realized how much I had needed her.

The evening was just a little cool, courtesy of a light breeze that puffed the curtains inward. My furniture had been arranged with Mimi's sure hand around the huge (by New York standards) living room. Mimi had given me the ground floor bedroom I had requested. It lay off the hall running from the living room to the kitchen.

Celeste's was not a grand house but a large old family home. All the rooms were big, with the original high ceilings. When Mimi mentioned having to turn on the furnace in a few weeks, we thought of the probable heating bill and exchanged grimaces of dismay.

Mimi yawned, crumpled an empty cigarette pack, and pitched it toward the wastecan. Siamese Mao intercepted the pack with a lightning paw and began batting it around between my rugs. Those rugs looked beautiful against the hardwood floor, I noticed with pleasure.

"Want to hear about Cully?" Mimi asked.

"I guess so." I kept my gaze carefully fixed on Mao. "Rachel's consented to live in little old Knolls?"

Cully's wife had strong and strange ideas about the South and small towns. Rachel was from New York. I'd seen them a couple of times when they'd come up to visit her family.

"He and Rachel just got divorced, too. The Houghton children don't have a very good batting average when it comes to staying married."

So Cully was divorced. I set my teeth against asking why she hadn't told me before. But there were some questions I couldn't repress.

"Why did Cully come back here? Weren't they living in Memphis? What happened?"

"He was living in Memphis. And he came back here to lick his wounds, like me. Except I have so many, I have to stay here all the time." Mimi laughed halfheartedly. "There's nothing like living in a town with a college, street, and library named after you. Anytime you have an identity crisis, you can just turn around and there's your name. Your *generic* name, anyway."

I pitched her a cigarette when she looked around to see if another pack was within reach. She caught it as gracefully as Mao. Mimi is always deft and quick. She is small-boned and dark, with black hair she wears like a lion's mane. She looked fragile that evening, and vivid, in a brilliantly patterned caftan. Mimi has never been afraid of strong colors.

"As to what happened, to answer your second—or third?—question. My theory about Rachel is that she was just doing an anthropological study about southern tribal customs. When she had enough material, she gave Cully the old heave-ho. I never understood that marriage, anyway. Of course I have a theory about that, too. I think Cully was searching for Mother's opposite." Mimi squinted at me through her smoke and jabbed the air to point out her own wisdom.

"Expound?"

"Oh. Well, Mother is still beautiful, resolutely unintellectual, committed to the social graces, and she's as conventional as they come. Her religion is being gracious. Rachel was—plain, to put it nicely. She'd gotten heavy into stuff like *The Dialectics of Sex*. And her idea of fancy entertaining was to pour some wine in the spaghetti sauce."

I laughed; I couldn't help it. Mimi's thumbnail sketches were an element of our intimacy. She had always sworn that no one else would remain her friend after hearing how nasty she could be.

"What Cully *missed* seeing," she said, carried away by the flow of her theory, "was that they are *both* bitches."

"*Shame* on you, calling your mama that," I said out of duty, though my mouth was twitching.

Mimi tried to look properly ashamed. She had weathervane reactions to her mother. There would be truces, sometimes for months, during which the two thought alike and got along very well; but inevitably an explosion would come—always when the partisan in Mimi was ascendant. The warfare never came completely into the open; it was a suspenseful guerrilla variety.

"By the way," Mimi said more soberly, "the college has hired Cully as a counselor for the students, and he's setting up a private practice. Don't holler nepotism, or at least not too loud, okay? A full two weeks before Cully decided he wanted to leave Memphis, our last counselor had some sudden health problems and told us he'd have to retire."

I was having my own thoughts. "Maybe Cully thinks I'm like your mother, and that's why he's always had such a thing about ignoring me," I ventured.

"Why didn't that occur to me before? I'll bet that's it. I can see a strictly superficial resemblance. Now there he is, a psychologist; and he's never figured all this out. Here we are, mere amateur analysts, and we have the whole thing solved in seconds. You're beautiful, and the image of the model is that she's a brainless nitwit. And you were brought up to have social graces, even though you may have lost them up north, I don't know." Mimi gave me a very wicked look. "So that might very well be." She picked up Mao and tickled the cat behind the ears. Attila, who had come back in, glared at this favoritism from behind a plant stand.

"I think you've just had this thing about Cully all these years because he's different around you."

"It is very true, Mimi-my-friend," I said heavily, "that your brother has always been 'different' around me."

When other boys were going to absurd lengths to bump into me accidentally, when other males were calling every dorm at Miss Beacham's until they found mine, when men were generally behaving like fools in my presence, Cully had stood resolutely untouched by The Face. Even worse (though less surprising) was his matching lack of interest in what lay beneath that face.

So I had had a mission since I was fourteen. My mission was to make Cully Houghton notice me. Since I am in most respects a normal healthy person, that ache of piqued vanity had subsided in recent years. I had recognized it for the childish thing it was. But the ache wasn't entirely gone. I had just begun to assess my power, and use it, when I met Cully Houghton. He had been my first—and for a long time, my only—failure.

"More power to you, if you're still attracted," Mimi said suddenly. "He needs someone. He really tried with Rachel. It just didn't work."

"Do you remember the expression on Rachel's face when I walked into your rehearsal dinner in that dress?" I asked.

"Are you still brooding about that?" Mimi said incredulously. "That was years and years ago."

"*You* can say that. You've never been on the receiving end of the polite freeze."

"Water under the bridge," Mimi said grandly. "And we'd better go to bed. You've got an appointment with your faculty adviser at eleven-thirty tomorrow morning. Barbara. Dr. Barbara Tucker to you, lowly student."

"Faculty adviser?"

"You've forgotten the ropes. She'll be your shepherd. Help you pick your schedule, approve your courses, et cetera. I zapped you through admission, but you have to pick out your courses and times, and Barbara should know by tomorrow how many of your hours from Elbridge have transferred."

"Look, Mimi, did you have to ram me down the college's throat?" I had known Mimi could get me admitted in time, but I had worried that scrambling in under her wing might make my presence resented.

"No, ninny. You had good grades, very good grades. Don't worry so much! There's been a slump in enrollment, so there was room for you. Even with the slump, there's no extra dorm room or parking spaces—those have been at a premium for years. Since you don't want either, they were practically panting. You'll like Barbara. I do. She's been here several years, and she's really fitted in well. She just got tenure. By the way," Mimi added delicately when I was halfway to my room, "you have to pay your fees this week. How's the money situation?"

"I'm a well-to-do woman," I told her firmly. "Don't even think of filthy lucre. I'm chipping in on the house expenses, of course. We'll have to sit down and work that out tomorrow."

"I think you have a fan," she remarked dryly.

I looked down to see Attila sitting before me, great green eyes fixed on my face in an unnerving stare. When the big cat was sure I was watching, he flopped over to expose a wide creamy belly and said, "Rowr."

"Don't be surprised if you have company tonight," Mimi warned me. "He's been sleeping on your bed ever since I set it up."

I observed Mao as she slept curled on Mimi's lap. Mao was a fancier's cat, fine-boned and graceful and purebred. I looked back at huge tawny Attila, who had the glow of mockery in his eyes and a generally self-satisfied expression. Since I didn't bend to scratch the proferred expanse of stomach, he rolled to his feet and began rubbing himself against my legs. I hoped there wasn't any unflattering significance in the cat's preference.

But I told the bathroom mirror that birds of a feather flocked together, before I crawled into bed with the cat.

I lay awake for a while, mulling over my good fortune. Just as I was drifting off to sleep, I thought about poor little Heidi Edmonds. I couldn't even recall the face of the dead woman on the sidewalk in New York. I could lose her in the city. But in little Knolls, I couldn't forget the tragedy of a girl I'd never seen.

I sent a wish for her recovery and well-being out into the ether, drowsily tickled Attila behind the ears, and blanked out with my hand still resting on the cat's broad back.

Chapter 3

I'D ALWAYS REGRETTED THAT CELESTE'S HOUSE didn't actually face the campus, whose landscaped gardens made a beautiful view; but the house stood only half a block away from the college's southwestern corner.

I borrowed Mimi's car for this first trip to the campus, since I didn't want to arrive for my appointment dripping with sweat. I should've realized the unfamiliar strain of driving would make me even more anxious than I already was. I bit my lip until I turned safely into the college's main drive. The campus was fully as impressive as I'd remembered—green and welcoming, if slightly frazzled near the end of the fierce summer.

With a glance I checked the campus map spread on the seat beside me, to verify the location of the English department. The college grounds were empty and quiet—in a dreamy calm before the storm of freshman students soon due for orientation. I saw the occasional parked car, so a few staff members had to be tucked away somewhere. But workers on the grounds crew were the only living souls I glimpsed.

I slid the Chevrolet awkwardly into the first parking lot I saw. I'd walked about ten feet when I realized, from a further study of the map, that I could have parked much closer to the English building. I hesitated for a moment, but it didn't seem worth the extra strain of maneuvering the car again. The gardens were always worth a visit, anyway. I shrugged to myself and set off down the concrete path.

Houghton's gardens were quite famous. When Mimi's great-grandfather had founded the college, he had planted them as a combination public service/tourist attraction. Photographs of the camellias and roses in bloom were always prominently featured in Houghton publicity material. It was easy to see why Houghton was a popular site for outdoor weddings. The sidewalk I now followed led through the heart of the gardens and emerged to one side of the library, crisscrossing other paths.

The foliage was dusty but lush, and the grass had been trimmed to a carpet texture. The day lilies were blooming, their rich orange flaring brilliantly against the dark green. It was good to see so much flora after New York. I bent to run my finger lightly over the curve of a petal. I felt a sort of grateful relaxation deep inside me. I knew the name of almost every plant; my mother had been an avid gardener before she turned to drinking.

I recalled all the times Mimi and I had sauntered through these gardens as teenagers, pretending we were real college coeds. At least that part of Mimi's dream had come true, though she'd been unfortunate in other ways. Now I was going to make it happen for myself. A real Houghton College coed. How young those kids were going to seem to me.

Thinking of the young faces that would soon surround me reminded me again of one Houghton student I would never meet: Heidi Edmonds, achiever, whose adventure had ended in getting raped and going back home defeated. As I strolled around a curve and arrived face to face with the library, I realized I was on the path where she'd been attacked. I turned to scan the camellias, the sidewalk; and then snorted at my own stupidity. But it did seem such agony should have left some mark. I saw only the lazy charm of the gardens, and heard only the whir of a bee touring the day lilies. Somehow that was more unnerving than a commemorative plaque would have been.

For the benefit of the bee, I suppose, I glanced down at my watch and stepped out a little faster.

THE IMMENSE DOUBLE DOORS SET IN THE CENTER of the ground floor led into a vaulted central cloister, cool and very dark after the glare outside. As I peered through the dimness, searching for some sign of stairs to the second floor, I wondered if the original Houghton architect had toured medieval monasteries right before he'd been commissioned for the job.

There were halls leading off to the right and left; they were empty. After some fruitless searching, I became absurdly frantic. Where the hell had they hidden the stairs? I wasn't going to impress Dr. Barbara Tucker if I turned up late. I took a few tentative steps forward, peering from side to side. My wooden heels made little tap! tap! echoes on the stone floor. The building was quite silent otherwise.

To my heartfelt relief, one of the enigmatic doors in the corridor to my right opened. A man came out and walked in my direction. (I'd been quite prepared to bellow for help if he'd turned the opposite way.) As he drew nearer, I saw he was about thirty-eight, with a slight belly preceding his legs and a tonsure fringed by blond curly hair.

"Excuse me," I said, louder than I'd intended.

He jumped. I felt embarrassed.

"Can I help you?" he asked politely, after he'd located me in the gloom.

"You're going to think I'm awfully stupid, but I just can't find the stairs." I winced. I was simpering. I hadn't simpered for years.

He laughed and came closer. I could make out a patrician nose and the slight suggestion of a double chin. I mentally prescribed laying off the sweets and starches for a few months.

"I think the architect wanted to hide something as mundane as stairs," he said. "I'm Theo Cochran, the registrar. Don't feel stupid. I tell an average of twenty people a year where the stairs are. There, see?" He pointed to the right. After a second, I was just able to discern the balustrade. It was composed of the same stone as the wall, and blended into it perfectly in the pervasive gloom.

"Oh," I said flatly. "Well . . . thanks a lot." Come on, Nick, manners. "I'm Nickie Callahan. You probably just processed my transcript."

"Oh. Mimi Houghton's friend."

Distinct lack of enthusiasm. Having an influential friend is not always a plus.

Theo Cochran stirred himself, probably remembering that influence. "We're glad to have you with us here at Houghton, Miss Callahan."

"Thank you," I said again. "I'm sure I'll be in and out of your office in the next week or so."

"So will the entire student body. The first week is always hell," the registrar said more pleasantly. He seemed to look forward to hurling himself into the fray. "Goodbye, now."

"Goodbye." I started climbing the stairs, my heels clattering. I resolved to remember to wear rubber-soled shoes to classes in this building.

I looked down the stairwell and saw the bare tonsure of the registrar moving away down the hall into the darkness. His progress was relatively silent. He must have made the same resolution.

It was impossible for me to blunder any more, since room 206 was just a few feet to the right at the head of the stairs. I checked my watch again. On the dot. I twitched my skirt and gathered myself in general.

"Come in," called a midwestern voice after I knocked.

"I'm Barbara Tucker," said a slim auburn-haired woman as she rose from behind a desk covered with every imaginable form of printed material: books, notebooks, forms, memoranda, catalogues. I blinked. The office seemed dazzling with light after the cavern below.

"Nickie Callahan," I said too heartily. I shook Barbara Tucker's hand and took the only scarred wooden chair that wasn't overflowing with books and papers.

The woman sat down, pushed her glasses up on her slight nose, and smiled at me. Her features were plain, but her skin was beautiful. I decided I liked her on the spot. I liked her smile, I liked the books stacked everywhere, I liked the plants that flourished in the two slitlike windows. I beamed back at Barbara Tucker in approval. There are some women who dislike and distrust me at first sight, on principle. She was not going to be one of them.

"So, you decided to leap back into the academic battle, Miss Callahan."

"Call me Nickie. I decided it would be a good idea to finish, and the time was right."

"Good decision. I remember Mimi told me you were a model, but I think I would have figured that out anyway."

I had to make it clear I was not a dilettante. "I used to be a model," I said carefully. "Now, I hope, I'm an English major."

"Okay, we'll start you on the road to a degree today," Barbara Tucker said briskly. She pulled my file from a crammed metal tray. "What's your goal? Do you want to teach?"

I took a deep breath and plunged. "No, I'm going to be a writer," I said, and couldn't stop myself from making a deprecating face.

Barbara brushed back her bangs and looked thoughtful. She didn't ask me how I planned to eat and pay the rent on a writer's erratic earnings; and she didn't laugh. She did smile again, suddenly. "You'll be the Don Quixote of the English department," she said. "Let's get you started."

For forty-five minutes we went over the hours I'd accumulated at my first college and made out a list of courses I wanted and courses I was required to take as an English major—certainly not a synonymous list. Finally we hammered out a schedule I thought I just might be able to handle.

But I kept reminding myself I'd been over six years away from the academic routine. As Barbara signed forms, I blew out a sigh of relief and apprehension.

"You're certainly going to be an interesting addition to the student body," Barbara commented cheerfully.

"Does Houghton have many older students?" I asked.

"Not that many, but you'll have some company, don't worry. And the older students we do have almost always make higher grades than the average-age student. They seem to have a better idea of why they're going to college."

That was heartening. I wondered again how it was going to feel, seeing those nineteen-year-old faces surrounding me. "I'll probably be a mother figure," I said ruefully.

Barbara whooped. "Believe me, Nickie," she gasped. "*No one* is going to think of you as a mother figure."

"What's all the merriment?" asked a voice behind me. I started, then twisted in the chair to look.

A man had stuck his head through the gap left by the partially open door. Now he looked as though he felt extremely foolish. "I'm sorry, Barbara, I didn't know you had anyone in here," he apologized.

"Come all the way in, Stan, and meet Houghton's newest sophomore-and-a-half," Barbara invited.

The man smiled a little shyly and edged into the room. He was a few years older than Barbara, whom I'd placed at around thirty-five. His neat brown beard was well salted with white and his face was seamed. He managed to look comfortable with himself.

As Barbara performed introductions (his full name was Dr. Stanley Haskell), I got the firm impression that the two were a couple. They shared the ease that comes of intimacy and long association; and Barbara seemed not the least disturbed when his eyes stayed glued to me.

They were obviously going out for lunch together. I quickly thanked Barbara for her time and gathered up my papers. Since Dr. Haskell was going to be instructing me in Chaucer (at eight o'clock Mondays, Wednesdays, and Fridays), I told him I'd see him in class and took my departure, my heels tap-tapping again down the stairs.

As I pulled the Chevrolet cautiously out of the parking lot, I spotted the two English professors at a stoplight at the edge of the campus. They were laughing. The sun was shining. I beamed idiotically to myself. Ah, love!

Mimi's narrow driveway led around to the back of the house, where it formed a wide apron, affording room to turn around; but she'd asked me to leave the car out front, since she meant to use it. I parked across the street from the house. The yard sloped up from the sidewalk, so I had to climb steps up to the yard, and then more steps up to the wide porch that girdled three sides of the house.

Panting a little from the heat and the stairs, sweating like a pig, I flung open the front door with that silly smile still pasted on my face—and there stood Cully.

. . . I was fourteen again. A tall, thin, black-headed boy, a lofty senior in high school, slipped into the chair opposite mine at the Houghtons' dining table. Hazel eyes summed me up and dismissed me.

"This is Mimi's brother, Cully," Elaine Houghton had said proudly. Mimi kicked me because I was gaping like a fool. I was abruptly sick, stricken with first love; and those light-brown eyes with little green streaks were utterly cool when they rested on me . . .

Mimi wasn't in the living room to kick me now, so I did the job myself—mentally, of course. Cully's eyes were just as cool now, though the rest of him had changed a little. He was still very tall and too slender, but a little gray streaked the black hair of his head and mustache. There were a few wrinkles at the corners of those eyes. His cheekbones and arched nose jutted a little more sharply; the parentheses from nose to mouth were deeper.

"Hello, Nickie," that mouth said calmly.

"Hi," I said, and slung my notebook down on one of the couches. "Where's Mimi?" Charm and grace, that's me.

"She and Alicia Merritt are in the kitchen planning the party."

"Alicia! What party?"

"Your party," he said, and relaxed enough to smile faintly.

Now that was interesting. Cully had been very tense.

"Mimi just decided she wanted to celebrate your arrival and have a housewarming at the same time," he continued.

We stood in uneasy silence for a moment.

"By the way . . ." He hesitated for an awkward length of time, and I stared. Cully *always* knew what he wanted to say. "I'm sure coming back here fitted in with your plans, but I'm glad you did come back to town and move in with Mimi," he finished.

Surely not for the sake of my beaux yeux.

The slap and the stroke, or the stroke and the slap. Cully had never said an unmitigated thing to me in our whole acquaintance. *I'm sure you came back to Knolls for your own, doubtless selfish, reasons, but I'm also glad it's what my sister wanted and needed.*

One thing I could say for Cully—he'd always adored Mimi, and the feeling was mutual. Now, I decided, Cully was angling toward something. But I wasn't going to bite.

Things had never, never been simple between us.

"I'm glad too," I said briefly. "Now when, and where, is this party going to be?"

"Friday night, here. I'm going to bartend."

"I'm glad to hear that," I said sincerely. Mimi had never mixed a decent drink in her life. Then my mind started racing. Friday was two days away. Some of our moving boxes were still strewn through the house. I was itching to make a list of things that had to be done. I began rummaging through my purse for a pencil and a pad.

"Listen, as long as we're alone . . ." Cully began, capturing my undivided attention.

"Yes?" I fixed my eyes on his. That usually either frightens men or inflames them. One of my photographers,

a romantic, had said that my eyes were exactly like opals—
a compliment that had pleased me no end, of course.

Just as a little voice inside me was protesting that I had
promised to stop using my face as bait—and I'd told that
little voice to shut up—Cully went on: "I want you to
watch out for Mimi."

I was back in the real world, with a thud.

"I'll tell you something in confidence—" He broke off
as Alicia Merritt and Mimi blew into the living room.

I had to jump and scream and embrace Alicia in the accepted fashion. If I'd done less, she would have thought I
wasn't happy to see her. Alicia was refreshingly the same,
her accent still one of the heaviest I'd ever heard. Her voice
dripped magnolias and molasses. When she exclaimed
"You sweet thing!" the product sounded like "Yew sweeet
thang!" I held our former schoolmate at arm's length to take
a survey.

"You look great, Alicia," I said. And I meant it.

Her short hair was more golden than God had made it,
and curlier; but her figure was definitely her own, and still
tempting as a ripe peach. Alicia had the happy face and assured manner of someone who has seldom in life denied
herself an impulse—someone who has pretty nice impulses, that is.

"How's Ray?" I asked, when I decided we'd gushed
enough. Mimi beamed in the background.

"Oh, he's just fine, Nickie. He still has that same old
job, though, and he's on the road all week. At least he
comes back home on the weekends. I'm glad I'm not the
jealous type!"

"You don't have anything to worry about," I assured her.

"Oh, I'm fat as a butterball," Alicia protested untruth-
fully. "And you're still long and thin and totally gorgeous.
It must be staying single that does it."

I'd forgotten Alicia's little needles, the way you tend to
forget little faults in otherwise nice people. For a second,
this little barb almost got to me. I was off guard and back

in the ambience of girlhood, and I actually found myself defensively totting up the proposals I'd received. Shame! If I'd been alone, I would've slapped myself for my regression. As it was, I had to clamp my mouth shut: I had been on the verge of retorting, "Oh, Alicia, I'm just so *picky!*"

"Where are you all living now?" I said instead, and promised myself something nice for my restraint. Earrings?

"Didn't Mimi tell you?" Alicia gave Mimi a look of mock reproach. "We bought the house two doors down from here, the other side of Mrs. Harbison, oh I guess about a year ago. So I'll get to see a lot of you! When I have a second, that is," she added, to my relief.

"Are you still in every club in town?"

"*And* on a bunch of college committees, too. Got to support the old alma mater, and I have to do *something* while Ray's gone!"

Alicia's energy was something of a legend. Underneath all the gush and flutter, which apparently she found necessary to assume, Alicia was actually a very efficient woman. Mimi had told me that in college Alicia had invariably made the dean's list. But if Ray's fraternity brothers mentioned that achievement to her, she would blink and giggle and tell them it must have been a fluke.

"You know," our old friend was saying now with a great display of roguery, "Mimi was on every board at Houghton, and they finally gave up and started paying her for it. I'm just hoping that some day this town will give *me* a salary for running it!"

"You sure deserve it," I murmured. I was tiring already. It had been a long time since I'd met Alicia broadside.

"Ray and I are going to start working on a baby," she told us cheerfully. "He says that'll keep me at home, if nothing else will. He thought buying our own house would do that too. But you know, I had the whole thing done over in no time."

"I don't doubt it for a minute," Cully said with a smile that robbed his words of any sting.

Alicia looped her purse straps over her shoulder and moved to the door. "Nick, I'm just thrilled to death you're back in town to stay. We'll see you at the party Friday night. Ray'll be back in time, and we'll be here with bells on. You call me, Mimi, you hear? If you need any help!"

All at once she was gone, leaving us standing in a daze, as if a tornado had passed close by.

"Still the same," Mimi said with a grin of half-admiration, half-regret.

I nodded. "What's all this about a party?"

"Oh, just some people you met when you used to stay with me, and some of the people from the college," she said smoothly.

"Like the entire English faculty?" I asked with suspicion.

"Oh, don't worry! Just the ones I really know and like. I'm not trying to butter anyone up for you."

"Oh. Okay," I said, feeling some doubt. "When is this going to be? What kind of party?"

"It kicks off at eight, and from the length of the bar list, it's going to be a drunken brawl," Cully interposed. "Listen, Mimi, are you sure this is everything you need from the store?"

A list I hadn't gotten to make. I eyed it sadly. Then I realized that Cully was going to the grocery for us, and I felt a jolt of amazement. I just couldn't imagine Cully Houghton doing something as tedious and universal as wheeling a cart through the supermarket to buy groceries. It occurred to me that I had perhaps been idealizing Cully a wee bit all these years.

"I'm sure," Mimi said firmly. "Listen, are *you* sure you've got the bar list?"

"Right here." He pulled the edge of another list from his pants pocket to prove it to her.

"Good. Thanks, Cully, that'll save us time. We've got to get cracking on cleaning up this house, and we'll have plenty for you to haul off to the dump, starting tomorrow."

"Maybe I should try to borrow Charles's pickup?"

"Good idea. Drop by his office and see if he'll need it. Generally he just uses it on weekends."

There was a little something about the way Mimi smoothed her hair . . .

"Charles?" I asked, after Cully had left.

"Oh, you'll meet him at the party. I've known him forever," Mimi said nonchalantly.

Right. Uh-huh. Here we go again.

But I swore to myself I wouldn't say anything. Mimi was always prickly in the first stages of any attachment. There are some lines even a best friend—or especially a best friend—shouldn't cross. I'd upset Mimi in the past with my criticism of her choice of men, before I'd gotten wiser. That was why Mimi was being so clamlike with me now.

I withheld my sigh until I reached my bedroom. Then I heaved it to the mirror, as if I were practicing "Exasperation" for a pantomime. We'll just see about *Charles*, I told myself grimly while I changed into my oldest cutoffs and my T-shirt with the paint stains. Reserve judgment, Nickie.

Mimi had excellent taste in clothes, furniture, jewelry, and (of course) friends, but she completely lost that taste when it came to men. Husband Number One had at least been harmless; Mimi had just gotten tired of packing ice chests with beer for fishing trips and whooping it up at fraternity parties. Richard had been more dangerous; an effete would-be painter who lived on an allowance from his parents—who could well afford it, granted. But he too had never denied himself an impulse, and his impulses, unlike Alicia Merritt's, were apt to be rather nasty. There'd been others she hadn't married, of course. I remembered best the cadet who had painted a glowing picture of an army officer's wife's life, and the budding rock star who'd wanted to have a baby (via Mimi) and name the child Acidstar.

At least apprehension about Mimi's latest involvement temporarily smothered my curiosity about what Cully had been going to tell me before Alicia and Mimi had come into the living room. I had the distinct feeling that whatever it was, it was something unpleasant.

* * *

FOR THE REMAINDER OF THAT DAY AND THE BULK
of the next two I hadn't time to think of anything but
Comet, Future, and Glass Plus.

After we'd taken the kitchen apart and put it back together, we turned our attention to the long living room that
extended the width of the front of the house as the kitchen
extended the back.

Mimi had tentatively arranged my heavy desk and
bookcases in the empty dining room across the hall from
my bedroom, but the living room was so scantily furnished
that we had to move them back out to fill one corner. My
two couches and chairs, which had filled my apartment
in New York rather tightly, looked like an island perched
around the fireplace at the right side of the living room. In
despair, we lugged down a couple of chairs and a table of
Mimi's that blended with my stuff well enough. The result
was passable.

Then Cully began to haul boxes and other moving debris, and we began to cook.

Of course Attila and Mao went wild in this maelstrom
of upheaval. They'd scarcely had time to adjust to the
move from Mimi's former home. The cats dashed between
our feet, pounced out of odd corners, and got shut in clos-
ets for indefinite periods. Thursday evening, when I called
the two to supper and only Attila responded, Mimi leaped
from her chair as if she'd been electrocuted and pounded
up the stairs at full speed. She returned in a minute, her
nose red with incipient tears, clutching Mao to her chest.

"I just remembered the last time I'd seen her she was
asleep in my underwear drawer, and then I pictured myself
putting the wash away and shutting the drawer without
even thinking about it," she explained in a shaky voice.
"Oh, God, she could've suffocated!"

To Attila's intense indignation, Mao had an extra treat
for supper that night. Mao accepted her close brush with
death quite placidly. In fact, when I asked Mimi if the cat

had been frantic when she opened the drawer, Mimi told me rather stiffly that Mao had still been fast asleep.

Cully was a great help; which, like his grocery shopping, surprised me—until I realized that he'd never watched *me* lift a finger to do anything practical, either. When he and Rachel had dropped by my apartment on their infrequent visits to Rachel's family in New York, I'd of course had the place spotless hours beforehand.

I volunteered to go to the dump bins with Cully on Friday morning, since his load was especially heavy. I perched up high in the pickup that the mysterious Charles (whose last name I discovered to be Seward; occupation, lawyer) had obligingly donated. It had been years since I'd been in a pickup. I felt very down-home.

"We ought to have a beer in our hands and country music on the radio," I told Cully as we bucked along the dirt road that led to the county landfill. It was good to get out of the hot kitchen.

"It *is* kind of fun," Cully admitted cautiously. He was shifting gears with a certain macho air that tickled me. I had a feeling that if he'd been alone, he'd have been going "Brroom, brroom," pretending to be a cross between Mario Andretti and the Marlboro man.

When we got to the dump and Cully had let down the tailgate, I heaved garbage bags with tremendous panache.

"That's the one with all the cat litter and the broken glass in it," he protested when I grabbed the gathered neck of the last bag.

I gave him a scornful look. Since Cully was not only a man and a southerner but also a jogger, he tended to be smug about his superior strength. Pooey on you, Cully! I'm tall and I exercise every day—well, almost every day—and I'm not going to play clinging vine.

My training in the control of my facial muscles came in handy. I managed to swing the bag off the tailgate and onto the pile of dumped garbage with the requisite gusto, but I was glad Cully had to shut the tailgate. That gave me a moment to hop back into the pickup and have a blissful second to relieve my anguish by some down-home cussing.

I let out a few more unprintables when I discovered I was bleeding. Some of the broken glass had pierced the bag, and me. I believed the cut was small; but as hand injuries will, it bled profusely, and I couldn't be sure. When Cully climbed in beside me, he may have had the hint of a smile on his face, but it vanished (fortunately for him) when he saw the blood.

"Charles has a first-aid kit in the glove compartment, since he takes this pickup when he hunts." He reached across me, his arm touching my knee, and pulled out the kit.

I was angry and embarrassed. "It's just a little cut," I said through tight teeth.

Cully was already pulling a gauze pad from the kit. He pulled my arm over as if it weren't attached to a body. Dabbing carefully, he blotted the blood with the gauze. His eyes flashed sideways once, but his look bounced off mine and back to the cut.

It came to me that Cully was a wound healer. That was a beautiful trait in a psychologist, or a brother, or a bosom friend; but fairly dismaying in an object of lust. If I could manage to survive a pretty bad car accident, I conjectured, I might even rate a kiss.

"What did you start to say to me that day that Alicia was over at the house?" I asked, just to remind him that I was indeed at the end of my arm.

"Oh." He was absurdly intent on the little cut. He got out a bandage and ripped off those irritating strips of paper that guard the adhesive. "I just wanted to tell you to be sure to lock up at night, and just sort of watch out in general for Mimi."

I frowned. "Maybe I'm being dense, but why?"

"Well, she's been through a lot lately; Grandmother and Richard and all."

Mimi was about as frail as an innerspring. Though Cully might not see her that way; after all, he was her dearly beloved and only brother. There's more here than meets the eye, I told myself wisely, and twirled an imaginary mustache until Cully looked up and caught me.

"What on earth are you doing?"

"There's something you're not telling me," I parried.

He straightened and looked thoughtful. I wondered if I could have my arm back, since it was obvious this was not going to be one of those electric movie moments when the hero suddenly gives way to passion after touching the girl, usually when she's dismounting. I didn't have a horse to slide off of; the best I could do was cut my hand.

"No," Cully decided out loud. He bent back over my cut, meticulously applied the bandage, and handed my arm back to me.

"No, what?" I asked nastily. My muscles were aching from the weight of the garbage bag, the cut began to throb, and there were about seventy-five things I had to do before I could retire for my much-needed preparty nap.

"It wasn't important anyway," Cully said, and started the pickup bucking along the road.

We were halfway home when I turned to him and said with absolute honesty, "Cully Houghton, you are one of the most aggravating and frustrating people I have ever known."

He looked considerably surprised, as well he might. I think it was the first time I'd ever said something really personal to Cully.

"That's interesting," he said after a moment.

We didn't speak again; but oddly enough, the silence wasn't uneasy. I blocked him out of my mind, and I was half asleep by the time we got home.

ATTILA WAS PRESSED IN A HOT PURRING BUNDLE against my leg when I woke up. He'd definitely adopted me, which showed sheer ingratitude to Mimi, who'd found him as a starving kitten and fed him to his present enormous size.

He sat on the toilet lid as I showered and dried my hair. The sound of the blow dryer made him nervous, but he tolerated it to satisfy his curiosity. He even endured my tuneless humming, the closest I will ever come to singing. The nap and hot shower had banished the worst of my soreness. The cut looked clean and small. I felt refreshed and in a mood to party. I tickled Attila under the chin, and he followed me to my vanity table to watch me put on my makeup.

I was thinking sweet thoughts about little furry friends when (via the mirror) I observed Attila carefully and deliberately shoving one of my earrings over the edge of the table. He tried hard to look innocent when he realized I'd caught him at it, but the look didn't come off.

"You're going to have to learn my ways," I said grimly, "if we're going to cohabit. *Bad cat!*" I whacked him on his broad beam.

He instantly bit me and began purring like a chain saw.

We stared at each other.

The cat's schizophrenic, I concluded. I knelt to grope under the bed for the earring. (Of course it had bounced under the bed—don't they always?) Attila descended from the vanity with a thud and dived under the bedspread to see what I was doing. He spotted the gleam of gold a split second before I did and quickly sat on my earring. We stared at each other again. It looked like a Mexican stand-off.

Fortunately for one of us, little Mao stuck her head around the door to investigate my room. Attila was off the earring in a flash, pursuing the smaller cat with yowls of fury.

Dressing went more smoothly after his departure. Soon I was all ready except for the top layer, and that required some thought.

Before going upstairs for her own nap, Mimi had advised me on what to wear: "Something that doesn't show a whole lot of boob. Wait till they get to know you, for that. But don't condescend, either; they'll all know where you've lived and what you've done for a living." As if I needed that advice, after my never-to-be-forgotten gaucherie years ago.

Now I searched through my closet nervously, sliding hanger after hanger across the rod in search of something absolutely appropriate. It suddenly occurred to me how ludicrous my anxiety was. I recalled some of the parties I'd dressed for in New York. Some—not a lot, but some—had been the kind that got written up at great length and talked about for years.

Unfortunately my old ego boosters (Famous People I've Drunk With, Publicized Parties I've Attended, Beautiful Men I've Dated) didn't seem to weigh an ounce now I was back home. They might as well have been social distinctions on the moon, for all they counted here and now. I gave myself the green light on being nervous. I had every reason to be.

I finally lighted on a dress that mingled every shade of blue and green and covered my chest pretty thoroughly without being in any way virginal. I pulled it on and got everything settled. Then I turned around in front of the mirror and looked over my shoulder. My partially bare back told me my tan was holding up pretty well.

"Great!" Mimi applauded from the doorway. She was wearing true red and she looked like a million dollars. She came and stood beside me, and I revolved to look at our reflections in the mirror. We had gazed into many mirrors together across our friendship's span of thirteen years. I liked this reflection better than any I'd seen.

We were as sharp a contrast as ever—Mimi small and dark, myself tall and fair. Some of the arrogance was missing in the way she stood and held her head; it had been pared off by the divorces. Some of the self-conscious power vested in me by my face had been knocked off my shoulders. Mimi was not so wild and willful. She was not so trusting, either. I was less defensive; and I knew now I would never conquer the world.

I don't know what Mimi was thinking during that long moment. Maybe her thoughts were traveling the same road as mine. But somehow I was convinced that she saw us as we used to be; not as we were.

She put her arm around my waist and hugged me close, then loosed me to lift my hair on my shoulders and rearrange it in a drift she liked better.

"Let's get this party rolling," she said briskly.

I blinked, and the moment was gone.

Chapter 4

PARTIES IN KNOLLS STARTED (AND ENDED) EAR-
lier than I was used to. About eight-thirty I decided that the
entire population of the town was crammed into Mimi's
house. At least the entire *white* population of Knolls—
some things hadn't changed much in the years I'd been
gone.

Aside from their uniform skin color, our guests ran the
narrow gamut of Knolls society. There were friends of
Mimi's with their husbands in tow, women I vaguely remembered, most of them giddy with the excitement of a
night off from the kids. There were plenty of college people. I met the cowardly college president, Jeff Simmons,
and found him charming. He had a beautiful head of
wheat-blond hair for which most women would've sacri-
ficed their microwaves. And there were people unaligned
with either college or society cliques, whom Mimi just
knew and liked. Town and gown and independent.

I hadn't been to see Mimi's parents yet, so I was glad to
see them come in the door. Sleek, dark Elaine was still one
of the most attractive women I've ever known. She swept

me up in a carefully loose embrace and brushed her cheek against mine, bombarding me with questions it would take me a week to answer. Not that Elaine intended to stick around and listen if I did. She was wearing a beautiful dress that revealed a lot of still-prime cleavage. If Elaine subscribed to Mimi's dictum, the people here tonight must know Elaine very well indeed.

Elaine's husband Don was close on her heels, as always. I hugged Mr. Houghton with far more enthusiasm. I'd always been very fond of him, a fondness compounded both of pity and of gratitude for his kindness. I believed it was not easy to be married to Elaine, and I sometimes thought it couldn't be too easy to be Cully's and Mimi's father. In social situations Don was always overshadowed by his family. But he did have his own flair; Don could make money, and he was shyly proud of that, I'd discovered years ago.

"How's the man with a finger in every pie?" I asked lightly.

Mr. Houghton looked pleased and embarrassed and altogether like a great teddy bear. He'd lost some hair and gained some weight since Mimi's last marriage, but his face wasn't deeply lined and he still had a bounce to his walk.

"Well, I can't complain," he admitted proudly.

I led Mr. Houghton over to the bar, where Cully mixed his father a gin and tonic. They shook hands with an odd formality, but they looked glad to see each other.

"What are you up to now?" I asked in a whisper.

"Well, Nickie," Don began slowly, taking a sip of his drink, "I've bought me a restaurant."

"Which one?" This was sure to be a secret. In addition to owning a big insurance agency, Don was a silent partner in many Knolls businesses.

Don whispered back the name. I recognized it as one of the few good restaurants in Knolls.

"You demon," I said with a grin. "You're going to own this town before too long." Don loved that kind of talk; he grinned like a twelve-year-old with a frog in his pocket.

We chatted for a while, and at first I enjoyed it thoroughly. But as usual, Don (bless his heart) began to bore me just a little after a while. I caught myself looking wistfully at guests I hadn't had a chance to visit with.

Mimi whipped up to rescue me in a swirl of red.

"Daddy! You let Nick talk to other people. You can have her over to lunch soon and hash over old times. There's Jeff Simmons over there. You better go tell him that Houghton needs some more insurance, after that awful thing this summer!"

Her father obediently headed in Jeff Simmons's direction, his face becoming purposeful as he thought of business.

"You've always been such a favorite of Daddy's," Mimi told me as she whisked me away. That pleased me, of course; Mr. Houghton had always been a favorite of mine, too. But this evening, as we'd talked, I'd caught a little gleam in his eye that was quite unwelcome in the father of my best friend.

I shrugged to myself. Oh, well, Don had always been an appreciator of women. He bragged about Elaine's looks all the time, as if he were personally responsible for her attractiveness.

Mimi introduced me to white-haired Mrs. Harbison, our next-door neighbor, who immediately assured me she'd "just dropped in for a minute." Mrs. Harbison's minute stretched to twenty as she filled me in on the details of her widowhood. Her house was as large as this one. I wondered how the old lady managed by herself. As I listened, I found out. Mrs. Harbison had few free moments. She gardened, kept the house up, canned, embroidered, played mahjong, and was active in the church. And she took some pains to find out what church I belonged to.

It had been so long since anyone had asked me that, I hardly knew what to say. I'd forgotten that this was always one of the first questions to be settled in the South. I remembered I'd been an Episcopalian once upon a time. I breathed a sigh of relief when Mrs. Harbison turned out to be a Baptist. She couldn't enlist me in any of her church organizations, and she was a little disappointed about that. To my dismay, she told me she'd be sure and tell a mysterious Mrs. Percy that I was in town. I assumed Mrs. Percy was Mrs. Harbison's Episcopalian equivalent, and I shook in my shoes. Church-minded ladies are as incontestible as gravity.

Mrs. Harbison finally wandered off home. I made my way back to the makeshift bar where Cully presided. We'd borrowed two sawhorses, laid some planks over them, and covered the whole with a tablecloth now sadly stained with spilled cola and bourbon.

"Got any Blue Nun left?" I asked.

"Coming right up," Cully said, and poured me a glass. He looked at me a little doubtfully, and I thought he was remembering that long-ago rehearsal dinner when I'd had too much to drink. I looked him straight in the eye and gave him the smile that had formerly cost so much per hour. For a gratifying second he looked stunned. I decided to leave while the going was good.

"See you later," I called gaily, and wriggled through the crowd to join Barbara Tucker and Stan Haskell by the mantelpiece. They were standing close together and alone, looking like a pair of shy sheep. It was obviously my duty as a cohostess to cheer up this corner of the party.

I bellowed at Stan and Barbara over the noise of the room and got them livened up. Soon another Houghton professor wandered over and began to deliver a neat character assessment of his department head. I fixed my face in attentiveness, but my mind drifted. I listened to the party booming all around me. This was my first southern party in years, and I began to notice a difference in it. The voices were certainly as boisterous, the throats as dry. Of course these voices had a different cadence, for the most part; some Houghton people from the North and Midwest added variety. But many of the topics of conversation I could hear were the same—the president, the economy, children, personalities.

But there was a difference. Finally I had it. Most of the people I'd known in New York were on their way up or already there, in one of the most competitive cities in the world; a city in which making the grade locally meant making the grade all over the world.

Incredibly, these people at this little party in Knolls, Tennessee, were more assured. They had a place; and by God, they knew it. With the exception of the imported college people, the crowd in Mimi's living room was interrelated, interbred, and interdependent. And with rare exceptions they would always be accepted in the place they'd been born to, no matter what any one of them did.

That had its advantages and disadvantages, like any other given condition. But this evening, in the flush of successful party-giving and the warmth of homecoming, that assurance seemed almost divine. In this society I felt an incredible safety that I'd felt nowhere else. I sank back into it as if it were a soft couch. Back in the fold. No need to prove myself. My struggle in New York seemed ludicrous.

Barbara shouted something in my ear then, and I snapped to. I couldn't make out what she was saying, but I did hear enough to tell her she was acquiring a southern accent. Barbara laughed so much that I realized she was certainly appreciating the liquor. She was flushed with the heat of packed bodies and a good dose of bourbon. Stan, her Chaucerian lover, looked mildly embarrassed by Barbara's noisy good cheer, but it appeared he was matching her drink for drink. Maybe later in the evening I would get to see shy Stan Haskell let his hair down. What a prospect.

Right now he was gesturing wildly to someone beyond my left shoulder. I twisted to see who it was. My rescuer from the cloister of the English and Administration building was making his way to our little group.

"Nickie Callahan, Theo Cochran," Barbara introduced us. "Nickie, Theo is our registrar at Houghton."

I beamed at Theo. "We already met, in the dark," I told Barbara. Barbara laughed immoderately again.

Theo smiled and nodded to me, then craned toward

Barbara. He was looking rather handsome this evening, in his Roman senator/well-fed way. "Congratulations, Barbara! On the tenure!" he said. "I haven't seen you since I heard."

"Thanks, I'm celebrating! Where's your wife?"

Theo pointed toward the farthest corner of the room. His wife seemed to be the intelligent-looking woman wearing a dress that would have made any designer throw up.

"How's Nell?" Barbara asked. I must have looked blank. Stan bent over to tell me that Nell was Theo's little girl. I nodded. There was that special inflection in Barbara's voice that signaled a delicate subject, so I sobered my expression appropriately.

"She's doing as well as we expect," the registrar told Barbara through stiff lips.

And that was the end of Theo's stay in our company. He stood there the second longer required for courtesy, then nodded curtly and moved off to rejoin his wife.

"You shouldn't have asked," Stan told Barbara. I got the feeling that perhaps I should edge away. Stan was obviously more than a little aggravated with Barbara.

She accepted his irritation as just. "You're right, that was dumb. Nell's his little girl, Theo's only child," she explained to me. "She has leukemia."

"Oh, that's horrible!"

"He doesn't like to talk about it at all. It was really stupid of me to ask. But I *do* want to know how she's getting along and show some concern. It's okay to talk to Sarah Chase about it—that's his wife's name—oh, didn't you go to Miss Beacham's?"

Bewildered by the abrupt change of subject, I nodded.

"Theo's wife is Sarah Chase Beacham."

"Miss Beacham has relatives?" I said in amazement.

"Well, a brother anyway," Barbara said. She was beginning to smile again. Stan took her glass and his own to get a refill, but I shook my head when he gestured toward mine. "Sarah Chase's father is Miss Beacham's brother. He's in education too. I think he's dean of men at Pine Valley Methodist College, and Sarah's brother is a high school principal somewhere, and she herself used to teach. But with this illness of Nell's—well, Sarah Chase just had to quit work. She's changed beyond recognition. She's older than you, so I doubt she was at Miss Beacham's when you and Mimi were."

I peered over at the woman again, trying to recall her face. Now that I knew her story, I thought I detected the lines of care, the grayness, that marked her features prematurely. But I didn't think I'd seen Sarah Chase Cochran, née Beacham, before. When Stan returned with two full glasses, I took my leave and began circulating through the crowd. Mimi made her way toward me with a man in tow. He was tall and solid, with heavy blunt features and a sensuous mouth. Her face looked more alive, more animated, than it had since I'd come home.

"Nickie, this is Charles Seward, young lawyer-about-town," she said lightly. "Charles, Nickie Callahan, my oldest and dearest." But I noticed that while one small hand lay relaxed on his arm, the other hand at her side was clenched in a tight fist. She was afraid I'd judge him as harshly as I'd judged the others.

She fluttered off immediately after the introduction, a technique of hers with which I was familiar. I called it (very much to myself) "Make Them Seek," and I'd never been sure if the practice was conscious or unconscious on her part.

"I've heard a lot about you, Nickie," Charles Seward said pleasantly.

He couldn't know that was my least-favorite conversation opener, of course. I ordered myself to overlook it and find some pluses in a hurry.

The young lawyer was tall, even taller than Cully, so I knew he was a recent arrival. (Late for Mimi's party—a minus, unless he had an acceptable excuse.) He was quite an attractive man, I thought. His brown hair was prematurely thin on top, but that gave him an air of gravity becoming to a man of law. His light-blue eyes looked even lighter against his deep tan.

"Have you known Mimi long?" I asked cautiously. I can converse in platitudes as well as the next person.

"Long enough to wish I was living here with her, instead of you," he said. Right to the heart of the matter.

"Whoosh," I said, and rubbed my stomach.

"I've been waiting four years for that creep Richard to leave. Before that I waited for Gerald to leave. What do you think my chances are?"

"There's nothing like getting down to brass tacks," I muttered. Why hadn't he stuck to platitudes? "Well, do you think you could hold off until I finish college?" I asked half-seriously. "I just moved in, and I hate the thought of changing addresses so soon."

"Sorry," he said, without a trace of sincerity. "I tried to catch hold of Mimi after she divorced Gerald, but I bided my time, since I thought she needed some breathing space. That bastard Richard hopped in and whisked her off before my eyes. I told myself then that if I got a chance, I was jumping in with both feet. And I have. And I'm sticking." He looked unnervingly determined.

Mimi's bruised ego made her a pretty susceptible woman right now. I hoped Charles Seward was the right man for her—because with his looks and his flattering determination, I figured Mimi might be a goner.

Charles grinned at me suddenly, and I blinked. If he wasn't so set on Mimi . . . I could see the young lawyer's attraction, yes indeedy.

"Well. Moving right along, are you a native son of Knolls?" I asked.

"Born and bred. Good family: father, mother, two sisters married to good men. Went to law school, joined my father's firm. All set. Now all I need is a wife just like Mimi."

Now *that* was a fixation. The Houghton children seemed to inspire them, I observed to myself. I glanced involuntarily across the room to Cully.

"Good luck," I said. I didn't know if I meant it or not. At least Charles Seward came from Mimi's world—a plus. He saluted me and plunged into the crowd, surely in search of Mimi.

Make Them Seek.

I stared thoughtfully after him and wished my wine glass was full.

"What do you think?" asked a voice somewhere over my head. Cully stood very close behind me. How had he gotten here so fast? He handed me a full glass and took my empty one. He must have taken a mind-reading course for his doctorate.

"I think his chances are good," I said soberly. "Do you like him?"

"Fairly well. He's a little too hearty for me. I haven't been impressed with Mimi's husbands so far . . . Charles is several degrees better than Richard or Gerald. Mimi didn't much like my wife, either. It looks like a pattern."

It was fortunate that someone hooted for Cully to return to the bar, since I had no idea what to say to that. I'd already opened my mouth to try, though; and it wasn't wasted effort. Alicia Merritt flew up to me, and we shrieked at each other for a while. I also got to visit—a little—with her husband, Ray, whom I dimly remembered as the boy who'd called Alicia every night long-distance while we were at Miss Beacham's.

Ray was a light-complexioned, sandy, solid type: Alicia's paperweight, I thought, inspired by the wine, He didn't seem overwhelmingly glad to see me. He'd always been one to mistrust the different, I recalled.

After the Merritts joined Jeff Simmons's coterie, I went back into general circulation, from time to time going down the hall to the kitchen to get more munchies for the table.

About midnight, the crowd seemed to be thinning out. Time for the babysitters to go home, I guessed. Cully had abandoned his post to talk to his father and Ray Merritt. Elaine was being mooned over by a youngish bachelor coach from the college. Mimi's red dress wasn't hard to spot; but Charles Seward wasn't looming over her, to my surprise. When we met by chance in the kitchen, Mimi told me rather proudly that he'd be working all weekend on a court case for Monday, and had left to plunge back into his preparations; so I mentally excused Charles for being late. Stan and Barbara said a slightly tipsy goodbye, and it seemed that Theo and Sarah Chase Cochran had already left. I'd never gotten over to her corner to meet Theo's wife, and I chided myself. As I was totting up the remaining guests, I saw Elaine neatly detach herself from the young coach and collect Don.

My facial muscles were aching from my hostess smile. I rubbed my cheeks as I surreptitiously began to check nooks and crannies, tracking down the glasses that people leave in such odd places. I took a few back to the kitchen as unobtrusively as possible, and there was trapped by a professor who wanted to talk about the Romantic poets, apparently with a view to getting my mind on the general subject. After I smiled him out the front door with a hearty handshake, I found a few more glasses and plates and exchanged chatter with a few more people.

So when I considered it later, I decided it was about forty-five minutes after the Houghtons left that the phone rang. I happened to be blotting up a ring on the hall phone stand, an old-fashioned arched one built into the wall. I lifted the receiver automatically and said hello.

"Nickie? Nick?"

Elaine Houghton. "Yes, ma'am?"

"I have something kind of nasty to tell you, now. You and Mimi lock up extra careful tonight, you hear? A friend of mine who rents her garage apartment to Barbara Tucker just called me, and the police are over there. Barbara Tucker got raped tonight."

"But she was just here," I said stupidly.

All the party drained out of my system. I found myself staring at the ring on the painted wood as if it were proof the news wasn't true. "Maybe she just got burglarized?"

"No. There's an ambulance," Elaine said crisply. "Besides, the police told my friend Marsha. I'm quite sure. Goodbye, now." She hung up.

I was close to the improvised bar just inside the living room. Cully was there, for once making himself a drink. I wobbled over to him and put my hand on his back. He turned sharply.

"What?" Then, more urgently, he said, "Nickie! What's wrong? Who was that on the phone?"

"Oh, Cully. Oh, Cully," I said out of a fog of alcohol, exhaustion, and shock. "Poor Barbara. He's gotten Barbara Tucker."

Mimi had sensed trouble with her built-in hostess antenna, and she arrived at the bar in a swish of red, her face stern at the spectacle of two people being upset and serious at a party. So I was able to tell them both what Elaine had said.

I thought of the woman on the sidewalk in front of my apartment building in New York, and wondered what was so different here, after all.

Chapter 5

EIGHT O'CLOCK IN THE MORNING WAS A HORRI-
ble time to schedule anything, much less Chaucer. I was almost stumbling on my way to the English building, trying
desperately to wake up and look alert. I wanted to start
briskly and keep the momentum going.

All the dreariness of registration, fee payments, orientation, book buying, had led to this first full day of classes. I
was actually beginning the completion of something I'd
quit years before.

Since the registrar's office was situated on the ground
floor of the English and Administration building, I passed
Theo Cochran's open door on my way down the hall. The
fluorescent light was gleaming on his bald head. He looked
up as I passed and gave me a little wave. It was nice to see
a friendly face among the herd of strangers, all depress-
ingly younger than I.

To say I was nervous was an understatement. Mimi had
been giving me rah-rah speeches for days, after I'd finally
admitted how scared I was about learning to study all over
again, being pitted against younger minds, handling the

workload poor Barbara had so cheerfully assured me I could bear.

Right classroom? I checked the room number on the door against that on my schedule. Right classroom, yes indeedy. I hesitated for a second. Then I grabbed my courage with both hands and pushed open the door—to be met by an audible gasp from a little guy wearing a Led Zeppelin T-shirt who was sitting in the first row of desks. That exaggerated gasp focused everyone's attention on me. I stared back at their smooth faces. Had I done something wrong?

"Wow!" said cocky little Led Zeppelin just as loudly as he had gasped. "You are some *kind* of woman, woman."

From sheer relief I started laughing, and after a second the others joined in. Even Stan Haskell chuckled from his post by the desk.

I sobered when I saw him. My amusement disappeared abruptly, as did his when he saw me watching him. He was grayer. The summer had gone from his face as surely as it was fading in Knolls. In a week, Barbara's shy lover had passed to the other side of middle age, too early and too fast.

I pitied him and I was angry with him; but I had resolved that on Mondays, Wednesdays, and Fridays from eight to nine he was going to be Dr. Stanley Haskell, my professor in Chaucer, period. I had to take this class. I had my own life, I told myself. My own goal. I had to stop thinking about Barbara Tucker. So I slid into a desk, whipped out a pen, and opened the virgin notebook I'd labeled "Chaucer."

MIMI, BLESS HER HEART, WAS READY WITH A glass of wine when I got home. I'd been studying in the library until five-thirty, when hunger rousted me out. Mimi's big push had been in the previous weeks, when she'd been assembling committees, organizing the year, and smoothing ruffled faculty and staff who ran atilt during the anxious preopening month. She would have a brief lull now, she had explained.

"How'd it go, Nick?" she asked sympathetically.

"Oh boy, oh boy. I'm going to have to work my tail off, Mimi." I threw myself down on the couch and accepted the wine gratefully.

"Well, you knew that."

"Sure. But knowing and doing are two different kettles of fish."

"Did you see Stan?" She settled opposite me, and Mao arrived to jump in her lap.

"Yes, first thing this morning." I told her about my resolution.

"You're going to have to do that, all right. But what a bastard. I just can't think of any other word for him, Nick."

"Well . . . yes. But I don't think he dropped Barbara like a hot potato because he's a *basic* bastard. Do you see what I mean?" Attila materialized on the arm of the couch. I took a long sip of my wine and tickled the cat below his chin. He began cleaning my knuckles ardently. Maybe he'd missed me today? More likely he was hungry. "You know I don't know them well, not nearly as well as you do. But I think he just *can't* talk about it to her. And if he can't talk about that crucial thing, they can't have a relationship. He can't even stand to see Barbara, he can't face any part of what happened to her."

"Why not?" Mimi had been especially sensitive to disloyalty ever since Richard left her.

"I guess he just can't." I lit a cigarette. "When I saw them together I thought they were a matched set, and you say they were in love for at least two years. But I guess Stan's just weak, or something."

"Like it was her *fault!*" Mimi interrupted.

"I'm not defending him," I said gently. "I'm just trying to understand, because I need to. I have to stay in the class."

"I'm not mad at you. I'm sorry," she said. "But you know how broken up Barbara is, and Stan acting like this is all she needs, right? Now is when she needs him most. Now is when he bows out. Remember how she kept asking?"

I didn't want to remember our visit to Barbara. I'd suffered with, and for, Barbara Tucker as much as our limited acquaintance would allow, since I'd so naturally liked her at first meeting. Now I was weary of the pain and fear her situation had given me.

But I couldn't help remembering. I heard again her bewildered voice asking Mimi if she knew why Stan hadn't been by. That had been the day after the rape, when Barbara was still disoriented and in pain.

When Stan had dropped her at the door, she told us, they'd both been sleepy from too much to drink. Stan started back to his own place to collapse. Barbara had climbed the steps to the front door of her garage apartment as usual—probably making a lot of noise, since she was clumsy from the bourbon.

The man had already broken in the back door. He was waiting for her in the dark. When she'd reached to turn on the light, she had instead touched an arm.

We could scarcely bear to hear it, but Barbara went on and on in a shaky voice. She had finally fainted. After the rape. When he hit her on the jaw.

But it wasn't over when she'd come to. It wasn't over for a while. Now it would never be over; never. That was what had shaken me to the core, so painfully that I'd recoiled from Barbara. What had happened to her could not be mended, healed, shoved aside, bought off, glossed over. It was irreparable.

In New York, I'd known women and men who'd been robbed on the street or burglarized. But by chance I'd never been close to anyone who'd been the victim of a personal and violent attack by another human being.

Like Heidi Edmonds, Barbara had never seen her attacker's face. She hadn't the slightest idea of what he looked like: eyes, hair, build, or anything.

But he had called her Barbara.

Mimi and I agreed later, once we'd gotten home and calmed down a little, that his knowing her name might mean a great deal, or nothing at all. If he'd been stalking her (Stalking? In *Knolls?*), he'd have easily found it out. On the other hand, he might be someone she knew well. She seemed sure of it. And that was so unthinkable that we just blotted it out.

Chapter 6

TWO MONTHS WENT BY WHILE MY THOUGHTS were turned to my books. Those weeks were so full of adjustments and assignments requiring all my concentration that the outer world just had to get along without my participation.

Alicia dropped by from time to time, and we went to dinner at her house. Ray seemed to like me more now that I was doing something as ordinary as finishing college. Whenever I talked about my life in New York, though, those pale eyes would flicker.

Mimi and I met Cully at the Houghtons' for a Sunday brunch. It was an uncomfortable meal. Mimi and Elaine sniped at each other from the underbrush, and Don still had that gleam in his eye that made me uneasy. Cully, too, was at his dryest that day. He said his counseling load at the college was much heavier than he'd expected—a lot of freshman students were already having qualms about attending college at all. They were homesick. He and I seemed to have established some kind of truce. The talk and feel of things between us was easier and more relaxed.

I caught him watching me at odd moments, and developed the notion that he was beginning to see me as a rounded human being, not just a beautiful dodo. But that was the only bright spot of the meal.

I decided to ruin the day good and proper, so I called my mother. She'd been to church, come home, and started drinking. Jay wasn't there. She tried hard to sound sober, but I knew she wasn't. However, she was proud of my going back to college, and she managed to ask correctly after the Houghtons and send a polite message to them. Mother also said one curious thing. She told me, quite out of the blue, that she hadn't told Jay where I was.

I was going to have to think about that.

Before I went to sleep that night, I decided that Jay might have dropped a hint to Mother, God knows why, that he'd gotten rough with me all those years ago. It also occurred to me that it had been a long time since I'd known Mother to hold off drinking long enough to get dressed and go to church. I tried to cancel that thought; I pinched myself in punishment. I would not hope.

Time ran through my fingers as my life with Mimi settled into a comfortable routine. Having two separate floors to live on made that much easier. We didn't collide in the bathroom, we didn't keep each other awake with lights or music or studying. Our most serious disagreement was the great debate about when to put the garbage out—the night before pickup was due, so we wouldn't have to surge out in our bathrobes at the crack of dawn, but the dogs often got it; or early in the morning, in which case the dogs still might get it, but not if we watched to shoo them off. We solved this knotty problem by alternating garbage duty instead of sharing it.

Because of our lavish cooking I gained four pounds, which Mimi swore became me. I thought I looked like I'd swallowed a cantaloupe.

Attila became quite possessive. He cuffed Mao unmercifully when the smaller cat ventured too close to me. I grew used to studying with a heavy load of tabby on my lap. When I was alone, I discussed things with Attila in disgusting baby talk. Mimi overheard me a couple of times and made graphic gagging noises.

Occasionally I heard from New York friends. Their phone calls seemed like communications from a foreign land. I was sliding back into my own. My speaking cadence slowed. I didn't wear camouflage on the street. My manners resumed their former polish. My way of thinking reverted (a little) to the labyrinthine.

But mostly I studied. I had to. If I wasn't reading, I was writing: not the novels of my dreams, but essays and term papers of one kind or another.

I dated a friend of Charles's once or twice. He was nothing worth working at, just good for a mildly pleasant evening; for one thing, he talked about duck hunting too much. But our double dates gave me a chance to observe Mimi with Charles. To my relief, she showed distinct signs of finally having developed a streak of caution and a sense of her own rights.

Sometimes she sang in a fair-to-middling alto as she got ready for a date, and sometimes she had that exalted, melted, "in love" look. But more often she seemed thoughtful. I was glad to see that; I hadn't brought myself to like Charles yet, though I was trying. And I did not, repeat did not, criticize him to Mimi. But perhaps she sensed my anxiety. He was courting her at such a furious clip that I'd become semiseriously concerned about finding another place to live in Knolls, in case Charles really did succeed in sweeping her off her feet and to the justice of the peace. Housing in Knolls was no idle concern. Because of the shortage of dormitory space, every doghouse and garage in town was rented during the college year. Barbara Tucker had had an awful time finding a place to live after she got raped. She just hadn't been able to stand her garage apartment any longer.

Poor Barbara. She was the only specter on a horizon I found full of promise, and she was becoming a very faint wraith. I was truly busy, desperately busy; and the tiny tremor in her voice reminded me that I should, must, treat her specially. She was of the walking wounded. She marched down the sidewalks of Houghton very swiftly, and very alone. Stan's defection had proved permanent. From a comment she dropped during one of our rare meetings, I got the idea she was seeing Cully professionally, and I hoped my surmise was correct. Cully's calm, restraint, and precision would be comforting to a woman in Barbara's situation, I thought.

Talk about Barbara's rape was no longer current in Knolls, partly because neither Heidi Edmonds (the first victim) nor Barbara had ever been figures in the mainstream of town life. According to Mimi, the feeling prevailed that the rapes were a campus problem—though plenty of residents strolled through the gardens, and of course Barbara's rape had happened off-campus. The scare had hit hard only among faculty wives and town women who worked at the college. These women watched what went on around them more carefully, and many installed extra locks. The female students went in pairs after dark, at least while the fear was fresh.

Mimi and I were conscientious about locking the doors every night, and I tried to do all my library work before I came home to supper. We decided we were doing everything we reasonably could to make ourselves safe. I distinctly remember the phrase "fortress mentality" coming into our conversation when we discussed security measures.

On the whole, this was a pleasant and rewarding period in my life. I loved it. I was living in a place I wanted to be, doing what I wanted to do, spending time with a friend I cherished. I was slowly making more friends. The ladder was gone; I didn't have to climb it, or scrabble to keep my place on it, anymore. I seldom turned on the bulbs of my mirror for that dark close examination.

Late October had never seemed so full of golden light.

Chapter 7

I WAS JERKED OUT OF SLEEP SO SUDDENLY AND
violently that the shock robbed me of breath. A hand was
clamped over my mouth. If I had had any air, I would have
screamed.

"Don't make a sound," whispered the figure that was
only a darker part of the darkness filling the room.

That figure was not Mimi or Cully or anyone who had a
right to be there. In the worst moment of my life I knew
clearly what was going to happen.

I couldn't breathe, I had to breathe. I lifted my hand to
knock his away, let me *breathe!*

"Don't move, I have a knife," he whispered.

He held it up into a shaft of moonlight he was careful
not to cross. I saw the blade, as he wanted me to.

Oh my God I'm going to die.

And I imagined the blood soaking the sheets, and God
bless Mimi, she would find me. I was going to die and I
wanted to live.

My heart was pounding so erratically and loudly that I
feared a heart attack, too—fear was going to kill me, fear

and the knife, fear or the knife. This was my end; this secret dark and hideous incubus was going to end Nickie Callahan, and my God I couldn't breathe.

There was hate filling the darkness around me, hate trickling down that shaft of moonlight. I was sick from the hate and the fear.

He moved his hand and I gasped air, air, oh Jesus, let me live! The hand had risen to gain impetus for the smashing blow it delivered to the side of my face. I choked on blood and pain.

"Be quiet," he warned me, and then he hit me again. And again.

Sometime before the fifth blow I was still conscious enough to begin to hate, for my hate to match his; conscious enough to want his death for the death he was dealing me.

I heard the ordinary sound of a zipper rasping.

He put the extra pillow over my face and he raped me.

I twisted my head to one side under the pillow's smothering pressure and breathed wonderful air for the minutes I had left. My arms were locked protectively across my chest. I could feel his head brushing them. I wrenched my mind away from my body. I loathed the thing that lay on me. What was happening bore no relation to anything I'd experienced before. This was not sex but punishment. He hated me. He was going to kill me. And I couldn't move to defend myself. If I moved I would surely die, and there was a chance, some kind of chance, there *had* to be . . . *a chance that I would live* . . . if I stayed still.

The incubus owned my life.

Where was the knife? Somewhere it was waiting to slide into me, between my ribs, ripping me, violating me in another way. Both his hands were occupied (*don't feel, Nickie*), the knife must be somewhere in the tangle of sheets.

But I couldn't move to find it.

My heart pounded erratically, on and on, frantically wanting an end to this. I knew the end would be soon.

Then it was over. He was off me, and I heard a fumbling in the dark as he zipped up his pants. My silent screams had compounded into such a noise inside me that I could barely hear the things he was whispering. I was glad of that. I had reached the bottom of humiliation and helplessness.

He hit me again, body blows now; over and over, and I thought it would maybe be better if he went on and used the knife. The fear would be over, the pain would end. I was going to die soon. There was no chance of my living. I could feel that rage, taste it in the blood in my mouth—my rage and his. He surely wouldn't let me survive to hate him this much.

He bent to my ear, bent to the air gap under the pillow. "I might come back, you superior bitch," he whispered. "Think about that. I might come back."

I suddenly realized that he meant to leave me alive this time—alive. This bastard was going to *permit* me to live; and I hated him, it throbbed in the blood pumped by my exhausted heart.

"Don't move, or I'll kill you, Nickie," he whispered again. "Do you understand?"

I nodded somehow; he must have seen the pillow shift.

Then a funny sound. It came to me that I was hearing gloves sliding onto hands.

A final "Don't move." I felt a stir in the air.

I was going to live.

He was leaving.

If I had gotten up, and to the window, perhaps I could finally have seen him. I couldn't move. Nothing could get me off that bed. My muscles were locked, and fear was still shrieking through my veins and arteries.

I had survived.

I stared into the darkness from under the pillow wet with my blood—but not my lifeblood. The fact that I was going to live filled the universe under that pillow.

But he might come back even now. I sensed he was gone; but he might be back, he might be just in the next room. Had he meant immediately? Or had he meant some night in the future?

Oh God I can't stand it if he comes back. I can't survive it again.

There was not such a thing as time. There was only breath after breath, one more breath that I had lived, then another . . . In. Out. Not dead, I'm not dead, alive alive alive. In. Out.

There came a breath when I was convinced he was gone.

In one convulsive shove I threw the pillow from my face and the chilly night touched my face. I stared into the dark corners of the room. Even the shaft of moonlight had vanished, covered by clouds.

It was really over. It had really happened. I smelled of it, to my sick disgust. I had lived through it. And I had to have help. I managed to roll. I stretched my arm. I found the switch on my bedside lamp.

Light. Blessed light, emptying the room of shadows that might hold him. He was truly gone; I would truly live. I was filled with an intense shock of astonishment.

Now. If I could get up. I looked down at my body and shuddered, feeling more naked than I had thought it possible to feel. There was damage. He must have worn a ring; maybe he'd put one on especially to cause more damage. I felt as sorry for my body as if it were a separate thing, not a part of me. My mind pitied my body for what had happened to it. It had to be covered, poor bleeding raped thing. I had to reach the closet to cover up that bruised body. I didn't want it to be naked anymore, ever.

But the closet was a few feet away. Need drove me. I swung my legs over the side of the bed, bringing them together in a tight protective parallel. Holding on to the bed table, I stood. I swayed for a second and caught myself. I shuffled forward, my knees trembling, and turned the handle of the doorknob. Opened the closet. My robe, my winter robe, the long one that closed up to the neck, that had a sash that I could tie tightly; that was what I wanted. It took me a long time to find that robe and get it on. I had to rest before I started for the hall. If my knees would just stiffen; come on, please, legs.

Raped. Oh Jesus God, *raped.*

I hadn't left the door to the hall closed when I went to bed. It was closed now. I opened it with infinite effort. It swung in silently, disclosing the blackness of the stairs and hallway.

And I wondered if Mimi was still alive.

The terror started all over again. My hand independently found a switch and pushed it up. The stairs leaped into light. Attila was huddled in a mass of wild-eyed panic on the landing. His tail twitched as he stared down at me. I couldn't climb the stairs; I tried to lift my foot to the first step, and failed.

"Mimi," I whispered. Louder, Nick, I told myself.

"Mimi," I said raggedly in a voice I didn't recognize as my own. I felt fluid running down my thighs. I gagged.

Then I screamed, "MIMI!"

An uncertain sound upstairs. Then a whole series of little thumps, a door opening. Attila turned his crazed eyes upward.

Alive and unhurt, Mimi appeared at the head of the stairway, buttoning her bathrobe. She stopped on the landing when she saw me. I stared up at her.

"Oh no," she said quietly. She brought her hands up to cover her mouth. "Not—oh, Nickie. Not you."

The tears that started down her cheeks ran over her hands. She jumped when she felt the wetness, dropped her hands to grip the banister, and crept down the stairs to me, hand over hand on the wood, like an old crippled woman. When she was level with me she looked at my face, into my eyes, and shuddered. I didn't feel anything, anything at all. I knew that would end, soon. And there was a lot to do before it ended.

"Call the police," I mumbled. Something was going wrong with my mouth. My knees gave way and I sat on the stairs. "Call them right now."

She moved past me. The cat streaked past her heels, mad with all this abnormality, wanting out. Away. I huddled close to the banister and crossed my arms over my breasts, pressing the bathrobe more tightly around me. I could feel blood moving down my cheek and couldn't—wouldn't—lift a finger to stop the ooze. I focused on the front door, directly across the expanse of living room from me. Soon a lot of people would be coming through that door. I dreaded the unknown process that was about to be set in motion; I dreaded the questions; I dreaded, most of all, the faces.

But my hate matched his. No matter what it cost me, I would endure anything to catch the man who had done this to me. Before the pain blurred my thoughts, I realized, with an eerie clarity, that nothing I had ever done in my life—nothing—could justify the punishment that had been meted out to me.

IT DIDN'T HURT MY CAUSE THAT THE HOUSE I lived in was Mimi Houghton's; that I was white; and that I had visible wounds to show. Even so, I was surprised by the Knolls police department. They were neither naive nor inefficient. The first car arrived within two minutes of Mimi's call. These were patrolmen. After a quick question as to whether I needed an ambulance, they began to search the house and the block. Then came the detectives, two grave middle-aged men in sports clothes with faces like road maps of unpleasant scenery.

They held some kind of colloquy with Mimi, and she vanished into my bedroom. When she returned, she squatted in front of me and took my hands.

"Come with me for a second, Nickie. Can you get up?"

Confused, but not caring enough to ask any questions, I let her lead me to the empty room across from my bedroom. She had a pair of underwear balled up in a bathrobe pocket.

"Honey, you have to put these on, okay? They're going to have to keep them and send them in to the lab."

I had to lean against the wall while Mimi tugged them on. She saw my torso. She had to sit down for a second, and she sobbed, deep racking gusts of air. I stood propped against the wall and observed her.

She got up after a minute. "Now, we're going to have to go outside, but the police will be with us," she said unevenly. She put her arm around me and I leaned against her, my own arms still crossed over my chest. One of the detectives came to my side as we crept through the living room and out the front door.

"We're going to see my doctor," Mimi explained carefully as they maneuvered me into a strange car. "For the evidence, and because you're hurt, okay?"

I nodded. If I had tried to speak, I would have started screaming and never stopped.

The examination I had to endure, I did endure. I clenched my teeth while the doctor treated the cuts and clucked over the forming bruises, then told me I had no broken bones and only two loose teeth, which was some kind of miracle. The doctor recommended a visit to an optometrist to have my eyes checked, told me I'd have one shiner, and then got out some kind of kit to collect evidence for the police.

In a nervous effort to make small talk, to fill the silence as I stared at him, he explained that he'd examined the student, Heidi Edmonds, the past summer; and also Barbara Tucker two months ago. The police had supplied him with some kits in case the rapist struck again. He'd gone to a training school, he told me, to learn how to use them.

I had a horrible vision of myself posing for an ad for rape evidence kits, an ad designed for some law-enforcement journal. I would be posed holding one and smiling, sitting on the examining table with an avuncular doctor patting me on the back. A stern and determined policeman would be visible through a partially open door into the hall.

I suddenly realized I was still in my bathrobe. Mimi was somehow in blue jeans, though I'd never been aware of her leaving my side to dress.

The doctor told me it wasn't necessary for me to go to the hospital, but if I wanted to check in for a couple of days of observation, that might be best.

"No." I would not have more people staring.

While I lay on my back on the cold examining table, I spied a clock on the wall. I realized, with a jolt, that it registered four o'clock in the morning. When had I been awakened by that hand over my mouth? I'd gone to bed around ten-thirty. Mimi had been out with Charles Seward; I vaguely remembered hearing her come in, but I had no idea of the hour. I'd gone straight back to sleep.

By the time the doctor had finished, the night was thinning toward dawn. We rode back in the detectives' car. We walked into the house to face more activity than we'd left. I saw men in my bedroom, dusting for prints. For the first time, I noticed that the screen was not on the window I'd left ajar when I went to bed—a window that looked out onto the encircling porch.

That must be how the man had entered my bedroom. It had not occurred to me to wonder before. While I was sleeping, in my own bed in my own home, he had stood there watching me through the window and then carefully removed that screen and entered.

I had thought I could sleep with an open window on a cool fall night. Despite Heidi Edmonds, despite Barbara Tucker.

There it was, the thing I was guilty of: I'd left a window open. I stood convicted of not fearing enough.

"There have been two rapes," I said informatively to the detective helping me get to the couch.

He jumped. It was the first time I'd spoken since the doctor's. "Yes," he said. "Maybe more. Some women won't call us, you know."

"Is this the same rapist?"

"After we've talked to you some more, we'll have a better idea. Oh—later we'll need your bathrobe, too, Miss Callahan. I'm sorry."

That was okay with me. I never wanted to see it again after this night was over.

Their questions had been few and brief so far, only aimed at determining how close the rapist might still be to the house. They'd decided right away that a doctor had to come first.

Mimi left the room. I faced the detectives on the opposite couch. Other policemen were coming up to report things in whispered conferences.

Then Mimi was back beside me, holding a glass of water and a handful of pills. "You have to take these," she said.

"What for?"

"Um, in case he had a disease," Mimi said wretchedly. "Dr. Cole said I had to make sure you took them pretty soon."

I had informed the doctor, in a very terse exchange, that I wouldn't become pregnant from the attack. I was on the pill. The very idea of pregnancy had filled me with such loathing that I almost vomited. Now I had to make sure I wasn't diseased. I took two of the pills from Mimi, swallowed them, drank, and shuddered. Then two more. Every time I thought I was through, Mimi handed me more. While I swallowed and shuddered, the detectives began questioning me, their voices quite neutral. I was grateful for that briskness; it helped keep me from collapsing.

And suddenly I became conscious. If it was possible to be walking and talking in a state of unconsciousness, I had been. I could remember my conversation with Mimi's doctor, but not his face, or his office, except the clock on the wall. I stared at the two detectives, seeing them individually for the first time. They had different faces, I observed. They were not interchangeable, as I would have sworn minutes earlier.

"What are your names?"

They looked startled, and glanced at each other.

"Tendall," said the gray-haired one.

"Markowitz," said the heavier man with brown hair.

They waited for me to tell them why I'd asked, or give some kind of signal. They were eyeing me warily; they were unsure of what I might do next.

"He called me Nickie," I said. "He knows me."

I had to tell them everything: every word, every act. And I had to hold myself very tight to get through it.

"I can stand this," I assured Mimi, apropos of nothing. "I lived through that. I can stand this."

Then my awareness began flickering again. It was like drifting in and out of anesthesia. At one point I became aware that the pills were all gone and the glass of water was empty. I must have finished taking the capsules. I took Mimi's hand. Until she gasped, I didn't realize that I was gripping it with unbearable force. When the detectives were asking me the most delicate questions ("And did he— uh—experience an orgasm?") I heard a nagging sort of noise that bothered me, and I glanced around vaguely to find its source. It was Mimi; she was crying.

I didn't want to cry. I was never going to cry . . .

And I went under again, only coming back to myself when a door slammed. Mimi was standing in front of me and the house was empty. I was in a different bathrobe.

"What time is it?"

"Six o'clock," she answered. "The police are all gone. They asked me to bring you to the police department to- morrow afternoon—today—to take pictures."

"Pictures?"

"Your bruises and cuts."

I began to laugh. I'd been photographed for years, for my beauty. Now I was going to be photographed for my cuts and bruises. "How much will they pay me per hour?" I gasped.

Mimi collapsed on the couch beside me and began laughing too. Then she began crying. I watched her curi- ously, my legs carefully parallel, my hands folded neatly in my lap. "I'm never going to cry," I told her.

Wisely, Mimi didn't respond to that. "You're going to bed in my room," she told me.

The thought of going to sleep, of being vulnerable again, made me begin to shudder. I'd been trembling since I'd crawled from my bed hours ago, but now violent mus- cle spasms began to shake me. "I can't get up the stairs," I said helplessly.

Mimi looked as though she was at the end of her re-
sources. "Do you think you can sleep on this couch?" she
suggested finally.

"Not alone, I can't be alone." The very idea made the
shudders intensify. I wanted desperately to bathe, to be
clean, even more than I wanted to rest. As soon as the idea
occurred to me, I knew I couldn't sleep until I washed the
uncleanliness off me, the filth he had left. "I have to bathe,"
I told Mimi.

"I'll help you," she said with instant comprehension.
"We'll have to use your bathroom, though."

That meant passing through my bedroom to get there. "I
can do that," I mumbled. It was increasingly difficult for
me to articulate. I could tell Mimi was having a rough time
just understanding me.

"Okay, here we go," she said bracingly. She put her arm
around me to help me rise.

I read the utter exhaustion printed on her face. "I'm
sorry, Mimi," I whispered.

"Shut up, ass," she said. "I can't cry anymore."

I kept my face turned away from the mirror over the
sink.

We got me into the bathtub, a tub filled with the hottest
water I could stand. I didn't realize how many cuts I had until I sank into the water. I became fully aware as soon as I
submerged. I hissed at the sting. But my God, it was a
blessed thing to wash. I dipped my head down in the tub as
the simplest way to clean my hair. The water became so
soapy with repeated latherings that Mimi finally drained the
tub and turned on the shower attachment to rinse me off.

After the bath, my mind was more at ease. I felt cleaner
inside and out; perhaps a particle of what I'd undergone
had been washed away. Some of my cuts had reopened in
the water. Mimi bandaged them. Then she found my nightgown and helped me into it. It had been a long time since
I'd worn one, and I only knew where it was because I'd un-
packed so recently. Mimi looked a little surprised when I
asked for it.

"I'll never sleep naked again," I said flatly. "I don't know how much of this will stay with me, but that is one thing I do know I will never do again."

Finally, finally, I was ready to stretch out on the couch, with Mimi ensconced on the one opposite. It was daylight. A few cars were moving on the street. The world had come alive again after the death of the night.

I knew when I put my head on the pillow that I wouldn't be able to sleep. I would mime it for Mimi's sake, since she was obviously at the end of her rope. I would keep watch over us.

The next second I was asleep.

Chapter 8

WHEN I AWOKE THERE WAS A MAN STANDING over me. I drew in my breath to scream.

"It's all right, Nickie," Cully said urgently. He knelt beside the couch. "It's all right. It's me."

After a moment my pulse slowed, my breathing eased. "Better in a minute," I whispered. We waited.

I could tell by the slant of the sun across the floor that it was afternoon. Cully was wearing blue jeans. I wondered why he didn't have a suit on, and realized it was Saturday. I felt slovenly in my wrinkled nightgown. I wrapped the light blanket around me as firmly as I could and swung my legs to sit up. My breath whistled in sharply. Movement brought pain. I stared at a dust mote dancing in the air until I had adjusted to this pain.

Cully observed me silently. He sat on the couch beside me. I knew what my face must look like by now; I turned it to him. Directly, deliberately, for once with no artifice, I looked directly into his eyes.

I watched his own face change. I had finally gotten to

Cully. The wound healer saw a massive gash in a human being he knew.

I watched him search for something to say. Cully, the articulate psychologist, was struggling for words. I waited, full of unused anger, my eyes fixed on his face.

He'd never been a toucher, by inclination and by training. But when the words didn't come, he touched me. He searched out a square inch of my face that wasn't damaged and he kissed it very gently.

I remembered thinking once that I would have to survive a bad car smashup to rate a kiss. Well, I'd done it. I turned from him, ashamed of my anger. It shouldn't be focused on him, of all people. He was the one man in Knolls I could acquit of being the rapist. No matter what the circumstances, I would have known Cully.

"Where's Mimi?" I asked quietly. It seemed an eerie echo from two months ago.

"Trying to calm Mother down. They're in the kitchen."

I told him bluntly that I didn't want to see Elaine.

"I know. We'll try to keep her out." Then he said tentatively, "I think I'm going to move in here for a while."

I felt a vast indifference. During the long night my edifice of pride and independence, my integrity, had collapsed after the voice had come from the darkness. Today another structure, called Cully, had slid to the ground. All the feelings I'd built up around Cully's image seemed to crumble in the space of five minutes. For the first time in fourteen years he was just Cully, Mimi's brother, comforting a female he'd known for years, his little sister's best friend.

Now I was a grown woman with no girl left. No structures at all, and I had to start all over again.

I didn't know the first thing about the man at my side. And I wondered for a bleak moment if I really knew Mimi. I suspected I didn't even know myself.

I had no frills left.

At this illuminating and painful moment, Elaine

Houghton went out of bounds and swept into the living room, Mimi on her heels with hands outstretched as if she were thinking of physically restraining her mother.

TODAY I LOOKED AT ELAINE BARE. I'D ALWAYS tended to think of her as a one-dimensional comic-book villainess. Of course, she was human—perhaps not a good mother, but capable of moments of generosity and sympathy. Elaine squatted before me, took one of my hands in hers, and said, "Nickie, I'm so sorry this happened to you. It upsets me no end that this has happened to you in our little town, while you're Mimi's guest." To her credit, she did no more than clench her teeth and swallow hard when she got a close-up of my face.

That's Elaine, I thought. Really sorry it happened at all, but even sorrier that it happened in Knolls in a family home. Obviously Cully had inherited his "slap, stroke" technique from Elaine. But almost in the same instant I realized I was being grossly unfair. Elaine had undoubtedly been scared out of her wits. Her daughter had been only yards away from a terrible crime, and perhaps had escaped being its victim only by being on the second floor of the house.

"I know you'll want to leave us now, and you've only been here a few weeks. Please don't think badly of us."

"Leave?" I said blankly.

"I hardly imagine you'll want to stay here," she said in surprise. "I mean, with everyone knowing . . . you'll be more comfortable where nobody knows."

"Why?" Fool that I was, I really couldn't imagine why. How could I get the support I needed, if no one around me knew me? Where should I go? Home to Mama, who would cry over me and then get drunk? Home to my stepfather, good old Jay?

Elaine began to lose her assurance. Her dark bird-wing brows contracted. "Why, Nickie . . . Who could you date here? I think you've learned an awful lesson, the hard way, bless your heart, but surely you'll want to start all over again somewhere else."

The three of us stared at her. Elaine rocked back on her haunches, a hard thing to accomplish in a ladylike manner in a skirt; but she managed.

Cully said, "Mimi, do you understand what Mother's saying?"

"Yes," Mimi answered wearily. She rubbed a hand across her forehead.

"What?" I asked. "What's she saying?"

"She means no one will want to date you here, since you're damaged goods now," Mimi answered. "I think she's hinting that you somehow brought your rape on yourself."

Elaine had drawn herself up. She was not used to face-to-face challenges. She was not used to open contempt from her daughter. She wasn't sensitive, but she would have needed a hide of iron not to feel her children's exasperation and dislike at this moment.

"Not exactly 'brought it on yourself,'" she protested. "It's letting them think they're equal, welfare letting them have anything they want without having to work for it or pay for it. And the clothes girls wear now."

"No," I said. "I don't believe this." I leaned back against the soft couch and shut my eyes. But there was a sinking feeling in the pit of my stomach.

"You probably just smiled at one on the street, and they just thought it was an invitation."

If Elaine Houghton felt this way, surely others would too. Elaine had never had an original emotion in her life. I hoped her comments would just evaporate; but they stuck to my skin, they congealed. I had more to face than I had imagined.

"Mother, go away," Cully said quietly. I could feel his arm muscles tense.

"Mrs. Houghton," I said, opening my eyes and leaning forward painfully. "Listen to me. You're Mimi's mother, and I don't want to be rude to you. But you have to understand how I feel. What happened last night . . ." I drew a breath. "Getting raped . . . was in no way my fault. If I'd walked down the street buck naked, I would still in no way deserve what happened to me. I am not ashamed. If my purse had been snatched, you wouldn't be saying what you've been saying. This was . . . another crime, a nastier crime. An act of hatred. But it was not my fault any more than a purse snatch would be."

As I mumbled this lengthy speech through swollen lips, I probed myself for the truth of what I was telling Elaine. I was formulating my thoughts as I spoke. It was true. I was not ashamed. But it was also true that I was horrified that even strangers to me would know approximately what had passed in the dark of my bedroom. It was sickening to conjecture that some people would look at me and try to picture my rape; perhaps secretly enjoy that picture, or think it served me right, in some mysterious way. There are a lot of black crevices in the corners of sympathy. Last night I'd fallen into one that had widened into an abyss.

"I don't know if you can see this," I said to Elaine and to myself. "But the man who raped me wants me to be destroyed by what he did. He wanted to hurt me; and he did. I couldn't do one damn thing about it. But he wants me to keep on hurting. I can do something about that. I *won't give him the satisfaction*." My fingers were clenched in fists by the time I finished. I meant what I said down to my bones, I meant it more than I've ever meant anything.

"Well," Elaine said briskly, "I think you're making a mistake, Nickie." She rose in one graceful movement and brushed her hands against her skirt. Washing herself clean of me. "You would forget a lot faster if you moved away. But you're a grown woman, and Mimi owns this house, so I guess there's nothing more I can say."

But of course there was. Elaine was deeply shaken, not only by the anger of her children but by what she must have seen as a NOW diatribe delivered by, of all people, a former model. Elaine's face was red; she was holding down her voice with an effort. "I personally feel you should get out of town and try to put this behind you. And may I add, Don agrees with me."

Mimi and her brother exchanged glances. Mimi had long ago told me that her father agreed with everything Elaine said, to keep the peace and because he loved her. He just did what he wanted after he'd completed his lip service.

"When you get over this being brave to impress people"—and Elaine glanced pointedly from me to Cully—"you may take my advice." Her face twisted with genuine passion. "Honey, how are you going to pass them on the street? Knowing one of them raped you? They'll all talk about it, you know. How will you be able to stand it? I bet half the niggers in town know who did it, but will they tell? Oh no, not on one of their own."

In the North I'd become accustomed to racism being more cleverly cloaked, among my chic acquaintances. I'd temporarily forgotten Elaine's earlier ranting about "welfare" and "taking things for free." Now I understood what she had meant all along. White men wouldn't date me because a black man had raped me, she thought.

"Mrs. Houghton, the man who raped me was white. I don't know anything else about him; but I do know that he was not black. I know from the voice."

That shocked Elaine more than anything else I could have said. She stared at me in utter disbelief. Then she obviously decided I was making my rapist white out of rampant liberalism. "You poor child," she said, and marched out the door.

"What can I say?" Mimi cried. "Nick, I'm so sorry."

"I wonder how much of what she said is true."

"Nothing!"

"A little," Cully said. Mimi made a violent gesture of protest, but Cully raised his hand to silence her. "You're going to notice changes in attitudes," he told me steadily. "But mostly it'll be because people won't know how to express sympathy to a woman who's just been through a rape. They'll be uncomfortable, because they won't know whether you want to talk about it, or maybe couldn't stand it being mentioned. It's almost like . . ." He thought for a moment. "Like you had an enormous green wart on the tip of your nose. No one here would ever dream of mentioning it to you, out of kindness and embarrassment. Even if you had that green wart removed, people *still* wouldn't say anything—for fear of admitting that it had disfigured you before."

I nodded. I could remember how it had been, when this had been the only country I knew. And I remembered, with shame, how uncomfortable I'd been when I talked with Barbara Tucker. I'd put her misery at arm's distance. I was guilty of more than an open window after all, I decided.

"Men, especially, may be uncomfortable," Cully continued, still speaking in his steady professional voice, but with his eyes averted.

Thanks, Cully. I'd already figured that out.

"They may feel guilty that one of them did this to you. Maybe they'll feel uneasy about how you're going to react to other men now—dating and sex and so forth."

"Gosh, it's great having a psychologist in the family," Mimi said savagely. She mimed gap-mouthed admiration.

"I need to be forewarned, Mimi," I said. "I'd never . . . naturally, I'd never thought of all this." Others were certainly going to invest a lot of emotion in my tragedy.

"You haven't exactly had time," she said briskly. "Now, I think you ought to try to walk around some, so you won't get stiff. The doctor wants to see you again this afternoon and take some x-rays of your ribs, just to check, and the police want to take pictures. We have to make a dentist appointment, too."

I didn't want to see anyone at all. I didn't want my face recorded. I wanted to stay in the house. I wanted to get dressed and study. I wanted to do anything normal, anything routine, to keep from remembering the night before. But there was my brave speech to Elaine Houghton to live up to. I rubbed my forehead. There was a gap, I thought, between my intentions and my desires. There was more to face now than I'd faced the night before, when I had seen the thread of my life held in someone else's hands.

The thread of my life was in my own hands again. I was *alive* to face those problems.

Gratitude raced through me for the precious life I had kept. I looked at the sunlight drifting through the curtains. I looked over at my books, piled on the desk on the other side of the room. I was deeply grateful to God that I would be able to open those books again.

I would pay a price for my life. I might lose some of the friends I'd just begun making, lose them in a welter of embarrassment and misunderstanding. But what did that matter if I was still alive?

At that second, I felt I would never lose the wonderful awareness that everything was new for me. I had thought my eyes would never see the world again. I decided I would never take for granted any action my live hands could perform. I looked at those hands, saw the veins still working to purify my still-circulating blood, flexed the muscles that worked so miraculously. I watched the bones move under my skin.

That glory, that beauty, didn't ebb, even when I stood painfully, even when Cully helped me hobble out to the kitchen for the most delicious bowl of Campbell's chicken noodle I'd ever tasted.

CULLY EXPLAINED SOMETHING TO ME LATER THAT day.

"I started to tell you twice, once the day I first saw you and again when we were on our way back from the landfill. I have a friend on the police force, a guy I used to hang around with in the summers." Cully, like Mimi, had gone away to school. "He told me that when Heidi Edmonds got raped, the police thought it was a fluke. A transient, or maybe a boyfriend no one knew about who got carried away. But then they began hearing rumors that another woman had been raped and just couldn't report it. And then another.

"So, my friend figured it wasn't a fluke. There really was a rapist in town. He got the police chief to come to me, with the idea I could give them some directions to look in. But there wasn't anything I could tell them that was helpful. I started to warn you, twice. But both times I decided I'd just frighten you more than I'd get you to be alert. I figured you'd be on your toes anyway, since you'd lived in New York. And after Barbara got raped, I didn't think I needed to say anything."

It wouldn't have made any difference, and I told him so. His face relaxed. "Cully, even if I'd locked my window, which I only *might* have done if you'd warned me, the police told Mimi the locks on those windows are so old a ten-year-old could get in. Don't ever think of it again."

I hope he didn't. I never did.

SUNDAY WAS ANOTHER OUT-OF-KILTER DAY. AFTER the bustle and appointments of the day before, it felt empty. Empty for me, anyway; Mimi was kept busy answering the telephone. No one, apparently, wanted to come by, because they weren't sure what shape I was in. But they wanted to express concern. Mimi said most of the callers sounded frightened.

I hunched on the couch, hearing the reassuring murmur of Mimi's voice in the background. I stared in front of me with an awful emptiness echoing through my whole body. *Emma* lay open on my lap, but I never turned a page. This crisis was too evil for gentle Jane.

I had always been healthy, so physical pain was new to me, and shocking. I couldn't move without a reminder of what had happened to me, though it was never far enough from my thoughts to make that necessary. The rape happened to me over and over again, that Sunday.

I discovered many things.

I discovered that pain requiring vengeance is very

different from accepted pain. The misery of my father's death now seemed equivalent to the coldest, grimmest day of winter, perhaps after an ice storm, when every forward step is shaky. But this pain had pinned me in the middle of the forehead, branding me with a sizzling *V* for victim.

I discovered I wanted to know his face. I wanted to seize that face in my hands and rip it, cause pain, draw blood. I wanted to say, "See! *This* is what you did to me!" I wanted to hang him naked and conscious in a public place, and say again, *"See! This is what you did to me!"* And I would never be able to do it.

But still I wanted that face, and I swore to find it. I swore before I went into the bathroom to look in the mirror for the first time.

I discovered then that my face was finally my own. I would never see or think of it as a separate thing again. I would also never again think of myself as beautiful. Even after the skin healed, even when the bruises faded.

I wanted to know his face.

I WENT BACK TO CLASSES ON MONDAY. IT WAS the hardest thing I'd ever done.

Two days had started the healing but made the discoloration of the bruises more lurid. At least my clothes covered my ribs and stomach. If any student at Houghton College, any resident of Knolls, had wondered who the rape victim was, they would wonder no longer.

That was why I had been beaten; so everyone would know.

As I left the shelter of the house, it occurred to me that any man I saw, any man I knew, might be the one who'd done this to me. He could examine his handiwork; he would be pleased with what he'd done to my face.

And he might be furious that I was apparently going to go on with my life. As that new fear occurred to me, my courage faltered. I clasped my books closer to my chest, as if they could protect me. My feet dragged. I was desperately tempted to turn back to the house, to hide myself from his eyes.

"No no no," I swore out loud, and slapped my chest with the books. Going back to the house today could easily—so easily—be the first step toward shutting myself in it for the rest of my life. I would not, could not, do it. That would give him what he wanted, on a platter. I'd felt that in his rage.

But more than that I did not know. Even under a requestioning by the tired detectives, I couldn't think of anything tangible to tell them, except that the man was white, solidly built . . . his weight had not been light on me; don't think don't think . . . and he had said he might come back.

"Common threat. Don't worry about it. They never do," Detective Tendall had reassured me. He hadn't looked at me as he said it.

Never? Tendall was fudging just a wee bit, I decided. Just a wee bit. So as not to scare me.

Here came a girl, a student. I was approaching her and would pass her. I looked neither to the left nor the right. I heard the sharp gasp as the girl went by.

Beautiful sidewalk, white and even.

In a few hours my classes will be over and I can go back home legitimately, I thought. I will study and I will take another shower and I will not think about Friday night. I will take a pain pill and I will sleep without dreams.

During that longest walk to class, as I caught the faces of those who passed me from the corners of my eyes, a film of that night played over and over in my head: the hand clamping over my mouth, the pillow over my face, the beating, the rape, the pain in Mimi's face. Over and over, as my feet moved forward, I relived that night. The projector in my mind was running that movie continuously, and I had no means to switch it off. I wondered if I would always watch that movie; the audible tortured thudding of my own heart on the soundtrack, the visual shaft of moonlight, the intangible presence of death.

I must've seen it ten times before I reached my classroom. I glimpsed Theo Cochran during one of the intermissions. He nodded to me silently, solemnly, from his desk beyond the open door to his office. He knew. I nodded stiffly back, the screen jumped, the movie sped on.

My tunnel vision was serving me well. But I felt the silence in the classroom as I entered; so different from the silence of admiration that had greeted me the first day. Led Zeppelin T-shirt wouldn't whistle at me now. I sat like a stone at my desk. I heard the sound of the class bell, then the belated footsteps of Dr. Haskell, half a minute late as he'd been ever since the first day. Those footfalls stopped short in the doorway. He had seen me. Then they resumed at a staccato pace to his lectern, and he entered my tunnel of sight. He was white. Every line in his face was deeper, all those grooves and seams etched into the flesh. He started to say something. He looked away.

Go on and speak, I begged him silently. Mention it. If you acknowledge it, it won't be so bad.

But the Stan Haskell who couldn't tolerate seeing even his lover after she'd been assaulted wasn't going to speak. To borrow from Cully's simile, he was going to pretend he didn't notice the gigantic green wart on my face.

That might have made some women feel better. It scared the hell out of me. If other people pretended it hadn't happened, I'd be left alone watching that movie in the dark.

"In our last class . . ." Stan Haskell began jerkily.

And there I was. Alone in the dark. A restricted audience; and no popcorn.

BARBARA TUCKER WAS WAITING FOR ME IN THE hall after class. She flinched when we were face-to-face. I was getting used to that. She drew herself together and laid her hand on my arm. I felt movement on either side; my classmates were departing very slowly, passing me reluctantly, as if they wanted to stop. Stan Haskell had brushed by as soon as he could, casting one unreadable glance at us.

Gradually I became surrounded by people, as though

Barbara and I had formed a dam to hold back their flow. We were all quiet for a long moment. Then the chunky blonde girl who sat to my right in class said, very formally, "I don't want to intrude on your privacy, Nickie, but you have my complete sympathy, and I hope they catch whoever did it. And I hope he resists arrest and I hope they shoot him dead. For Dr. Tucker, too." She said this in one breath, touched me gently on the shoulder, and marched off down the hall. There was a chorus of "Right" and "Me, too," and then a loud and shrill "Kill the son of a bitch" from my dear Led Zeppelin T-shirt.

"Sisterhood, Nickie," said a tiny girl named Susannah with great earnestness. I tried to smile, which caused a cut on my lip to open and bleed. The militance that had filled the hall altered to sick horror.

"Thank you," I mumbled, so the poor things could go.

Barbara's hand on my arm began to urge me toward the women's bathroom. She awkwardly pulled a tissue from her purse with her other hand and dabbed at my lip as we reached the door. We sat on a hideous brown couch. Barbara gave me a cigarette and lit it. Her face twisted.

"For God's sake," I said furiously, "don't cry."

"Neither of us needs that, I know," she said. She gulped a few times. "Okay. Do you think there's any chance they'll catch him?"

"Minimal, in my case. No fingerprints. No one saw anything, least of all me. Except maybe Attila the cat. It was too dark."

"Same here. The first thing the police asked me was, 'Is he black?' " Barbara said grimly.

"White. I could tell by the voice."

"Me, too. I think I'm so damn fair-minded. But you know, that's the first fear I had when he grabbed me. Is it a black? The great racist bogeyman rises again." She brooded over that for a moment while she put out her cigarette with a vicious grinding motion. "What's made this thing a nightmare for me is how Stan hasn't been able to handle it. I haven't seen him away from the college since it happened."

Right now, I didn't give a tinker's damn about how Stan Haskell was handling it. I was worried about *me* handling it.

"He can't deal with it at all," Barbara continued. "I can't fathom his attitude. He's a caring man, he surely believes in the equality of women, but he can't come to terms with me being raped at all."

"Cully says some men are just embarrassed," I offered. Then I remembered that I'd suspected he was counseling Barbara, that he must have formulated the advice he'd given me from his experiences with her.

There had been a flatness in my voice that had penetrated to Barbara. She flushed. "You have enough problems without me burdening you with mine," she said.

I realized I was doing it again. Shoving her off. "Barbara," I said, "we share something pretty unique. I can say this to you, I think. Screw Stan. Let him grow up on his own. He's not tough. We are. We're here. We're going on. Not all men are like him. You've lost something that must have been pretty wonderful. But we're here, alive."

She sensed what I was saying, but it didn't satisfy her, of course; I'd had no right to expect it would.

"Anyway," she said finally, "I couldn't go to bed with him, or anyone, now. Maybe after a long time. With care. A lot of care."

That hadn't been a prime concern of mine, since I hadn't any partner. But I suddenly wondered how that was going to be for me.

We had been wandering through our separate fears for a couple of minutes when Barbara roused herself to ask me how I was physically.

"No broken bones. The dentist tomorrow—I expect a lot of dental work. The eye doctor said Saturday that there wasn't any permanent damage to my eyes, just bruising. I'm sore, and stiff, and I hurt like a sick dog. But I'll get over all that. Mostly, I'm just mad. Barbara—do you hate?"

She flipped the clasp of her purse open and shut a couple of times. She pushed her glasses up on her snubby nose. At last she looked at me directly; I saw something naked behind those glasses.

"For the first time in my life, I frighten myself," she said.

"I know exactly how you feel. What can we do about it?"

"There must be something. I'm torn up inside. Sometimes"—and she pushed a wisp of hair behind her ear—"I can't believe that I can walk and talk and teach class and tell people good morning . . . and all the time I'm carrying this terrible cancer inside me."

"We can pool what we know. We can think, we can figure."

"The police are professionals at that."

"It happened to *us*."

"I'll tell you one thing I know that I don't think the police took much stock in. He knew me. He didn't just know my first name. He *knew me*."

I took a deep breath. "He knew me, too."

"All right," Barbara said with a briskness she hadn't displayed in a long time. "We'll do it. Think about everyone you know. Write names down."

"I'll make a list," I said. This was going to be a different list from any I'd compiled before. "We'll compare. It's a pity Heidi Edmonds isn't here at Houghton anymore."

I straightened up. I felt my shoulders brace. Even probably futile action was better than no action. In my heart I was quite sure that the trained, professional police would do the best job possible. And in New York, our plan would have seemed laughable. But here in Knolls . . .

"I think mad is a good way to take it," Barbara was saying consideringly. "The little girl—she really was, you know—who got raped last summer; she got *sad*. Heidi was one of Stan's students. He told me she became so frightened she wouldn't even go to the bathroom without someone to go with her."

"Oh, I'm scared all right," I said grimly. "It takes an hour and sometimes a pill to get me to sleep. Then I keep waking up. But going away isn't the right thing for me. It may yet get to be too much for me here, but I'm going to try to stick it out."

"I have to stick it out here, I have no option," Barbara said. "The job. Speaking of the job, I have to go meet a class." She gathered together the paraphernalia teachers and students carry with them everywhere. "If you ever need me, call me. Anytime."

We clasped hands briefly and tightly. When I left for my next class, I felt better. I was not alone in that darkened room anymore.

And I made it somehow through the rest of the school day.

WHEN I GOT HOME, A LOCKSMITH WAS PUTTING new hardware on all the windows and doors. Mimi was following him from room to room, a cigarette lit but disregarded in her hand. I was appalled by my mental estimation of the cost of this. I cornered Mimi to tell her I'd pay for it. With one terse phrase she turned me down. When the locksmith left, a check tucked in his pocket and a smile on his face, Mimi asked me if I was ready to move upstairs with her. I'd been sharing her king-size bed for the past two nights; she had been as restless as I.

"No," I said. "I'll keep my bedroom. And sleep in it, starting tonight."

"That's crazy," Mimi said bluntly. "There are two rooms upstairs you could have. All it'll take is a little time and muscle."

It was foolish of me to insist I would sleep in my own bedroom. Sheer bravado, rather than courage. Having determined I wouldn't let this get me down, I was bullheaded enough to persist in any resolution, however ill-reasoned. I should've made some concessions to myself, given myself a little leeway. I should have known my life would never again be exactly as it had been.

"With all those locks you put in," I insisted, "no one in

the world could break in unless he was a professional and had lots of undisturbed time."

"Then, Miss Martyr," she said tartly, "Cully's going to sleep in the dining room right opposite your bedroom."

"There's no need for . . ."

"Just cut out this heroine stuff," Mimi said. Her voice soared high and thin. I saw her hands shake when she lit another cigarette. "You may be willing to be an iron woman, but my God, I'm *scared*." Even the cats, sleeping together peacefully for once, lifted their heads at the warning note in her voice. I felt very small: as my father used to say, "knee-high to a grasshopper."

"Mimi . . . I'm sorry. I've just been so set on overcoming this thing that I hadn't thought about how you must feel." I shut my eyes (they were watering) and bit my lip. Which of course promptly bled.

"Okay, you don't have to flagellate yourself," she said unevenly. "You have enough on your plate right now. You're doing great. Just don't carry it too far. I want Cully to move in for *me*. And he wants to. Just for a while, okay? Charles wanted to move in instead"—and her mouth turned up in a lopsided smile—"but I told him the town had given us enough attention as it was. Besides being good for us, I think the move would be good for Cully."

"What do you mean?"

We had migrated into the kitchen. Mimi began washing dishes. She paused in her task, her hands immersed in the soapy water. She sucked in her lips, a sure sign that she was thinking heavy thoughts. "Cully is a psychologist, but that doesn't mean he's immune to the syndromes he treats in other people," she said finally. "I think he's probably very good professionally. He's always in control, he always knows what he wants to say. And he can keep so calm and detached. Boy, is he good at detachment!" Mimi screwed up her face expressively, and I laughed a little. I picked up a dish towel and began drying.

"I bet lots of people think he's a cold fish," she continued soberly. "But he's not, underneath. He's as vulnerable as anyone else; and maybe more tender than average. Rachel's leaving him hurt, just as bad as Richard's leaving me. But I wailed and cried to you, and now it doesn't ache quite so much." Mimi's crooked smile lit her face. "Cully, now, hasn't wailed and moaned at all. Mama thinks that means he's glad to 'get shuck' of Rachel. Well . . . he may have fallen out of love with her, but he had shared a life with her, and he had a lot of pride involved in that marriage."

"Being a psychologist wouldn't help in that situation," I said as I put the glasses away in the cabinet. "You'd feel like everyone was saying, 'Ha, ha, look at the pro who can't even counsel his own marriage back into shape.' "

"Exactly." Mimi nodded vigorously, the dark cloud of hair flying. "So Cully really needs to feel all male and effective right now, and I do want him here. I think it's a good thing for all of us. Really, won't you sleep a little better with a man in the house?"

"I think, frankly, that I'd sleep better with a shotgun in the house. But since I'm not about to buy one and have no idea how to fire one if I had it, Cully will have to do." I imagined briefly how Cully would react if he knew he was running second to a shotgun. Then I handed Mimi the last dirty cup and saucer and headed toward the living room to try to read my assignments. My body was reminding me at every step that it had been abused, and the damn movie was still playing. Studying wasn't going to be easy, but I had to start sometime.

"Hey," called Mimi as I reached the door. I turned.

"I just want you to know, you're a great woman. Now don't come hug me or anything," she added hastily as I took a step forward. "Or I'll cry again. But I just wanted to tell you that. You should already know I feel that way, but sometimes I want to tell people things I'm sure they know."

"I love you very much, Mimi," I said, and left the room. My eyes were watering again.

Chapter 9

So Cully moved into the house, in a limited way, the next weekend. Since Celeste had left the dining room suite to a niece, the room opposite mine was already empty. Mimi and I had made an exploratory trip to the attic in search of furniture for Cully's room and had discovered a bed set that apparently had been stored up there for years. We managed to haul the mattress halfway down the stairs, but I was too sore to get it any further. Fortunately, at that point Alicia breezed in. She willingly helped Mimi drag the mattress out into the backyard to air. Until her arrival, our labor had been a hasty chore of sweat and curses, and pain for me. With Alicia on the scene the old house rang with giggles and a stream of comments flavored with her heavy accent.

"I hope you all have a beer in the icebox to pay me for that!" she gasped, after the box springs had followed the mattress out into the yard.

"Sure," I said. "We have two six-packs left over from the party." I creaked into the kitchen and bent stiffly to peer into the refrigerator. The bruises on my torso and face were assuming a fainter but wider spectrum of colors now that most of them were almost healed. I had all the hues of a sick rainbow. The deepest cuts were still scabbed, a healthy but hideous development.

It was a temperate early November day. The sun, radiant in a clear sky, was a blessing, not the curse of full summer. The leaves were turning in a halfhearted southern way; a light breeze fluttered them from the oaks. There was peace in that day, and calm; I think we all felt it as we sat on the porch drinking our beers.

"Is Cully going to see his private patients here, Mimi?" asked Alicia idly.

"No, he'll go back to his apartment for that."

"Good. You don't want those folks coming in and out here. I reckon it might be one of them that did this to Nickie." Alicia inclined her head toward my bruises.

Mimi's eyes met mine in surprise. "Why do you think that, Alicia?"

"Oh, it stands to reason," she said calmly. "Any you-know-what who can do a thing like that"—and she crossed her expensively trousered legs tightly—"has got to be sick in the head." Alicia stared out over the serene backyard where Celeste had spent so many hours. The roses were still blooming, but reluctantly, tired of the task. Mao was industriously stalking an oblivious cardinal. "Not that that's any excuse. You hear all the time about criminals with four and five convictions getting back out on the streets in no time. Remember Cotton Meers, out on work release two years after he shot his ex-wife's boyfriend? And us—the people who pay the taxes that pay those judges—we're the ones out here with 'em. We pay over and over. Not them, not the criminals. Oh no, they're sick and they have to be *cured*. Pooh. Some people are just *bad*. Born bad. Not sick—evil. Cure them, hell. They should be *removed*. Like rabid dogs."

I'd heard this view before, of course. Reactionary as it sounded, there was a lot of truth in it. I couldn't deny that the man who'd raped me was genuinely sick; of course he was. Any man who could do what he'd done to a woman who couldn't defend herself, a woman totally unwilling, was sick. Did I want him treated, rehabilitated, freed? Did I pray, if his problem was plain and pure evil, that he'd find the Lord? No-siree. I wanted him to hurt. I wanted him to *suffer*. If that couldn't be arranged, I was willing to settle for just plain death. Nothing like an experience with face-to-face violence to provoke a gut reaction, I thought. And my gut reaction was definitely eye for eye, tooth for tooth. At the same time, and at risk of sounding pompous even to myself, I admitted that a big dose of this vigilantism would ruin my country.

"You know," I began, after Mimi had fetched three more beers, "I wonder if the kind of man who'd do this would ever voluntarily go for help? I doubt, myself, that he's among Cully's patients. Maybe he can justify, in his own heart, what he did to me. He must be able to." I was thinking of this for the first time. "Otherwise, how can he live with himself?"

"He probably didn't even give it two thoughts," Alicia said with disgust. "Don't you waste your time trying to understand an animal like that. Besides, I read two magazine articles that both said rapists have the lowest cure rate of any offenders under treatment. Animals."

Animals don't rape—only men rape; but I decided to let that point go by. I knew what she meant.

"How do you feel about what happened to me, Alicia?" I asked curiously. Alicia gave an impression of transparency, but I'd discovered just now that her true feelings were very different from what I'd expected. Civilized Alicia had let her savage vein show.

She stirred uneasily in her chair. I realized I'd asked a northern question; or not so much northern as unsouthern. Her lips were disapproving. But the beer, or the sweetness of the cool day, or us being women together, made her answer honestly. "I'm scared to death," she said bluntly. "I'm scared to death. You know I'm by myself most of the time, with Ray on the road so much. Why did it have to happen to you, so close to my house? If it had been a nigger woman in the subdivision"—I noticed Mimi wince—"well . . . that kind of thing happens all the time down there. It was bad enough with that little girl this summer, worse when it was Barbara Tucker. But then it had to happen two doors down from me—to someone I've known for years."

After all this directness, Alicia covered her face with her hands, to let her features re-form behind them. She sighed, uncovered, and looked directly at me for the first time that afternoon. "Sometimes I think I'm just *mad* at you since it did happen to you—not to someone I can forget about," she said. We stared into each other's faces for a long moment. Her blue eyes dropped; she sighed. "There, I've gone and said it and probably hurt your feelings, and that's not Christian. You shouldn't have gotten me in a corner, Nickie. I'm real fond of you, but you shouldn't have gotten me in a corner. You just forget what I said. You have other fish to fry than worrying about what I think. I'll just go on with all my committees," she said, making a wonderful wry face, "and run this town till I have a baby."

She reassumed her brightness like a favorite sweater. "Got to run, now," she said cheerfully. She rose, gathered up her beer cans to deposit in the kitchen on her way through the house, dropped a sudden kiss on the top of my head, and breezed away.

"I did wrong," I told Mimi.

"You didn't do wrong. Your crisis just spread. The old 'stone in the pond' image. They always do, crises. It's not just yours. It's everyone's."

"That makes me feel guilty."

"Then you are a true southerner, despite your Yankee ways," Mimi told me solemnly.

We both laughed, startling Mao's intended victim, who gave a wild squawk and flew away. I realized it was the first time I'd laughed in a week. Mao looked at us reproachfully; Mimi promised him an extra dollop of 9-Lives at supper. Then Cully's car pulled in beside Mimi's on the gravel apron, and he emerged with an armload of clothes. The afternoon melted away in toting, lifting, and arranging.

After supper (I made chicken-fried steak, one of Cully's favorites, in his honor) we pulled on sweaters and returned to the porch to watch the dusk. Darkness was closing in faster and faster as the year drew to a close. After we had settled in the lawn chairs, due to be stored for the winter, none of us spoke. We were three people who had known each other for a long time and were enjoying each other's silent companionship, the evening, our place in the world. For the first time, I thought that true peace might come to me again, that the even glow of my life before the rape might resume.

IN THE NEXT TWO WEEKS CULLY BEGAN ADJUST-ing to us, and we to his male presence. (That meant, chiefly, that we remembered to be dressed when we left our rooms.) Since he wasn't due in his office at the college until nine, he went out to jog at seven-thirty every morning. I had the bathroom all to myself to get ready for my eight o'clock class.

Houghton's committees were recovering from their beginning-of-the-term exhaustion and churning with projects. Mimi was spending hours on the telephone at work and at home, reminding people to attend this or accomplish that. If I listened, I could hear her every evening while I studied in the living room. I'd never understood exactly what Mimi did, but her job title was College Coordinator. As she explained it, she had to know what every club and committee on campus planned in the way of activities and projects, allot them a date and room for meetings and whatever similar help they needed, and handle the needs of the campus. For example, if the Chi Omegas or the Chess Club wanted to "beautify" the campus one Saturday, Mimi might suggest that an ornamental bridge in the gardens needed painting. If the Recruitment Drive Committee wanted to meet in the Executive Conference Room on the same night the Campus Entertainment Committee wanted to use it, Mimi settled that, somehow, with a characteristic combination of tact, common sense, and steamrolling.

Apparently there was a lot more involved, but these were Mimi's main functions. She also served on several committees herself, simply because she was a Houghton and therefore had a strong interest in the college.

I heard a lot about Mimi's job in the weeks following the rape. My fund of small talk seemed to have dwindled away. Mimi filled in the gap while I waited for a new crop to grow. Cully chipped in with anecdotes about the iniquities of his predecessor, who'd given students some rather strange advice, to hear the stories Cully told. Now that I could observe Cully from a more detached point of view, I discovered he had a deep-buried sense of humor and a lot of patience.

Although all of us may have been thinking of what had happened to me, and who might have done it, my two housemates never discussed it unless I brought it up. Cully and Mimi listened whenever the terror and anger got to be too much for me. I tried not to drag on them, to leech them; I only went to them for help when I couldn't stand my own company anymore.

A week after Cully moved in, I walked in my sleep. He found me looking up the staircase from the foot of the stairs, trying to raise my leg to mount them. I only half-woke when he told me gently to go to bed. I obeyed in a stupor; I only recalled the incident the next day when he cautiously asked me how I was feeling. I don't think I ever walked in my sleep again. But sometimes when I went to bed very tired or anxious, I would wake about three o'clock with my heart pounding, sweating in the chilly night. Most of those nights I could go back to sleep. If the fear or the rage didn't keep me awake.

The detectives dropped in again after a week, to ask me if I'd remembered anything else. I had nothing to tell Mr. Tendall and Mr. Markowitz. They didn't seem to expect much.

Charles's lawyer friend didn't ask me out again. I was not surprised, and not much hurt. Charles himself was very awkward around me when he came to pick up Mimi or to eat supper with us. He treated me like Mad Aunt Letitia taking an outing from her attic; he humored me. But at least, as I kept reminding myself, he was trying to be kind.

I tried, too, even though it nearly cost me my expensive new dental work. I ground my teeth together frequently. The depth of my irritation did surprise me a little. I'd been halfway to liking Charles Seward before I'd been raped. (Everything was divided into two phases for me—before the rape and after.) Now Charles's mere presence filled me with uneasiness. Don Houghton's, too. I couldn't understand it. Don was sweet; he suffered through acute embarrassment to tell me how sorry he was I'd been "hurt."

Other men didn't affect me that way, so why Charles and Don? What did they have in common? At odd moments I wondered, but I could never figure it out. I dismissed it as a fluke.

Barbara and I met in her office on a Thursday afternoon, which was a free afternoon for both of us. I'd been compiling my list in odd moments. Sometimes in the middle of a class a name would hop into my mind, and I'd surreptitiously whip out my pieces of paper and write it down. The list was dismayingly long, despite the brevity of my life in Knolls. I'd met so many men the times I'd stayed with Mimi years before. There were so many male students in my classes.

Barbara's list was even more staggering. She knew almost all the male faculty members and at least a couple hundred students. She knew fewer townspeople, but she'd met some, of course, in her years at Houghton.

I guess the same thought crossed both our minds as we stared blankly at the little pile of paper: Our project was impossible. Swiftly I tried to imagine factors that might make our failure less sickeningly disappointing. The depth of our outrage would fade with time. It had to; human beings who wanted to remain mentally healthy could not carry such a crushing load. The rapist might get caught tomorrow, go to trial, get a heavy sentence . . .

But Barbara, who had managed words on paper for years, had other ideas. "Our old friend process of elimination," she said, her crisp midwestern vowels snapping clearly. "Okay!" She pushed the brown frame of her glasses back up her snubby nose. "How old was the voice?" she asked me.

It was like a pop quiz. "I would say—thirty or over," I answered slowly. "Past youth, way past youth."

"Same here. There, we've eliminated the students, except for the overage ones."

I began to feel more optimistic. "I only know two students my age or older," I said. "Two vets. Dan Kirby and Paul Scotti."

Barbara closed her eyes. "Don't know Paul Scotti," she said finally. "Dan Kirby's in my Victorian Prose class."

"Then we have one name."

"And we've eliminated about two hundred fifty men."

"In one fell swoop."

We'd both had the foresight to list students separately. Barbara threw away two sheets of her list and one of mine. "What else do we know that could eliminate some more names?"

I pinched my cheek to help me think. "White. Since we talked about that before, I presume you didn't list any blacks." Barbara nodded. "Heavy . . . and not extremely tall or short. That should knock out a few people."

"The short part, anyway. I thought he was average or maybe a little taller."

"And you were standing up, so you'd know better than I would. Strike the shorties and the very skinny men."

Excluding the students except for Dan Kirby, my list consisted of twenty-six names. Barbara said hers reached fifty-one. This purge of too-short, too-thin men pared my list to twenty, Barbara's to forty-two.

"Compare, now they're manageable," I suggested, and

handed over my list. I watched Barbara's pen move down
the columns. It hesitated over some names, drew a decisive
line through others.

"Cully Houghton's not on your list," she said at one
point. "He's on mine."

"He was with me when you were raped, Barbara."

"Oh. Okay." A line, thank God.

At last she threw down her pen and lifted her glasses to
rub her eyes.

"How many?" I asked anxiously.

"Nine," she said. "Just nine. That match."

I hadn't thought the list could be narrowed so quickly.
At first I felt elated. Then I felt sick.

"Let's check before we meet again, to see if either of us
forgot anyone. For example, did you include your postman?"

"Oh," I said slowly. "Mr. McCluskey. No."

"But I don't know him. So he cancels out. Anyone
else?" I shook my head.

"Then let's stop. I can't stand much more of this."

"I know what you mean." It had its own peculiar ghast-
liness, our little project. I began to gather up my things. I
asked, "Did you know the dectectives before?"

Barbara's hand froze in the act of passing my marked-
down list back to me. "Oh my God," she said. "I knew John
Tendall. Yes."

"I met him at a security lecture he gives at every orientation," I told her bleakly. "I just now remembered."

Barbara rubbed her forehead. She added John Tendall to
both our lists. Ten names.

Jeff Simmons, college president
Jeffrey Tabor, cashier
Don Houghton, businessman
Charles Seward, lawyer
Ray Merritt, salesman
Theo Cochran, registrar
Randy Marquette, English professor
J. R. Smith, English professor
Dan Kirby, student

John Tendall, detective

"We've both got to think," she said, as I stuffed the piece of paper in my purse. "We're doing the best we can," she added obscurely.

"I'll call you as soon as I'm sure I've got every single name on there," I said.

She smiled up at me. She looked small and frail behind her big littered desk. The deep auburn of her hair made her face seem even whiter.

"We're doing the best we can," I agreed. And it did seem to me quite an achievement. In thirty-odd minutes we'd managed to establish that our assailant was one of ten men. In making those sweeping eliminations we were able to do what the police could not, because we both were convinced that the man who raped us knew us. Now we couldn't even try to persuade the detectives who were handling our cases. One of them was on the list.

IN FACT, WHAT THE TOWN WAS DOING AT THIS time was figuratively holding its breath and waiting for the next rape, though none of us realized it until afterward. Heidi Edmonds had been raped in early August. Barbara had been raped in early September. I had been raped in the latter part of October. And there were the rumors from Cully's policeman friend, rumors of at least two victims who hadn't gone to the police. Cully confirmed one rumor on a night when Mimi and I were wondering out loud if the attacks were evenly spaced.

"There was one in late August," he said, and gave each of us a look to assure our silence.

"He must be counseling her," Mimi murmured over the after-supper dishes. We would never mention it to Cully again. But among his books I noticed several new ones on rape and the treatment of offenders and victims. So it was true that Barbara, myself, and Heidi Edmonds had an unknown companion or two—or three, or even four.

"We should form a club," I told Barbara bitterly one day

as we sat in damned-together closeness at a table in the noisy student center. "Think how we could narrow down the list!" The count still stood at ten, though we'd rummaged our brains for men we might have forgotten initially.

Barbara didn't answer. Stan Haskell had just come in, and her eyes were following him with a mixture of anger and grief. He was with a young anthropology professor who had the kind of quiet pleasant looks Barbara had. Stan picked women of a type. Surely the rapist did too? Perhaps Barbara and I should concentrate on what we had in common, what our near-fatal attraction was, rather than on our list. There was a pattern, I was convinced. There had to be a pattern, a reason. But maybe we two were too close to see our similarity. It might take a less involved person to spot it.

As I walked home a few minutes later I was praying, an infrequent activity for me until recently. I was praying that some nice man would ask Barbara out. Then, self-engrossed human that I am, my thoughts shifted to some reading I had to do, and from there to a letter I'd gotten the day before from my mother. She'd hinted heavily that she and Jay Chalmers weren't getting along too well. And she'd written it sober, I could tell. A couple of months ago, she'd been able to hold off until after church. I had already written her back, the longest letter I'd sent Mother in years. I hoped. I was afraid to hope.

I climbed the stone steps to the front yard, then the wooden steps to the front porch, with an ease and absence of pain that pleased me. Almost well.

"Mimi?" I called. She sometimes came home to lunch, walking for the exercise; so she might be in the house even if her car wasn't there. I hadn't glimpsed the bumper from the street, as I could if the car was parked behind the house.

"I'm up here," she called from her floor of the house. She came down in a clatter, dark hair bouncing on her shoulders. She was carrying Attila by his middle, so she was angry. The cat had a guilty, smirky look about him. His big green eyes went from my face to Mimi's with false affection: I adore you, don't punish me.

"This durn cat turned over my bath powder, and now I'm late," she said breathlessly. She handed the culprit to me. I gave him a severe shake, but then I hugged him. I'm a born sucker.

"You want me to get it up off the floor?" I offered.

"No, I got it. That's why I'm late. I'm going to run over to Alicia's instead of walking back to the college. She's due at the same meeting in"—Mimi glanced at her tiny silver watch—"five minutes. I've got to run. I'll cut through the backyards, maybe I can catch her going out the door."

Carrying a struggling Attila, I followed Mimi through the kitchen. I put the cat out and then opened the refrigerator to see if there were any pears left.

"Her car's still there!" Mimi called back triumphantly. She thudded down the back steps. She would cross through old Mrs. Harbison's yard to Alicia's back door.

I'd washed a pear, dried it, and turned to lock the back door behind Mimi when I heard the sound. I knew immediately it was coming from Mimi, though I'd never heard her scream before. I dropped the pear, ran out the back door, flew down the steps, and crashed through the hedge. I glimpsed Mrs. Harbison looking out her kitchen window as I sped across her grass. "Call the police!" I shouted, and saw her begin to turn.

Mimi was screaming no longer: She was stock-still on the steps to Alicia's glassed-in back porch. She was holding the door open with one hand. The door was smeared with something like rust.

I didn't want to see what Mimi was seeing. I checked my pace abruptly and stood gasping four feet away. Mimi's head turned slowly and her eyes met mine. The brown of her irises stood out shockingly in her face, which had turned a dirty gray. I felt my scalp prickle. Against my will, my feet moved until I stood beside my friend.

Alicia's eyes were also wide and staring. Her face was

even grayer. She lay in a crucified sprawl on the floor of the porch. We didn't need to check her pulse or breathing; even I could tell she had been dead for hours. Because I couldn't bear to look at her, I raised my eyes and stared through the length of the house. As though I was locked in a dream, I slowly recorded the fact that Alicia's front door was ajar, its dead bolts pulled back. And I thought, Barbara and I are right. Alicia knew him, too. She let him in.

WE HAD TO WAIT FOR THE POLICE. WHEN THE PA-trolmen arrived, they asked Mimi to check briefly to see if anything was missing. I didn't suppose for a minute that the police really thought the killer had been a panicked burglar. But I guess they had to be sure. After all, it was the first time the rapist had actually killed anyone.

The sunshine was horribly bright in Alicia's living room. It shone with autumn gilding on the blood spots on the pale gray carpet, traced with golden color the rusty handprint on the newel post. I wondered how this house, lavished with Alicia's care, could tolerate her death so easily; how the sun could bathe the evidence of her last moments with such gracious light. Her mortal fear, the annihilating terror I knew so well, had remained behind her: I felt it.

She had fought for her life every inch of the way. She had almost made it. Almost.

The trail of her last moments led through the house. Spots of blood on the carpet inside that open front door. The handprint on the newel. One of her slippers. A knife scar from a thrust that had missed her and scored the wall. Splotches of blood trailing through the kitchen. And finally her body, collapsed inside the back door, blood from her hands smeared beside the locks as she'd fumbled to work them; had unlatched them but had not been able to get out that door. Alicia had nearly made it out into the yard, where she could have hidden in the shrubs until her screams brought help.

I had seen Alicia's intact underwear under her bathrobe,

pinned askew by her fall. So she'd been spared rape but she'd lost her life, oh Alicia! Her terror and desperation were as thick in the house as a fog. I was frightened for myself, in the part of me capable of selfish thought. It was too soon for me to tolerate this. But I had to, since Mimi was still upstairs.

My old companions Tendall and Markowitz appeared at the back door, surveying what lay there before crunching around to the front door on the gravel of the driveway. Then Alicia's body was hidden from my view by the police technicians who gathered around her.

She would have hated them seeing her as she was.

The detectives came in the front door, taking care not to touch the knob or sill. They weren't surprised to see me. Someone must have filled them in. They nodded but were too engrossed in their job to pay me much mind. I stared at John Tendall to watch his reaction, so I could report to Barbara; he was on the list. He simply looked preoccupied and professional. He had thick gray hair, meticulously groomed. With his deep tan and flashy sports jacket, he looked like a smalltime hood rather than a police detective. Markowitz was just as finicky with his hair—he favored sculpted waves of the Jerry Lee Lewis school. He was beefy and pale, with sharp eyes staring from a blank face. They were both workmen absorbed in a technically tricky job.

I was increasingly concerned about Mimi. The police shouldn't be keeping her so long. She needed to get out of this house. Just as I rose to look for her, she appeared on the stairs. Her face was a horrible color now, even her lips; white as the dresses we'd worn when we graduated from Miss Beacham's—Mimi, Alicia, and I. Mimi was shaking so hard she looked like she had palsy. One of the patrolmen had to help her down the stairs. I instantly got myself to the foot and waited there with arms uplifted, as if to receive an infant. I had no more grief to spare for the handprint on the newel post. Alicia was dead. Mimi was alive, and Mimi was going to collapse very soon.

Even as I had my arm around her and we turned to go,

Markowitz was asking if Mimi knew how they could get in touch with Ray.

"Call Ray's mother, Mrs. Ralph Merritt," I said briefly. Later I wondered how I'd managed to dredge up that long-buried name.

We had to leave by the front door, of course. There were neighbors standing on their front porches looking at the police cars. People in Knolls were as curious as people anywhere, but they were ashamed of it. For a few seconds no one came to help me—not out of fear of involvement but for fear of seeming nosy and meddlesome. Finally old Mrs. Harbison (who could consider herself a member of the situation, so to speak, since she'd called the police) hobbled down to give me what assistance she could. It was enough. As soon as the old lady saw I could manage and that Mimi was safely deposited on one of the couches, she left after one quiet question.

"Is Alicia dead?"

I nodded silently. I remembered what I'd long ago learned from Mimi: Alicia had given Mrs. Harbison a ride to church every week. Alicia had called the old lady every time she went to the grocery store, to see if Mrs. Harbison needed anything. Now the old lady was shaking her head from side to side, and tears began trickling through the papery wrinkles as she turned to leave.

Mimi was crying convulsively, unable to speak or move. When I thought I could leave her, I called Cully at the college. Ten minutes later he came into the house like a whirlwind. He folded his long arms around his sister and held her to him.

I was unnecessary, and I needed to be by myself. I sat in the kitchen breakfast nook with my hands folded and my legs tight. I stared out the bay window into that lovely serene yard, at the last blowsy rose blooms. The blooms bent their heads waiting for the executioner frost. Time passed.

Cully came to sit opposite me. He blocked my view of the roses. "I found some tranquilizers left over from her breakup with Richard," he told me.

"Good."

"She's asleep."

"Good."

I poured Cully a cup of coffee heated up from the morning. I put it in front of him gracelessly and sat down again. He stared blankly for a moment at the steam rising from the cup, as if he couldn't identify the drink. He lit a cigarette and smoked it, and drank the coffee.

After a while I got a cup for myself.

"She fought hard," I commented. I imagined a pin lying in front of me; I would pick it up, if I could, and stick myself with it, to raise some feeling. I was only a loose-knit bag of perishable bones and skin.

Cully's hand covered mine, which lay fisted on the table. I looked at the black hair that grew in a pattern on the back of his hand. If I was ever called on to identify Cully's body, I thought, I would know it by that pattern.

"She fought, that's why she died," I said. "I was too scared to lift a finger, so I lived. He knew her. He knows me."

I was so alone. I opened my mouth and words came out, but I didn't know what they would be. The cool clean autumn air came through the window over the sink. It was polluted with the scent of those last rotting roses. That smell would be with me for the rest of my life.

"Look at me, Cully," I said, though he had been looking at me all along. It was I whose eyes were lowered. I raised them now. "I'm not beautiful anymore, Cully. Look at my face."

His own face was full of pain. He looked paler than ever, the lines from nose to mouth deeper.

"It could've been me lying there, Cully."

"No."

"Dead, Cully."

He was on his feet and he hauled me off the bench with a violent yank. He kissed me. His fingers wound in my hair as he pulled my head back.

While, two doors away, the ambulance came to cart off

what remained of Alicia, while Ray Merritt drove home to find his wife butchered, while the police took pictures and scattered fingerprint dust over Alicia's beautiful furniture, while Mimi slept a silent drugged sleep, Cully and I made sure we were alive, alive, alive.

ON SATURDAY MORNING, WHEN MIMI GOT UP after sleeping in spells throughout the previous afternoon and night, Cully had left to get some warmer clothes from his apartment. The bite in the air that morning was a definite warning of winter. I got one of my heavy blankets out of the hall closet and put it on the end of the bed, after I'd pulled on my new winter bathrobe. My emotions were in chaos, a nauseating mixture of joy, grief, and fear. The joy was temporarily banished by the sight of Mimi's face when she stumbled down the stairs and asked me for some coffee.

She was shivering with cold and looked white and drained; but Ray Merritt was as close a friend as Alicia had been, and Mimi was convinced she should rush to his side. It took me a long time to dissuade her. I think her own weakness finally did the trick. I could tell there was something pressing her, something besides grief and shock; but I wasn't about to ask her what it was. She would tell me when she chose.

After two hours and four cups of coffee, Mimi quite abruptly told me she thought Charles Seward, her young lawyer, was the rapist. "Because," she explained wearily, "when we went out on a date last week, and then one time before you were raped, we really had a wrestling match in the car. I hate to talk about it. It sounds so—high school. But this thing last week. When he stopped in front of the house, he just—grabbed me, and then he was just all over me."

Charles Seward was on our list.

"Ah—you didn't want to do it?" I asked hesitantly.

"Not in front of the *house*." Mimi summoned some outrage. "Not in the damn *car*. I mean, I've always assumed that sooner or later I'd sleep with Charles, but not then. I've been jittery about what happened to you and Barbara, and when he grabbed me like that, I got scared all of a sudden. I kind of yanked backwards, and he grabbed harder. It was much worse than the little tussle we'd had before, right before you . . . anyway, I really got scared. I hauled off with my free arm and whacked him in the face. That calmed him down. Which was good for *him*. Because next I was going to grab for his *balls*!" Mimi managed a shaky smile, and I did too.

"Mimi, did he ever say anything about what was happening?"

"Not then, because I got that car door open and got into the house as fast as my legs could go," she said flatly. "He called me the next day, and I hung up on him. I'm sure he has plenty to say; I don't know if I want to listen."

We eyed each other. "Do you think—really, truly—that it might be Charles?" I asked dubiously. If Alicia had lived to help Barbara and me, he would have been on her list, too.

"I was scared to death," she answered indirectly. "My God, what if it *is*? A man I've been dating for months, someone I really care for. What kind of person does that make me, by the way, that someone that creepy would want to date me?"

Mimi's nose turned red, her eyes watered, and a couple of tears trickled forlornly down her cheeks. She used her napkin to blot them. She resembled an abandoned kitten far more than the lioness her mane of hair usually suggested. Mao jumped in her lap and wailed for attention. Mimi hugged the little cat with a passion that startled the animal, and turned all her attention to tickling Mao's chin.

I had realized that the man who'd assaulted me was someone I knew, but I'd realized it in an abstract way. I hadn't really felt it in my gut. The fact that Alicia—who had told us only two weeks previously how tightly locked she kept her house, who had told us how frightened she was—had opened her door to her killer was the strongest possible confirmation that Barbara and I knew our incubus in another guise. Now that I had a name, Charles Seward, to fit into the nightmare, I did feel it in my gut. I pictured Charles's face above me in the darkness, Charles's hand holding the knife. A man, not a demon. Not "it" but "him."

"Should you tell the police?" Even I could hear the doubt in my voice.

"What?" Mimi asked angrily. "That I had a tussle with my date in a car? When I was upset and nervous anyway? Can't you hear them soothing me down? 'Now, now, Miss Houghton'!"

Of course I could. "And it might not be him, anyway," I muttered. Charles felt wrong, somehow, no matter how uneasy I'd been around him lately.

"Of course it might not," she agreed, still with that edge of hysterical anger.

We fell back to gazing into our coffee, lost in separate trains of thought. There was a knock on the kitchen door. I jumped, and Mimi almost dropped her mug. Mao sped toward the living room with a startled yowl.

The knock sounded again as we looked at each other, shamefaced. Shaking her head, Mimi rose to answer. There were no clear panes in the kitchen door. We were going to have to quit opening it blindly, I decided, even as Mimi twisted the knob.

The man at the door was Charles Seward. Mimi's back stiffened; I heard her breath whistle in. Her fear, rational or not, leaped across the room and infected me. There was a sharp snap. I looked down. My fingers had broken the handle of my coffee cup. Suddenly the tableau seemed surrealistic: Mimi frightened at the door, her face searching for the right expression; I at the table in my bathrobe with coffee trickling down it; and a young lawyer at the door, not menacing but surely—sheepish.

"Mimi, please let me talk to you, please just listen to me for a minute." Charles spotted me sitting in the breakfast nook. His hands made a quick gesture of helplessness. "Nickie, please—I need to talk to Mimi alone."

Ordinarily I would've vanished instantly. This wasn't ordinary. Old Mrs. Harbison next door couldn't help us if she wanted to, I thought quickly. The Carters on the other side were gone; I'd seen them pull out in their car. There wasn't any telling when Cully would return.

I gauged the distance to the knife rack above the counter, all the way across the kitchen, and wondered if Mimi could slow him down long enough for me to reach it. At the same time, it was almost impossible for me to believe I was contemplating a situation in which I would have to stab Mimi's boyfriend.

But when Charles took a step forward, my muscles tensed to move. At that moment, as if on cue, the front doorbell rang. My breath came out in an explosion of relief. "I'll get it, Mimi," I said in an odd bright tone, as if Mimi were an unstable child.

I almost ran, but restrained my pace to a brisk walk. I perceived that we were trying to make the scene *normal*; both Mimi and I were eerily trying to pretend that we supposed nothing lay behind Charles's appearance except a man wanting to make up with his woman. Why were we doing that instead of screaming bloody hell and attacking Charles? Was this some form of passive defense, pretending Charles meant us no evil so he would take our cue and do us none?

I peered through the panes in the door . . . Theo Cochran. I hadn't exchanged more than a few words with Theo since the party. I was so anxious about the situation I'd left in the kitchen that it didn't surprise me at all that Theo was calling at Mimi's rather early on a Saturday morning. I swept the door open and ushered him in with an enthusiasm that must have bewildered him.

"Come right on back," I babbled. "Mimi's out in the kitchen and we're having coffee. Come have a cup with us."

"Well, thank you," Theo said with evident surprise, pulling off his jacket and gloves. I shut the door and sped past the registrar to lead the way to the kitchen, moving so swiftly he had to hurry to keep up.

Mimi was still blocking Charles's entrance. When she

heard our steps behind her, her shoulders sagged. Charles's expression of gaping astonishment changed to one of frank resentment as I came to stand by Mimi. I abandoned poor Theo in the middle of the floor. When Mimi felt my shoulder touch hers, she said quickly, "Thanks for dropping by, Charles. I'll—be in touch later." She took a step forward, forcing him to retreat onto the porch. Then, with a horribly social smile, she shut the door in his face. We stood there shoulder to shoulder until we heard Charles's feet cross the porch and descend the steps.

Behind us Theo Cochran shuffled, reminding us that he was there and waiting. Mimi recovered first and turned to him with a dazzling welcome. "How nice to see you," she said shrilly. "Have a seat, if you don't mind sitting out here in this messy old kitchen. I'll get you a cup of coffee; or tea?"

"Thank you, tea," he murmured, and slid into the place I had occupied on the bench.

Mimi grasped my hand for a moment, squeezed it, then went to fetch Theo Cochran his tea.

THEO EXPLAINED HIS MULTIPLE MISSION. AS REG-istrar, he was automatically a member of the Recruitment Drive committee, which was supposed to have met the day before when Mimi had gone to pick up Alicia. There had been a quorum present without them, so the committee, of course not knowing anything of Alicia's death, had proceeded to vote on a number of projects. Now Theo's thoroughly bureaucratic soul was in turmoil. He realized, I heard him tell Mimi, that this was an awful time to come to see her, but he'd really come to talk to her as a college official and a member of the committee; some of the measures passed had been most important. Now a new member would have to be appointed . . .

I overheard most of this from my room, where I'd scrambled into my clothes and then thrown the door back open while I was changing my sheets. I didn't really trust anyone right now, even proud, portly Theo (he was on the list), and I was worried, after I caught the drift of the conversation, that Mimi would be angry and grieved all over again at Alicia's demise being discussed in terms of committees and resolutions. I needn't have worried. When it came to the college and mention of the word *committee,* Mimi became all business. Theo's visit was even therapeutic for her. People might perish, but Houghton College kept rolling on.

I didn't listen to the ensuing discussion or what they decided. Changing the sheets had put me in mind of more interesting things. I wondered when Cully would be home. I was half-afraid to see him again. He'd been gone this morning before I was really awake.

Their voices jogged me back to earth. They had risen and moved closer to my door.

". . . to tea," Theo was saying. "Sarah Chase has been trying to get you this morning, but our phone's out of order, so when she found I was coming over . . ."

"Thursday? I'll call her, Theo, I know we'd love to come; but of course I have to find out about the funeral." Mimi's voice was thinning again now that she was thinking of Alicia. Theo should leave.

"I'm sorry, again, for intruding," he said. "I tell you, I'm mighty worried about Sarah Chase. I wouldn't let her go out at night to her bridge club, but another woman picks her up and brings her home. It's terrible how this seems to be happening to Miss Beacham's graduates. Had that occurred to you?"

"What?" Mimi was startled. They were almost outside my door now. I looked up sharply.

"Well, Nickie, you know, and now Mrs. Merritt. It's made me kind of extra anxious about Sarah Chase, as I'm sure you can understand."

Barbara hadn't gone to Miss Beacham's.

Theo's back was to me. He happened to look in the open door of the former dining room, now Cully's room. I saw his shoulders stiffen at the sight of men's clothes dumped on the bed.

"I think Theo must be something of a prude," I remarked after Mimi had shown him out.

"Oh, you noticed. He didn't say one word, but he kind of snorted," Mimi said with a grin. "Someone'll tell him it's just Cully. Wouldn't Theo have made a perfect English butler?"

I pictured the registrar in a swallow-tailed coat, and laughed. Mimi settled herself on the foot of my bed and relayed Sarah Chase's invitation. "Isn't that sweet?" she said. "Tea! Thursday afternoon, okay?"

I thought about my class schedule. "Fine with me," I said. "But . . ." I turned back to my vanity and fussed with my comb and brush. "When's the funeral, I wonder?"

"Tuesday. There's a delay because of the autopsy," said Cully from the doorway. My heart gave a ridiculous lurch. "But Mimi, I'm afraid, has to attend the inquest this afternoon. The coroner called before you two were awake."

"Inquest," Mimi said. The remainder of the spark that had animated her during Theo's visit, as she'd gotten to talk about normal life instead of violent death, was extinguished. She was face to face with Alicia again. "I expected Ray to call me himself. Maybe this morning. But I guess . . ."

I guess we have to go to the funeral home, I told myself reluctantly. It seemed to me we'd been through enough; but after all we were alive. We had to pay for that, I supposed.

"I think the body will be at the funeral home by Monday morning or evening," Cully said. "I saw Alicia's aunt at the filling station. But the inquest this afternoon will be real short. Don't worry about it, Mimi."

She seemed to wilt under my eyes. I sat beside her on the bed. We huddled together holding hands like children. Cully folded down on my left.

"But why Alicia?" Mimi whispered.

I decided to take that literally. "Exactly." Mimi needed something to think about, and I needed another viewpoint. "Why me? Why Alicia? Barbara? Heidi Edmonds?"

Mimi straightened. "Right." She understood me instantly.

"Why you all, out of all the women in Knolls? You're beautiful, Nickie. Alicia was attractive in her own way, but no one would say she was beautiful. That girl this summer, she was just an average-looking girl. Barbara's plain, really, unless you know her."

"Alicia's lived here all her life," Cully muttered. "Nickie just came back here, hasn't ever before really lived here." His eyes narrowed with concentration.

"As Theo said, Alicia and I, at least, are connected through Miss Beacham's," I observed. "We went there."

"That's so," Mimi said. "He did mention that. I went to Miss Beacham's too." She shivered.

"Along with Theo's wife, as he was saying," I thought out loud. "But I don't think Heidi Edmonds went there, did she? You would've known and told me so, Mimi. And Barbara didn't, of course."

"Strike that pattern."

"Cully, isn't there bound to be a pattern?" I touched his sleeve.

"I think so, but I can't be sure," he said. "I've never had a patient with a record of rape offenses. I've never studied it before. I am now doing extensive reading on the subject," he added grimly. "There are all kinds of classifications of rapists, with all kinds of motivations, of course. Rapists most often do follow some kind of pattern, but it might be something as vague as simple availability, or women who look under twenty-one, or women who have gray hair."

"Well, we weren't all equally available," I pointed out. "Heidi Edmonds was in the open, and Barbara was in her apartment and he had to break open the back-door lock."

"Which was as flimsy as anything can be and still be called a lock," Cully interjected. "No expertise required."

"He broke in here via the window. The open window. Just a screen to remove. Even I could do that," I observed. "Alicia, well, obviously he used some trick. What on earth would make Alicia open the door at night—I presume she was killed at night?—to someone when Ray wasn't at home?"

"It was at night. Her aunt told me Alicia had called her mother at ten-thirty Thursday evening," Cully said. "Alicia said then that she had a breakfast meeting scheduled for eight the next morning. She never got there."

We all thought about Alicia unlocking her front door at night.

"Ray!" Mimi said suddenly.

We turned horrified faces to her. For the first time, I thought about Ray being on the list. But oh, not now; now that Alicia had been killed, surely we could strike him?

She said hastily, "No, no! I didn't mean he could have done it! I mean that she'd open the door if someone told her something had happened to Ray."

"Or to her mother," Cully suggested.

"Not even for that. She'd have been suspicious right off the bat. Her mother lives with Alicia's older brother, and the brother would've called if anything was wrong with Miss Celia. It *had* to be something about Ray. She's always been scared to death he'd have a wreck on one of his sales trips."

"Even then," I said slowly, "I think it would have to be someone she knew. Or a policeman. Even if the man at the door said he was from the police, when she went to the door she wouldn't have seen a uniform through the peephole. So she wouldn't have opened the door, right?"

"Not if he said he was a detective," Cully said.

I thought instantly of John Tendall.

"I think she would've been suspicious of any stranger, no matter what he told her he was," Mimi said firmly. "She had a good head on her shoulders, even though she didn't sound like she did half the time. She was very much on the alert, remember? She was really scared. She'd have been on the lookout for a ruse like that, I'm sure. Maybe not; maybe at the words 'Ray is hurt, he had an accident, let's go to the hospital,' she would've thrown open the door to anyone. But I don't think so. I think the only thing that would have made Alicia open that door was recognizing someone she knew."

Chilled and frightened, we hunched on the bed. The

picture in my mind was in their minds, too: "Alicia, honey, I just hate to tell you this, but Ray's been in a wreck just out of town. I happened to go by and the police asked me if I'd get you to the hospital." Yes. The combination of a familiar face and an urgent summons would have added up to enough to make Alicia open the door.

"Okay. Recap," Cully said briskly to break the mood. "The access to each of you varied in difficulty."

Yes, Professor. We nodded.

"You don't have physical traits in common. Not all blonde, not all blue-eyed, for example. One married; the rest single. But you're all connected with the college. Two students, one teacher, and one committee woman."

"Yes, I guess you could call Alicia 'connected with the college,' " Mimi said slowly.

But so, to some extent, was everyone on the list. "All white. All kind of upper middle class," I offered.

"That's the loosest tie imaginable," Cully said.

"But it's something. It looks like the Miss Beacham connection goes down the drain with Barbara," Mimi said, "but I'll ask Theo to check Heidi's record sometime next week to make sure she didn't go there." She scrambled to her feet. The talk had done her good, as I had hoped. Positive action, mental or physical, healed Mimi like aloe on a burn.

Cully slipped his arm around me. I leaned against him. Mimi looked from one of us to the other. "It finally happened, huh?"

I caught myself actually ducking my head, and Cully (I peered at him sideways) looked embarrassed.

"It's about time," she said brusquely. "Well, I better go get dressed. What time's the inquest, Cully?"

"In a couple of hours."

She patted me on the arm and whisked out of the room. We looked at each other a little shyly.

"Well," he said finally, in a tone almost as brusque as Mimi's, "I'm scared to death of you, you know that? Rachel bruised me pretty thoroughly. It won't be easy for me, for a while. But I can't be less brave than you."

Not exactly a romantic declaration. But I was satisfied our night together hadn't been a fluke triggered by emotional overload.

From the thunder of the pipes I could tell Mimi was running a bath upstairs. Cully's hand touched the nape of my neck, brushed it with long fingers. He rose and shut the door.

Chapter 10

THE NEXT DAY BARBARA AND I HAD ANOTHER grim little meeting. This time I went to her apartment. Like her office, it was crammed, but even more pleasantly—full of plants and books and clear, mild colors.

"Do you like it here?" I asked as she made some hot chocolate in her tiny kitchen. The building was a four-unit cube tucked in between private homes on a dead-end street. Someone with an empty lot had decided to make a little extra money—prezoning, of course!

"It's okay," she said as she got mugs from a cabinet. "I like having other people in the same building, now. I never liked that before."

We settled in the little living room with our steaming mugs. We talked of this and that, awkwardly. Apparently Barbara was as reluctant as I to buckle down to our task.

"I'm getting almost too frightened to go on with this, Nickie," she said abruptly. "I don't know if fear douses the rage or just replaces it. I can only hold so much."

"I've about reached my capacity, too," I admitted. "Everything's changed since Alicia was murdered."

"We'd better do it before we lose our courage. Let's try to take one more step."

We seemed to gather ourselves in unison before we hauled out our creased bits of paper.

"The list," Barbara said as clearly as if she were reciting poetry. "Jeff Simmons. Charles Seward. Don Houghton. Randy Marquette. Theo Cochran. Ray Merritt. Dan Kirby. John Tendall. J. R. Smith."

"What happened to Jeffrey Tabor?"

"I remembered Jeffrey was definitely out of town the night of Mimi's party. That's why he couldn't come to it. I didn't just take his word for it," Barbara said with a faint smile. "I asked his friend who shares his apartment."

"So that leaves nine."

"Did Alicia know J.R., Dan, or Randy?" Barbara asked.

"I don't know, Barbara. How could we find out?"

She looked rather daunted. "Well, we can't ask them, can we? Gosh."

"Let's see. Dan's new at Houghton, and he commutes from Hill Run, he told me. He just got out of the army. I think his wife's family is in Hill Run. He's from Arkansas. So the chances are very slim that Alicia knew him."

Barbara weighed that. Then, after an emphatic shove at her glasses, she crossed Dan Kirby's name off her list.

"Minus Dan," she said. "Eight."

I scooted down in my armchair and laced my fingers over my stomach. Barbara twirled her pencil between her fingers as though it was a miniature baton. We both brooded over other possible eliminators. So suddenly that I jumped, Barbara grabbed her telephone and dialed.

"Hi, J.R.," she said. "This is Barbara Tucker. Fine, thanks . . . and you? Good, good. Listen, how'd you come out in that poker game?"

J.R. answered at length. Barbara rolled her eyes in exasperation, then instantly switched to a smile so the words would come out right when she spoke. "Great! Thirty-four dollars, huh? Did Randy play? Oh. Oh, Cindy won't like that, you're right!" Barbara widened her eyes at me significantly. "You played that late?" she burbled into the phone in a very un-Barbara-like manner. Again a mumble from the other end. Then Barbara was nodding at me vehemently, and I took the list from the coffee table and drew lines through two more names.

"No, I don't want to learn to play right now. Just curious, you'd talked about it so much. Right. Well—sure, give me a call sometime. We'll do it. Sounds like fun. English professors need all the extra income they can get, right? Bye, now."

J. R. Smith was a jovial individual who taught me Archetypes in the English Novel with a kind of infectious zest. I was glad he was apparently cleared. I looked at Barbara expectantly.

She was a little pink in the face. "I guess I'm going to have to learn how to play poker," she said, and looked not unwilling. "I remembered J.R. was having a bachelor party for Randy Marquette Thursday night, since Randy's marrying—well, he married—Cindy from the admissions office Friday night. The poker playing was over when Randy fell asleep on J.R.'s couch at four in the morning. Considering the liquor, I don't think either of them could've gotten back up to go out after that. And there were only six men there, since not everyone's willing to meet Friday classes with two hours' sleep and an A-one hangover. So I think that if one of them had slipped out for any length of time it would have been noticed."

"Sounds like it," I agreed. "Besides, there would have been blood, with Alicia. To clean off." I took a deep breath. "So," I said as evenly as I could. "Six."

For a full hour we tried to think of other qualifiers that would eliminate one of the six. We couldn't come up with any. We even left Ray on the list.

"By the way," Barbara said as she walked with me to my borrowed car, "I take it you haven't mentioned this project of ours to anyone?"

"Not *hardly*," I said, like one of my young classmates. "The only people I would tell are Cully and Mimi. And since their own father is on the list . . ."

She nodded. "Not that I really think for a minute that someone sweet like Don Houghton, or for that matter someone as dignified as Jeff Simmons, our mighty college president, for God's sake, could ever do something like what was done to us."

"That's just it! Do we know *anyone* on that list who acts anything like the disgusting beast who did that to us? Who could knife Alicia to death?"

Barbara knew the answer too well to say it out loud. If we were right, the beast had to be there, lurking beneath a civilized skin that covered someone we knew.

We looked up at the clear cool sky. It was sweater weather in the afternoon, coat weather in the morning—my favorite season. This would have been one of the best years of my life, if only . . . For a second the filth was magically washed away. I drank in freedom with the air. Then I tensed my forefinger against my thumb and thwanged my cheek. No point in going down *that* dead-end street. Hippity hop, back to wonderful old reality.

Barbara was too used to my habits by now to comment on my cheek-thumping. "Six," I reminded her before I drove away.

She just looked forlorn.

PROBABLY BECAUSE OF HER FAMILY'S FAR-FLUNG influence, Alicia's autopsy had been concluded and her body released to her family—and Grace Funeral Home—on Sunday. We decided to pay our respects the next evening.

I was dressed and ready, and Cully was in the shower, when Mimi caught me alone in the living room. She looked uncharacteristically drab in the plain dark dress she saved for funerals and funeral home visits.

"Don't tell Cully my idea about Charles," she said without preamble. "It's not like we really know anything. And to tell you the truth, Nickie, I'm worried about what Cully would do if he believed Charles was the rapist."

Cully the rational, a vigilante? Farfetched. I stared at Mimi with dismay and a crawling suspicion. This was awfully like manipulation. Was she using Cully as a lever to keep me quiet, to protect her lawyer?

I didn't suspect Charles because of that bizarre episode in the kitchen the previous Saturday. I suspected Charles because he was on the list. But I couldn't tell her that, and I also wanted to find out what she was aiming for. "What if it *is* Charles, Mimi? We can't possibly let him do it again. Think of what this man has done."

"We don't *know* anything," she hissed. The shower had been cut off; Cully would hear us if we didn't keep our voices down. "I may have just gotten scared Saturday morning for nothing. If Charles gets hauled in on suspicion and he's innocent, the mud will stick and he'll be ruined. Besides, don't you see, I know Charles. And I can tell you don't like him, even though you've tried not to say anything."

My heart plummeted. This was the fruit of those years before I'd gained more tact, more wisdom, in my relationship with Mimi. She couldn't discuss her feelings for Charles with me with complete honesty. There was some mystery here that she didn't think she could share with me, because it was between her and a man she loved.

"I know he couldn't, wouldn't, do that to a human being." How often had Barbara and I thought of that, in scanning the names of the men on our list? "Besides, if he was the rapist, he wouldn't have just tussled with me in the car. He would've raped me. I couldn't have stopped him. Nick, I've thought about it ever since. We were just scared and maybe hysterical that morning. That was my fault. That whole weird little episode was something we made up." She twisted her fingers together. She looked at me and said, sadly, "Don't ask me to tell you what I know, Nick. But since from the look on your face I can't persuade you any other way, I have to tell you that I *know* Charles didn't do it."

That crawling suspicion came a little further out of its hole. Mimi had never, never lied to me, in fourteen years. But she was acting so strangely. I was totally bewildered by

128   Charlaine Harris

this whole scene. I couldn't have answered her if I'd known what to say. To my relief Cully entered the living room then, with the car keys in his hand.

As we rode through the dark streets of Knolls, I pondered. All Mimi was asking was that we keep those moments when Charles was standing at the door from Cully's knowledge. Maybe she did fear that now Cully and I were lovers he would feel obliged, in true southern fashion, to avenge his womenfolk's ordeal if he knew the identity of the rapist; for the ordeal had very much been Mimi's as well as mine. I had deep doubts about Cully ascribing to that attitude.

There really was no hard evidence indicating Charles was my assailant. There was no hard evidence against anyone, unless the police had dug up something; and they were hardly likely to tell me if they had. All I had was the list. And Mimi was definitely right about another thing: The panic we'd felt that morning when Charles came to the door could easily be written off to the tension and fear that had permeated our lives for so long.

So whatever she knew or didn't know, Mimi was right. I would not tell Cully about that stupid little incident. As we drove through the night silently, I whittled away at the knot of pain and confusion she had caused me, until it was only a canker of uneasiness.

I looked across the front seat at Cully. He glanced my way at the same time. The normal austerity of his face vanished in a smile that made him irresistible. I hoped I wasn't using Cully as a kind of emotional aspirin. He would be willing. He was, after all, a wound healer.

Grace Funeral Home was housed in an old mansion with pillars. It was a freshly painted, carpeted, well-kept-up place. Ordinarily, I'd have rather admired it for the gracious air it gave to a grim business.

Ray Merritt and Alicia's mother, Celia Anley, were standing close to the door to receive mourners. Ray was gray and ghastly, Mrs. Anley so rigid she looked like a mannequin. Mimi quivered when she saw them, and I knew she was afraid of what they'd ask her. Neither Ray nor Celia had been permitted into the house until it was cleaned by good and loving neighbors. Cully had told us that; he'd heard it from Alicia's aunt at the filling station.

When Ray's eyes met mine I knew I shouldn't have come. I had lived through it. I knew without doubt that he was wishing I'd died in Alicia's place. If the attacker had to kill, Ray Merritt wished the victim had been me, not Alicia. At that second, Ray Merritt was struck from the list, at least as far as I was concerned. He'd never liked or trusted me. If he had been the rapist, I would have died instead of Alicia, without doubt. I started to extend my hand, saw Ray wouldn't touch it if I did, and quickly moved on to Mrs. Anley, whom I'd met years before. Alicia had had at least one brother, but I knew she'd been the only daughter her widowed mother had.

"I'm so sorry." I felt I was expressing regret that I was alive, rather than sorrow that Alicia was dead.

"Bless you, Nickie," Mrs. Anley said.

She remembered me, then. I waited for the chill of condemnation I'd seen in Ray's face. Instead, Mrs. Anley hugged me and led me aside. "Don't mind Ray," she told me quietly. There were traces of Alicia in the shape of her mouth. Though Mrs. Anley had become very heavy, the likeness was there.

"He doesn't know what he's doing right now," she continued. She sighed. She gathered her thoughts. "There's a choice," she said slowly, not looking up at me anymore. "Not always. But for Alicia there was a choice."

I was mystified. I shifted nervously, twisted the cuff of my navy dress, and waited.

"From what I've heard . . . you chose to endure it, and live through it. My daughter"—she spoke slower and slower—"chose to fight. I'm not saying she chose to die, but she chose to take that chance. It proved to be the wrong choice, for her . . ." I had bent lower and lower, to catch her near-whisper. Suddenly Mrs. Anley was finished, and she turned to resume her place by Ray.

I stared after her. How much "choice" had I had? I simply hadn't been able to move. I'd been awakened from a heavy sleep, precipitated into a situation already established. I was sure Alicia had wanted to live fully as much as I had. But if it comforted Mrs. Anley to believe that Alicia had had some freedom of will in the matter . . . Then I was enlightened. Mrs. Anley was *proud* that her daughter had fought so hard. That was the only warm feeling left to Alicia's mother: pride, that her daughter had gone down fighting every inch of the way. Death before dishonor.

Cully and Mimi were comforting Ray, who'd begun to cry in the unpracticed way of men, with great heaves of his shoulders. I was standing conspicuously by myself. I felt, ridiculously, that everyone in the room was looking at me sideways. The One Who Got Away.

With a rush of relief I spied old Mrs. Harbison, our next-door neighbor, standing by an archway leading to another room. I scooted over to her as swiftly as I could manage, hoping to blend with her into a clump of mourning. Poor old lady, she was sandwiched between houses evil had visited. She was wondering, I discovered, if it might come to her house next. She told me that right after she left the funeral home she planned to depart for a prolonged visit to her married daughter in Macon. I told her I thought that was a great idea.

The open archway led into another, smaller, room. I hadn't looked in, since I was concentrating on Mrs. Harbison. Now the old lady inclined her head and said, "You ought to go see her."

I had no idea what she meant, but I turned obediently and stepped through the archway. And there, to my absolute horror, was Alicia in her coffin. I thought I was going to scream. I flinched backward, but Mrs. Harbison had a firm grip on my arm and steered me forward relentlessly. The old lady had no doubt that I wanted to see Alicia "laid out"; in her time she must have seen so many people die that viewing the faces of the dead was simple routine.

All too soon I was by the gleaming coffin looking down

at Alicia. Her face was colorless and smooth and still. Of course . . .

For the first time the absolute immobility of the dead struck me. The complete absence of movement, even the tiny movements of breathing, seemed so remarkable to me that I couldn't turn away. I wondered briefly if I should, after all, have gone in to see my father. And I wondered how the mortician had managed to fix Alicia up. I felt an eerie professional curiosity about the makeup he'd used. Why had Ray wanted the coffin open? Why on earth had the family consented to lay Alicia out in front of anyone who cared to take a look? It seemed the worst invasion of privacy I'd ever witnessed. I was appalled; but I was also spellbound. She'd looked so awful when I'd last seen her: mouth open, eyes wide, legs sprawled, covered with blood. What I was seeing now, I forced myself to admit, was better—and, after the initial shock, strangely comforting.

Here was no woman frozen in final pain and fear. This was a serene Alicia: clean, her hair arranged, her face turned to one side to cover a scalp wound I remembered. She had the dignity she'd had in life. She was presented as she would have wanted. But I swore to myself on the spot that I would put something in my will about closing my coffin.

I was only vaguely aware of Mrs. Harbison wandering away. When I finally looked up from the face I'd last seen smeared with blood, I met Don Houghton's eyes. His face was smooth and still and white. I shuddered. He looked at me steadily, with an unwavering disregard of what lay literally between us. "It's always a shock, isn't it?" he commented.

Maybe it was the carefully dimmed lighting, maybe it was the overwhelming presence of death, or my own horror at seeing Alicia—but he didn't seem to be the same Don Houghton I'd known for all these years. Not the same man who'd taken us to the zoo in Memphis, the man who'd borne so patiently and lovingly with his difficult wife. I would rather have looked at Alicia's corpse than at the face of this stranger. When I lowered my eyes, I observed as if from a distance my own hand gripping the rim of the coffin so tightly that my knuckles had turned white. I snatched my hand away.

This man is also on the list, I thought. There was only one list in my life, a list of names. And this man, the father of two people I loved, was on it.

"In the midst of life . . ." Don quoted ponderously.

I glanced up involuntarily. He was looking down this time, at Alicia. "I always liked that girl," he said simply. He walked around the coffin, passing within two feet of me as he went through the archway.

Thank God Cully is so tall. I spotted him immediately and flew to him like a bird homing to its particular tree. He was engaged in low-voiced conversation with a group of college people: Barbara, the Cochrans, Jeff Simmons, a couple of familiar faces I couldn't label. I jerked at Cully's coat. He swung round with a surprised look. When he saw my face, he mumbled an excuse over his shoulder and moved me away.

"I have to get out of here," I said through clenched teeth. He saw I meant it, and quickly asked Theo to get Mimi home; and without waiting for an answer he whisked me out the door and into the parking lot, just in time. I sped to a clump of bushes on the far side, and I vomited.

"Romantic, huh?" I gasped between heaves. He wisely kept his mouth shut. I loved him so much for that that I could have kissed his hands. But love and throwing up, fear and throwing up, don't blend. In the end, all you think about is throwing up.

That night Cully's training paid off in spades. He didn't ask me any questions on the way home. He just murmured soothing things about a hot bath and bed, exactly what I'd been dreaming of myself. I leaned back against the car seat in a jelly of exhaustion. Things gradually quieted down internally.

It wasn't just the eerie conversation with Cully's father that had upset me so violently, or Mimi's painful withdrawal, or Ray's hostility, though all had contributed.

When I'd looked down at Alicia's still face, I had seen my own. I had seen my longer, thinner hands folded on my waist.

It had been a vile moment, worse than a glimpse of my mother dead drunk, worse than the leer I'd seen in my step-father's face; worse, even, than my rape. During that long ordeal, I'd known my enemy. He was right there on me. Now I didn't know who he was, whether he was observing me, or whether his hatred of me was spent or active. I'd finally reached the end of my rope. My reserves of courage were exhausted. My almost-faded bruises seemed to take on new life. My gums around the loosened teeth ached. I thought I tasted blood in my mouth again.

As I brushed my teeth in the blessed solitude of the bathroom, I decided it would suit me just fine if nothing ever happened to me again in my life. Nothing more distressing than misplacing my keys, nothing more elating than successfully matching some drapes to a rug. Yes, that would suit me just fine.

To make myself feel better, I let myself dream dreams I normally would have dismissed from my mind. Would Cully ask me to marry him? Given the example of my own mother's remarriage, the misalliance of Elaine and Don Houghton, and Cully's and Mimi's washouts, it was amazing that I wanted to contemplate marriage. But the dreams fed you as a child are almost impossible to dislodge. Those dreams can be very comforting when just being an adult is a burden.

As I soaked in the bathtub under a mound of bubbles, I conjured up a vision of myself in candlelight satin and a picture hat (I'd worn a wedding outfit like that in a show once), marching down the aisle to meet Cully—who was in a tux, of course. The whole tableau was fuzzily framed by an old-fashioned church full of flowers and people who wished us well. Mimi was beaming by the minister, her arms full of flowers—but not wearing a hat like mine, I decided judiciously; Mimi would look like a fool in a picture hat . . .

By the time I was ready to switch off the bedside lamp, Cully tucked in beside me, I had designed Mimi's whole outfit and selected my china and silver. Cully's love for the wounded, his air of remoteness, had completely vanished in my vision—as had my memory of the years I'd knocked on the doors of his awareness in vain.

As I sank into sleep, Cully's breathing even and quiet beside me, I almost fantasized myself a virgin again for the wedding night.

THE FUNERAL WAS SCHEDULED FOR TUESDAY AT two. When I got up that morning it was raining, a cold autumnal rain. I let Mimi give me a lift to my first class; I didn't want to start the day soggy. I had been debating whether or not I should go to the service. I decided, after slogging between my second and third classes, that I couldn't. I'd already come up with a rebuttal to the argument I expected from Mimi. But when I got back to the house and announced my decision she only nodded.

Cully had an appointment that would keep him in his office till the last minute, so Mimi left alone. She was drawn with exhaustion: Her eyes looked hollow. Her emotions had been burned away by their intensity. Our conversation, what there was of it, was strained. We all needed time to heal. I wondered if we would have it.

The house was silent except for the patter of the rain. After I watched Mimi's car back out of the driveway, I tried to settle at my desk with a stack of work. I was doing well in most of my classes so far, particularly well in my English classes. I'd been so afraid that what I'd been through would ruin my grades that I'd actually been working much harder. Desperate concentration helped keep the wolves at bay.

I was supposed to read *Macbeth* for my Shakespeare class. It was fortunate that I was already familiar with the play, because I couldn't bury myself in concentration. I tried the devices that usually worked, but nothing seemed to help. The cats were having a running (and vocal) battle, both irritable at being trapped inside by the rain. I kept imagining Alicia's funeral and feeling guilty I hadn't gone, if for no other reason than to bolster Mimi. We might be estranged, but love is a habit as well as an emotion.

After I'd run through all my rational reasons for feeling restless, I discovered the true one. I was alone in the house for the first time since I'd gotten raped.

When I realized that, I closed my Shakespeare and began to piece together a conspiracy. If Mimi wasn't home, Cully was; if neither of them was in the house, it was while I was at school or studying in the library. Since I hadn't consciously been avoiding an empty house, it occurred to me that the other two had been orchestrating their departures and arrivals to ensure I wasn't alone. In an instant I was sure of it.

Well. I was alone now. I listened to the drip of rain off the eaves, and stared out the side window into the soaked vegetation between Mimi's and Mrs. Harbison's empty house. I shivered a little and pulled my sweater closer around me, doubled over my breasts. I couldn't sit there at the desk a moment longer; not with my back to the silent room.

I prowled the house. Attila had curled up to sleep in my clothes hamper, but Mao drifted at my heels. Upstairs, downstairs, from the kitchen to my bedroom. Back into the living room. All my favorite colors were there, my own harmony in the rugs and furniture; but I took no pleasure in it, in the fineness of the workmanship and wood. I stood at a front window and peered out at the houses across the street. They looked forlorn and dismal in the steady mist.

A man was slogging down the opposite sidewalk, his collar pulled up and his head covered with a plastic-treated rain-hat. I eyed him with idle curiosity, not recognizing him as any of the regular neighborhood walkers. A persistent cuss, to be taking his constitutional in this weather. Only when he was exactly opposite my window and had turned to look at the house did I recognize that the man was

John Tendall. I started to open the front door and call to him to come share tea or hot chocolate—that's how desperate I was. Even flashy Tendall, the detective, whom I associated with that horrible night, seemed preferable to the hush of the house. I caught myself with my hand on the doorknob.

"You fool," I said out loud. "That's right. Just ask a man into the house when you're alone. A man on the list, yet. Real intelligent." My fingers dropped from the knob. "Smart, Nickie Callahan." It made me feel a little sick, calling myself a fool because I'd been prepared to be friendly, been at the point of extending the trust one automatically feels toward familiar people.

Come to think of it, what was John Tendall doing walking in the nasty chilly rain? Especially when almost every other resident of a certain segment of Knolls was sitting in the church a few blocks away? I'd turned to sit at my desk, but now I moved again to the window to watch. Tendall had paused to stare at Alicia's house. Then, as I watched, he trudged away through the rain.

Maybe Tendall, the dedicated detective, was pondering the crimes. Maybe he'd wanted to stare at my house and Alicia's to refresh his memory. Maybe he was revisiting the scenes of his crimes.

My thoughts began the same old round. Barbara and I called each other, or saw each other, almost daily. We were still trying to come up with a way to further narrow our list, which remained at six. I'd told her I thought Ray Merritt was out, but she argued quite rightly that we had to have something more substantial than a gut feeling to drop him from the list. We'd temporarily reached a dead end. Maybe I should try again from the other end.

Back to the same old question. What did we, the victims, have in common? A young, inexperienced student. A college professor of thirty-plus. A former model, now writer-to-be and struggling student. An efficient young matron.

Already eliminated: build, hairstyle, access, age. Could be eliminated: Let's see. Income. Background—Alicia's and mine similar, but Barbara's father was a small-scale farmer and her mother a nurse, and Heidi Edmonds's father was a minister, I recalled. Oh—religion? No. Alicia had been a Baptist, I was an erratic Episcopalian, Barbara a Lutheran.

But there had to be a pattern, a rhyme and reason. This violence, this hatred, had a specific focus. I had to know that focus for my own peace of mind. I might tell myself and everyone else that I was blameless. And I was; of all the usual things rape victims are accused of: leading men on, wearing sexy clothes, being alone outside at night. As if such harmless behavior meant the victim should expect to be raped in consequence. As if lack of wisdom, incaution, merited such a punishment. But always at the back of my mind was the niggling idea that maybe I'd offended somehow, had trodden over delicate ground. In some innocent way, some blind way, I'd aroused that violence, and I wanted to know how.

I couldn't recall any disagreements I'd had with anyone in Knolls since I'd arrived. No arguments, aside from classroom discussion, came to mind. Those were hardly heated enough or long enough to provoke a reaction of that intensity, and they'd often as not been with other women in the class.

When Mimi and Cully finally pulled into the driveway in their separate cars, I was ready to talk. I wanted to hear voices and ideas other than my own. They wanted to talk, too; anything to wipe out the memory of what they'd just witnessed. They had taken the afternoon off to attend the funeral, so they were home for the day.

Cully kissed me. "You were right not to go," he said, and went to the kitchen to bring us all some wine. We settled in the living room. I asked him what he'd heard from his policeman friend about the progress of the investigation.

"He hardly tells me everything," Cully warned. "But I reckon they've checked all the obvious things. Men registered at the motels on the nights of the crimes. Drifters. Anyone in town or close by who has a record of violence or sex offenses. So far, almost everyone they've checked has an alibi for one, or all, of the incidents. The people who don't have alibis seem to be in the clear for other reasons: extremely short, which doesn't tally with anyone's impressions, or mentally deficient, which doesn't either. Or something. Thank God, Ray's in the clear. He was miles from here with witnesses at the time Alicia must have died."

So casually, another name was gone. That left five: Jeff Simmons, Charles Seward, Don Houghton, Theo Cochran, John Tendall. I had a fact for Barbara.

"No one's seen anything strange on any of the nights the guy's been at large," Cully was rambling on. "That's not too surprising when you consider how early this town goes to bed. No cars parked where they shouldn't be, no fingerprints, just physical evidence collected from—" He stopped short.

"From me and the others," I said quietly.

"What physical evidence?" Mimi asked suddenly. She'd been drinking her wine very fast, in silence. "I don't want to upset you, Nickie, but I don't really understand what that means."

I focused on a snag in my hose. "What they got off me, with a kind of sticky-feeling pad," I said after a moment, "was a pubic hair that was not mine. And—saliva samples, I think, and—semen." My fingers plucked the snag into a run.

"Some men secrete their blood type in the semen," Cully told Mimi quickly in a blessedly matter-of-fact way. "Some men don't. But getting a blood type is a good corroboration. This man was a secretor, as it turns out. And from Alicia, I believe, they got some skin and blood from her fingernails, since she fought."

"I haven't noticed anyone going around with a big scratch across his face," I said. But I'd watch from now on. What would Alicia have grabbed for? Not his face, dummy. His hands. His knife. Of course. I'd seen what shape Alicia's hands were in, the palms . . .

"But none of this is any good, is it?" Mimi said abruptly. "Until you catch the bastard. To match all this evidence up with. It can't help catch him, right? It'll just help nail him if he *is* caught."

"That's right," Cully said.

The rest of the day was just something to get through. Neither Mimi nor Cully could come up with anything we victims had in common. I lay awake long after Cully had gone to sleep. I was facing the fact that the man who had harmed me would probably go free. Quite possibly he would go forever unpunished for his violation of my life and body.

Then I had an idea so galvanizing that I sat up straight and drove my fist into my pillow. I shook Cully by the shoulder.

"Hunh?"

"Cully, wake up!"

"You okay, Nickie?" He rubbed my shoulder.

"I'm fine, Cully. Listen—did your police friend tell you what blood type the guy is?" I held my breath.

"What? Oh. Yeah. Let's see."

Dammit, Cully.

"Not a big help," he mumbled finally. "O positive. Real common."

"Go back to sleep, sweetheart," I whispered. "Everything's okay." He was snoring in two minutes, but I waited ten before I crawled out of bed to call Barbara.

I knew she'd be awake.

Chapter 11

THURSDAY MORNING BEGAN MARVELOUSLY. CULLY woke up feeling frisky. Hugging my wonderful plan to me, I was glad to respond. The room was cold. Cully and the bed were warm. My first class had been canceled because of a conference my professor was attending, so I didn't have to be at school until 9:45. Everything was going beautifully until I giggled when Cully's fingers brushed a sensitive area. In mock reproof, he lay a hand over my mouth.

I was instantly blind with fear. I struck his hand with all my strength, my breathing seemed to stop, and there went my heart, racing racing for the end, oh God I'm going to *die* . . .

"Nickie! Nickie!" Cully's face was over me, white and shocked. "Oh my God, honey, I forgot! I'm sorry!"

I managed to gasp, "Wait. Wait a minute." I fought desperately to control my lungs.

He had frightened me so much that for a few seconds I hated him. His black hair rumpled from sleep seemed ludicrous rather than endearing. For an abysmal moment I thought: What is he doing here? I don't know this man.

There was no sap left in me, nothing left that wasn't burned and shriveled from the blaze of fear and hate.

"I'm not going to hurt you," he said very quietly.

I stared at him. I believed nothing.

"I'm not going to hurt you." Then for the first time he said, "I love you, Nick." But he said it in his "calming" tone, professional and even. He put his arms around me, to cancel out that voice. I shuddered. "I wouldn't hurt you for the world," he whispered. And I began to warm. I located myself correctly in the day and scene. Weak daylight was sliding from behind drawn curtains. This was my Cully.

"I care for you," he said. He kissed me on the neck. I stared at the ceiling over his shoulder. Very slowly, he began to caress me again. I responded as best I could. I was trying very hard not to disappoint him, not to disappoint myself. When we finished, it had only been an exercise to me; to prove to myself I could still do it. I hadn't had a problem with sex before, and had counted myself lucky. The nightmarish flashback had been triggered by something as small as his hand over my mouth.

Cully kissed me very gently and adjourned to the bathroom. I lay wondering how many more such incidents were lying in wait for me. After a while, Cully came out and got dressed without talking. We both had a lot to think about. He sat on the side of the bed.

"Cully, I don't think I'll ever get over it," I said bleakly when I saw he was waiting for me to speak. Then I was furious with myself. I'd cried for help, knowing he couldn't resist that. I would not become an object of pity to my lover.

He had been badly frightened, too, so now he was ill at ease with me. "I wish I could stay here with you now," he said to me directly. I searched his eyes. "I can't. I have appointments this morning I can't break." And he hadn't had his morning run, either. "But you're not alone, Nick. I'm with you."

"You're with a lot of raped women right now," I said as lightly as I could. Underneath the blanket, I dug my nails into my palm. Maybe you're pretty sick of coming home to another one, Cully.

"Nick," he said, and pulled me up and put his arms around me. We sat like that until he felt me relax against him. "I'll be thinking about you all day," he told me.

I thought he meant it. Those were good words to leave me with. They infused some warmth into the outer edges, the area where I dealt with other people; and some of that warmth seeped a few layers deeper, to where I dealt with people I cared about very much. But my core, in which I lived as a solitary homo sapiens—that was still cold, still alone, and would be for an incalculable length of time. I had a mission to accomplish.

In that silent chilly room, I knew for the first time I would never be the same woman I'd been. Unconsciously, I'd been expecting to feel a "click" someday; after the police caught the rapist, when I was sure Cully loved me, or just any old time. And I'd imagined that after I felt that click I'd be just the same as I had been before that dark night. I'd forgotten what had frightened me so much when Barbara got raped: my conviction that what had happened to her was *irreparable*. Until this moment, I hadn't applied that to myself. "Dumb old Nick," I said out loud and with immense sarcasm. And I slapped myself hard.

At that instant I quit waiting for the click.

Before I could brood any longer, I jumped out of bed. I moved briskly as I dressed and gathered the books I'd need. Just feeling my body moving and working revived that incredible wonder at being alive. As always, I outlined my day while I brushed my hair. A 9:45 class. Out at 11:15 for the day. A meeting with Barbara. A paper due in—I squinted at the calendar by the dresser—a little over a week, right before Thanksgiving. And all my midterms were over except the one a dilatory professor had scheduled for Tuesday. So I needed to spend some time in the library studying before Mimi and I went to tea at Sarah Chase Cochran's in the afternoon. Also time to write my mother a letter, another fabrication that would omit all the important things. She'd sent me a thank-you note for the birthday present I'd mailed her, a sweater and blouse, and in it she mentioned that she'd gone out to dinner with some friends of my father's to celebrate. And again she hadn't mentioned Jay. Instinctively I throttled the rising hope, as I had for the past month. No point in dreaming about a sober mother, a mother without Jay.

Jay would just love it if he knew someone had "gotten" me. What I should have done all those years ago, I decided, was rocket out of that bathroom with . . . well, no, not a plunger, not heavy enough . . . but *something* . . . and bam! Beat the tar out of him!

It pleased me so much to picture Jay cowering (or even quite battered) that I wished passionately I'd had the guts at seventeen to do it. The fantasy was so vivid and satisfying that for a few happy minutes I felt I *had* done it. Even the bite of the November wind couldn't diminish my smile. It was the first time in ages I'd gone to class with a real smile on my face.

Despite the morning's humiliation, despite the beast still at large, in spite of everything, I suddenly knew that in some mysterious way I was going to win.

"YOU TAKE—LET'S SEE . . ." OUT CAME THE ragged list, which never seemed to leave Barbara's purse. "Um. Don Houghton, that'll be easier for you. Charles, likewise. I have Jeff Simmons and Theo. I don't know what to do about John Tendall."

"That'll be the hard one," I said soberly.

"I don't know. I think Jeff Simmons is worse. I spent fifteen minutes this morning, when I was supposed to be grading papers, trying to think of a way to ask the Houghton College president what his blood type is." Barbara wrinkled her nose and her glasses slid. I pushed them back up before her hand could reach her nose. She looked at me comically, and we both laughed.

"I feel good," I confessed.

"Me too." Barbara took a bite from a cookie. "I don't know why. What we're doing is dangerous."

"Not unless *he* knows about semen containing blood secretions," I pointed out. "Not the world's best-known fact. Out of all of them, only Tendall will be aware of that, I imagine."

"It *would* have to be the most common blood type," Barbara said ruefully. "I'm O positive myself."

"I'm A negative."

"The school has a blood drive every year. A mobile van comes by. Stan went with me last year to give. His type is O negative."

"Even though he was never on the list, I'm glad," I said after a moment. "That would have been too horrible." It had gone without saying that Stan couldn't have leaped out of his car and beaten Barbara to her apartment.

Barbara looked straight ahead. "Yes," she said. "So we work on our five."

"You think the blood van went to the police department?" I asked.

She thought. "I seem to remember that it did," she said uncertainly.

"Stay here a second." I fished a dime out of my purse and went to the phone booth in the student-center lobby. I flipped through the tiny Knolls phone book.

"Police Department," said a bored voice.

"Detective John Tendall, please."

Click, click. Buzz. "John Tendall speaking."

That flat voice called to mind some unpleasant memories. I screwed my eyelids tightly shut. "This is Elsie Smith from the blood bank, Mr. Tendall," I said rapidly and nasally. "We have an urgent call for B negative blood. Can you come in and donate?"

"There must be some kind of mix-up," Detective Tendall said. "You people need to get your records straight. My blood type is O positive."

"Oh. Oh, my goodness," I fluttered, "I've pulled the wrong card. Thanks anyway."

"All right," Tendall said, and hung up.

I returned to our table and reported to Barbara in triumph.

"Good for you!" she said, and grinned.

"But he's still on the list."

"What if he'd said, 'Okay, I'll be right down'?"

We laughed before we simultaneously realized that if Tendall was the guilty man, his discovery that the blood bank call was phony would've put him on the alert.

"But I'll take my laughs where I can find them, nowadays," Barbara remarked, and I had to agree with her.

"What if they're all O positive?" I said dismally.

"Then it'll be my turn to think of something," Barbara said. She folded her list. "Having worked down from a few hundred to five, I'm not about to give up."

"That's the spirit. Yea, team!"

We clumsily punched each other on the shoulder like hearty men, and went our separate ways.

"WHITE GLOVES, DO YOU REMEMBER?" MIMI smoothed back her mane and smiled at me before she returned her attention to driving. The Cochrans lived close to the college, she'd told me, but on a little suburban loop behind the big houses that faced the college.

"But we carried them, we didn't wear them."

"I still have four pair tucked away under my nightgowns," she confessed. "One pair has little pink rosebuds at the wrists. I can't imagine when I'll ever use them, but I just can't bring myself to throw them away."

"I threw mine in the fire one night when I was trying to liberate myself from southernness."

"Why on earth would you want to do that?"

"Now, Mimi, you know there was a lot of garbage we had fed us along with our grits and pralines." A figure of speech—neither Mimi nor I would touch grits with a ten-foot pole; though pralines were another matter.

Mimi pursed her lips thoughtfully as she mulled this

over. "Oh, sure," she admitted. "But you know, we're a dying breed. We've got to preserve what we are. You never hear a real heavy accent anymore, except every now and then, like Alicia's. You never heard anything like the way Grandmother said 'water.' Six syllables, at least. It's Johnny Carson's fault."

"*The Tonight Show*? Johnny Carson is responsible for the decline of southern accents?"

"Sho 'nuff," Mimi said with a wild grin. "Have you ever heard Johnny Carson say 'water'? Nothing to it!"

Mimi was still expounding on her latest theory when we pulled into the driveway of a very modest ranch-suburban house, the kind you don't even have to enter to know the floor plan. She stopped in midsentence to glare at a stamped metal eagle, her particular abomination, which was nailed above the front door.

Sarah Chase Cochran met us at the door with a kind of subdued frenzy of hospitality. Over her shoulder, I glimpsed Barbara looking rather relieved to see us. I was surprised to see her until I remembered she didn't have any Thursday afternoon classes to teach.

Mimi was playing hooky from her job. She'd told me that she put in so much phone time and committee work at night and on weekends that she felt perfectly justified in leaving her office a couple of hours early every now and then.

"I'm so glad to see you," Sarah Chase was saying. "It seems like I never get to see you all anymore, so I just thought, well, I'll have Mimi and her friend over to tea so I can get to sit down and talk to them."

I perched on the lumpy plaid couch beside Barbara and answered the usual questions, posed to me in a gracious stream—how I liked Knolls, did I miss New York, how I felt about coming back "home," how wonderful it was that I was living with Mimi.

Then Sarah Chase began catching up on Mimi's activities—she must have already covered Barbara—and I had time to look around me.

It was the kind of house only a strong personality can vanquish. Sarah Chase's wasn't strong enough. From the green shag rug to the smell of polish and cooking, from the decent bargain furniture interspersed with inherited antiques to the truly beautiful silver tea service that Sarah Chase lugged in presently with considerable effort, it was the kind of milieu that hopes to state, "Just here temporarily, soon moving up."

But Sarah Chase and Theo were somewhat beyond the age at which they should have moved up. The Cochrans were a few rungs behind on that invisible ladder, and Sarah Chase knew it. She was facing it with dignity. I wondered if it was their daughter's awful illness that had kept the Cochrans down, that had given Sarah Chase the look of someone who's beaten but won't leave the ring.

On the fake mantel stood a picture of a girl I assumed was Nell. She was a plain child but had a liveliness about her face that made her attractive. I wondered if Nell was in the house. I recalled the frozen look on Theo's face when Barbara had mentioned Nell's illness at the party, and decided not to risk asking.

But Mimi braved it. Mimi is awfully good at expressing grave concern. She has a special look for it that isn't insincere though it's predetermined. I have accidentally glimpsed the same expression on my own face, in mirrors. So I guess we learned it. The brows draw in to form a pucker above the nose, the mouth assumes a sober line, and one looks directly into the eyes of the object of concern.

"She's back in the hospital," our hostess said with a tiny shake of her head. "St. Jude's, in Memphis. Of course, we don't expect . . ." Her voice trailed off.

Didn't expect Nell to live? Didn't expect miracles? Didn't expect Nell would ever come home again?

With my new empathy for suffering, I felt a fraction of what Sarah Chase and Theo must have been enduring. Their only child was in the process of dying and they were helpless. I glanced at Barbara and saw from her expression that the same thing was crossing her mind. We had a raw surface for pain. We understood helplessness. In a minute, Sarah Chase would see that empathy too. Though I barely knew the woman, that silver service somehow told me that she'd hate to be the object of raw emotion.

I plunged clumsily into school reminiscences. Soon we were dredging up little anecdotes from our years at Miss Beacham's. Sarah Chase told us, with more sparkle than she'd yet shown, how it felt to be a student there and at the same time be related to the founder. The Founder.

"I remember taking Theo to meet Aunt Martha for the first time," she said with a little smile as she handed around the cookies and nuts again. "My Lord, was he scared! And in awe, too. Of course, my whole family talks about Aunt Martha like she was God Almighty. I think we nieces and nephews thought she *was,* when we were little."

"How did you meet Theo?" Mimi asked smoothly. She was determined to keep up this line of talk, since it was obviously cheering to Sarah Chase.

"Well, we were at college together. My whole family is in education, so naturally," she said, with a deprecating wave of her hands, "I was going to be a teacher too. And Theo wanted to be in the administrative part of education . . . we were in a lot of the same classes. It just kind of happened." She shrugged and smiled and looked almost pretty.

"Is Theo's family in education, too?" Barbara asked gamely.

"No, he's a first," Sarah Chase responded a little too brightly; so I knew that Theo had pulled himself up by his bootstraps.

I began to admire Theo Cochran. I knew what it was like to start out at the bottom, unknown, in a profession that depended a great deal on grace and favor and contacts. Mimi was fond of Theo, though she thought him a fuss-budget. He'd modernized Houghton's record system thoroughly, and was adored by the ladies who worked for him.

There are lots of good people in the world, I told myself. That was all too easy to forget nowadays. I compared my grievance against fate to the one Theo and Sarah Chase bore. For once, the violence that had been done to me seemed petty. After all, I'd survived it, and it had been over in maybe fifteen minutes. The Cochrans' ordeal might drag on for years.

"I tried to call you Saturday morning about the faculty Christmas party," our hostess was telling Barbara. Mimi looked startled; then she gave a shrug and turned her attention back to the conversation. It did seem a little early to start planning for Christmas. We hadn't even had Thanksgiving yet. But when a large party was being planned, which had to take place before the faculty scattered for vacation, I supposed you couldn't start too soon.

Barbara was explaining she'd been out shopping. "Where's it going to be this year?" she asked. There followed a logistics debate on the amount of food, liquor, and tables necessary, which degenerated into a discussion of the character of the faculty wife who'd planned the party the year before.

Theo came in just as they'd settled the whole thing. I was wondering what the other committee members were going to say when Sarah Chase and Barbara presented them with a fait accompli. Mimi, forgetting to mind her expression, was looking faintly bored and stealing glances at her watch.

"Good afternoon, ladies!" Theo said cheerfully. He kissed Sarah Chase with surprising vigor and looked at us (grouped graciously around the silver) with considerable satisfaction. Whatever else we were—Mimi, Barbara, Sarah Chase, and I—we were bona fide ladies, modern version; and there we were, sitting properly around Theo's living room chattering. I understood his pleasure now that I'd seen his home and knew more about him; but that obvious satisfaction made me want to say something shocking or sit with my knees askew. I pinched myself surreptitiously for penance.

"All quiet at the college?" Mimi asked too brightly. She had been getting ready to leave and now felt obliged to stay a few more minutes.

"Yes. Even if Mimi Houghton played hooky this afternoon, the walls were still standing when I left." Theo filched a cookie off the plate, and Sarah Chase smiled at him and shook her head in mock admonishment. The affection between them was alive and touching.

"Oh, by the way," Theo told Mimi, "I checked this afternoon, and Heidi Edmonds didn't go to Miss Beacham's."

Mimi and I absorbed this without surprise or comment. Barbara looked bewildered. I made a sign to her that I'd explain later. She responded with a look indicating she had something to tell me. I wondered if she'd extracted Theo's blood type from Sarah Chase.

"Oh, I'm so relieved these awful things aren't related to Aunt Martha's school in any way. Theo had thought of it, and he told me you'd thought of it too," Sarah Chase said.

Mimi thanked Theo for checking. "I know it was a long shot, but we were just trying to think of anything we could."

Theo looked sober, almost grim, and I knew he was thinking that Sarah Chase was out of the pattern and perhaps safe, since there was no Beacham's tie-in. He put his hand on her shoulder and kept it there. Poor old Theo, with all his troubles. It would be a pleasure to mark his name off the list.

"Listen, what are you all doing for Thanksgiving?" Mimi said to switch the subject.

"We're driving over to Aunt Martha's," Sarah Chase answered. "I'm afraid this is our Thanksgiving to keep her company. She has nieces and nephews to the feast on rotation."

Mimi and I had to laugh at the thought of Miss Beacham marshaling her relatives as she'd marshaled the girls in her care.

"What about you, Barbara?"

"Nothing in particular. It's too long a drive to go home for just a couple of days."

"Well, come have your turkey with us," I urged her.

"Okay. I'd love to," Barbara said happily. I realized

she'd been dreading a lonely holiday that would remind her at every minute of Stan's defection.

"Be prepared to eat more than your share," Mimi warned her. "Cully and Nick are going out to a party the night before, so they may not be in shape to really dig in!" Mimi turned to Sarah Chase. "Are you sure you can't come?" she asked.

"I wish we could; it's sweet of you to ask, isn't it, Theo? But Aunt Martha's Thanksgiving is a command performance. We'll be leaving early Thursday morning and coming back Friday. We get to pick up Nell at the hospital in Memphis. We got permission. She just loves Aunt Martha; whenever Nell's in the hospital, Aunt Martha goes to see her every day."

With that amazing piece of information, Mimi and I widened our eyes at each other and rose to take our leave. I was glad to go. I was oddly restless and uneasy. Maybe the thought of Nell Cochran oppressed me.

Barbara got up hastily, too, and after a search for her handbag (which had worked its way under the couch) we were all out the door in a flurry of "Enjoyed it" and "Please come see *us* next time."

A chilly mist brushed my face and made my hair go limp as we walked to the car. Barbara shuddered and stood for a second looking at the sky. A Scottie was lifting his leg against her car tires. She sighed. "Thanks again for the Thanksgiving invitation," she said gratefully.

Mimi had slung her purse onto the front seat and had one leg inside. "Listen, why don't you come over Wednesday night before Thanksgiving?" she asked Barbara suddenly. "Since Nickie and Cully are going out, I'll need help wrestling with the damn turkey. I have the worst time getting the legs out of that metal brace, when I'm ready to pull the innards out. And we can share some wine."

"Okay," Barbara said after a moment's hesitation. She was obviously afraid that Mimi was only asking out of pity. "What time?"

"Seven-thirty, I guess."

"I'll bring the wine, and you have to let me know what I can cook and bring for the Thanksgiving table," Barbara said firmly.

Mimi gave her a brilliant smile. "Sure I will," she said. "I look forward to it, the whole holiday." Then Mimi scooted out of the weather and into the front seat. I folded my longer legs and got in more slowly.

"What was it that surprised you when Sarah Chase and Barbara were talking about the Christmas party?" I asked Mimi curiously, after she'd negotiated the driveway.

"What?" she asked blankly.

"You had a pretty strange expression—"

"Oh, that," she interrupted. "Well—" Suddenly the Scottie shot across the road in front of us, I gasped, Mimi slammed on the brakes, and we began to skid on the mist-slick blacktop. We screeched to a stop about a foot from a mailbox. The Scottie scampered across a lawn, quite un-hurt, and Mimi swore for half a minute while belated adrenaline made my mouth taste metallic.

"You better get one of those bumper stickers," I advised when Mimi had started driving again. "One that says 'Warning: I brake for animals.' "

"Might not be a bad idea," Mimi said dryly, and then, glancing at the sky, added, "Oh hell, look at that rain." It hit the windshield as if someone had thrown a bucket of water at us.

The heavy gray of the sky, the wind, and the cold rain turned the day into one of those classic early-winter nasties.

Cully was already home. He opened the kitchen door as we scurried from the car. The kitchen light silhouetted him in the doorway; and the sight of that tall thin outline filled me with a rush of love that made me a little short of breath. I found I was too thankful for the warmth Cully and I had begun to share to ask any more questions about motivation or permanence. I came out of the cold rain into the warmth and comfort of the kitchen. "If I were watching a movie, I'd call that symbolic," I murmured to the cats as I hung up my coat.

IT WAS CERTAINLY OUR WEEK FOR BEING ENTER-tained. Mimi had to answer the phone just when Cully was saying that Elaine and Don had invited us over for Friday night. I nodded assent glumly. I'd seen Elaine a few times since our confrontation a few weeks before, but though we'd made our outward peace, we were both well aware we just plain didn't like each other.

I passed Cully another biscuit, and reflected idly that Mimi must have taken her call upstairs, since I couldn't hear her voice in the hall.

"Are you all right?" Cully asked me. "After this morning, I mean."

His concerned face reminded me of the awful flashback. "I'm fine," I said firmly. "There may be something else lurking in the woodwork for me; I don't know. But to tell you the truth, I feel better now than I have since it happened."

"I hated to leave you today. I'll make it up to you tonight." There was a slight hint of conspiratorial wickedness in his thin mobile lips that made me tingle.

I gave him a parody of a lewd wink; he laughed.

"Are you going to be around this evening?" I asked as he began clearing the table. Since he was gone so often in the evening, tending to his private practice, he'd slipped into the habit of clearing the table and putting the leftovers away, so all the dishes were lined up to wash and dry.

"No, two appointments. I should be home around nine."

Mimi didn't get off the phone until Cully had been gone about ten minutes. She went directly to the sink, turning on the water with unnecessary force.

"What are your folks doing for the holidays, Mimi?" I asked, after I'd told her about our Friday night dinner at their home.

"Oh, I forgot to tell you. Ever since Cully and I graduated from college and went our own way, they've been spending Thanksgiving in the Bahamas. It's a yearly rite now. They thought about canceling their reservation after we both got divorced, but when Mother mentioned it a few weeks ago I told her they should go on and go. She and Daddy were looking forward to it, and we can perfectly well have our own Thanksgiving."

Thanksgiving has always been my favorite holiday, so I was glad to have dinner with Elaine Friday night instead of sacrificing the big feast. Mimi seemed to be in one of her "fond of Mother" moods, so I didn't voice my relief. It occurred to me that Mimi might be so fond of her mother right now just because she wouldn't have to spend Thanksgiving with her. I'd have been jumpy about spending a whole day with Don, anyway, since he was on the list. I hadn't seen him since the weird scene over Alicia's coffin. I shuddered when I thought about it, and told my thoughts to move right along.

I went on drying dishes mindlessly, content not to think for a while. Gradually I became aware that Mimi was quiet, too. We usually talked during this unpleasant chore, to make it go faster. Things had gone so well between us that afternoon that it had almost seemed as though nothing had ever gone wrong.

"Cully gone to an evening appointment?" Mimi asked.

"Yep."

"He's probably meeting another woman on the sly," she said bitterly.

That kind of nastiness, out of the blue, wasn't typical of Mimi. It was so ugly and unexpected that I put down my towel and stared at her. Surely she wasn't brooding any longer about Richard's defection to the long-haired lady in Albuquerque?

"I'm sorry," she said curtly. "Male junkies."

"What?"

"I once heard a lecture by a woman who worked for *Ms.,*" she explained, "and she called women in our culture 'male junkies.' She said most women's magazines were about how to attract, keep, and entertain men. Or—having caught and kept—how to entertain and feed those men's children."

"Was that back when you were in college?"

"Yes, but we still are, Nick. We still are! Look at the way we were brought up. Every woman, but especially southern women. All brought up that way. You remember teen magazines? Everything down to how to tie your hair ribbon—for your *date*. If you disagreed with him, you were supposed to keep your mouth shut. Unless the disagreement was about whether he could stick his hand up your skirt. Then, and only then, you were supposed to disagree. That was why you had to carry change in your purse, to call your folks when he dumped you out of the car for resisting him."

This was the woman who'd saved four pair of white gloves? "From the magazines I've read lately, that seems to have modified quite a bit," I said mildly.

"Yes, maybe. But the old way is almost impossible to shake. You have to fight it all the time." Mimi scrubbed the pot she was holding as if she were indeed fighting it. "It's been impossible for me to uproot, just like monkey grass when you let it take over the garden. You pull it up one place, it comes back another. Propitiate, manipulate, never confront. And forgive, forgive, forgive! It's like a knee-jerk reflex!"

"Yeah, but you know what you do in a knee-jerk reflex, don't you? You kick at the guy with the hammer!"

That made her laugh. But I could still see the traces of regret around her mouth when I went to my desk to start studying. I'd known that Mimi's two aspects warred between themselves, but I'd never seen it get this intense. I was worried about her. But I concluded that, as always, Mimi would tell me what was on her mind when she chose. I couldn't figure out if she was angry with someone else or with herself. Both, I decided.

Barbara called about eight-thirty. "I didn't have a chance to tell you this afternoon, but Jeff Simmons's blood type is AB," she announced. "It took me thirty minutes' conversation to work around to blood types in some semblance of a normal manner."

"So. Four," I said slowly. "I thought you might've found out Theo's from Sarah Chase."

"It seemed like an abuse of hospitality," Barbara said. "If we'd met anywhere else but her house. I just couldn't."

"I see what you mean," I said. But I wondered if we'd make any more progress if we let the smaller scruples stand in our way. I listened to Mimi's footsteps moving around her bedroom overhead.

"Are you really determined?" Barbara asked suddenly.

"I was just wondering if I could ask you the same question."

"It's more awful, isn't it, the more we go on? Sometimes I'm tired of being so angry. Sometimes I just want to put it all away in a drawer somewhere. But then, when I really remember . . ."

"I know." I took a deep breath. "Should we go on?" I honestly didn't know how I felt. One day, one moment, I was up, hot on the trail. The next I was down, wanting only, as Barbara said, to shut it all away in a drawer, to begin to forget.

"I don't know. I just don't know."

"Maybe we should finish what we've started," I said.

"Like cleaning our plate of something we don't like to eat?" There was the faintest tinge of amusement in Barbara's voice.

Maybe I was being childishly stubborn. I pulled off my reading glasses and rubbed my eyelids. I searched around for a principle on which I could base a decision. Instead, I thought of Mimi, who in this continuing siege of fear and suspicion was being driven further and further away from me. It would put the nail in the coffin of our friendship if Barbara and I discovered somehow that Mimi's father or the man she loved was a rapist and a murderer. On the other hand (and I rubbed my eyes until I saw flashes), if Theo or John Tendall were to attack Mimi—after all, she was the same kind of woman . . .

I had a glimmering, then, but I let it slide away as I slogged down my original muddy path of thought.

. . . and if she got raped, then . . .

So I found the principle. "Other women," I said succinctly.

"Sure," said Barbara. "How could we live with ourselves?"

"So that settles that." I wasn't exactly pleased with our final decision, but I was relieved to have it over with.

"What if all the rest really do have O positive? I was just joking this morning, but they might turn out to. What do we do then?"

"Hell, I don't know. We line them up and ask them to drop their pants."

Dreadfully, we both began snickering.

"That was pretty sick," Barbara said when she'd wound down. "But we'd have a chance of recognizing the one."

"Like you said today, I take a laugh where I can find it, now." I heard Mimi at the head of the stairs. "So you've got one more to go, and I've got two. Let's get to work," I said hurriedly. "See you." I hung up.

"Nick, I'm going out for a while," Mimi said. Suddenly she seemed to recall something, and looked concerned. "When's Cully coming home?"

I glanced at my watch. "He should be here any time. He said about nine, and it's almost that now." I realized what she was worried about. "Hey, I can be alone and not go to pieces," I told her gently.

"Oh. You figured it out." She grinned. "We thought we were being so clever about it."

"It took me a while," I assured her, and grinned back.

"Nick, you know how—well, I'm sort of proud."

"Yes, Miss Mimi Houghton." I was still smiling, but I could feel my smile begin to wane. Her face had turned completely sober.

"You know I told you I knew Charles isn't involved in all this." She gestured with her hand to indicate me and the direction in which Alicia's house lay.

I nodded, trying to keep my face expressionless.

"I did that all wrong, but what I said is true. I'll tell you all about it, when I can stand to."

"Okay, Mimi." What else could I say?

Then she was out the back door to her car. I was shaking my head as I locked the door behind her.

THE HOUGHTONS' DINING ROOM HAD CHANGED very little since the night I'd met Cully more than fourteen years before. Elaine bought the best and took care of it. Just as she'd picked the best husband for her and had taken excellent care of him, I decided during the delicious dinner. I could have carried the idea further and further and my understanding of the family would have profited from it, but I called myself to order and reminded myself of my mission.

It wasn't easy to find an opening into which I could insert the odd subject of blood types. The gleaming wood of the table, the heavy sheen of the silver, the flowers in the crystal bowl, all reproached me for my tawdry problem. It hardly seemed possible that the rich striped upholstery of Elaine's chairs would consent to hold the bottom of a woman who had been raped. But that was just as real as the table or the silver, I told myself sternly. I braced and waited for the right opening in the conversation. Don himself provided it.

"Honey, have you heard how Orrin Sherwood is?" he asked Elaine.

"Not too good," she answered with that ominous little shake of the head that means death is in the offing. "That wreck was just a terrible thing. His wife won't even leave the hospital to lie down at home for an hour or two. She says Orrin's got to see her face if he opens his eyes, Miss Pearlie told me."

"I didn't hear about that! What happened?" Cully asked. "Orrin's worked for Father for, oh, twenty years," he told me. Elaine frowned slightly.

Don proceeded to describe the circumstances of the wreck, which I barely heard, poised as I was to spring.

". . . and he'd lost a lot of blood, way too much."

Thanks, Don. Ready, set, go. "I guess that's what they wanted the blood for the other day," I interjected. "They called this boy in one of my classes, he was telling me. The hospital was short of that blood type. He went in and gave."

"Gosh, if I'd known that, I'd have given some," Don said with deep chagrin. "I do wish they'd said something while I was at the hospital! Orrin and I were in the army together, and it seems to me we found out then that we had the same blood type. What type was the boy, the one who told you this, Nickie?"

"He didn't say," I managed to get out, feeling worse and worse.

"Let's see . . ." Don thought, his fork poised in midair. Elaine waited patiently, her face turned to him with apparent interest. "I think I'm just plain old type O, universal donor," Don decided. "So Orrin must be something else, since the hospital surely wouldn't run out of O." He was really sad at missing the opportunity to help his friend. My heart sank. Another type O.

"Aren't we all?" said Cully. "I know I am."

"Oh, it's been so long since I had you two, that's the only time I had mine typed," Elaine reflected. "Your daddy and I had to find out about that Rh factor. You know, it causes trouble for the baby if the parents are different."

Mimi nodded to show she was listening, but she looked faintly bored. Then she brightened. "Charles," she said happily, "can't give blood. He faints at the sight of it." She seemed happy just to say his name.

During the inevitable exclamations this quirk of Charles's engendered, I told myself rapidly that even if Don did have O blood, so did John Tendall. And probably Theo, too. But that peculiarity of Charles's bore out Mimi's assertion that Charles could not be the rapist. All of us had bled to some extent.

"Is it just his own blood, Mimi? Or anyone's?" I asked, just to be sure.

"Oh, anyone's. It's been embarrassing to him for years because he likes to hunt so much, and if someone he's with cuts himself, Charles has to look the other way."

Why the hell hadn't Mimi told me that earlier, instead of going through all that hocus-pocus about swearing not to tell Cully we'd suspected Charles? Then I caught on. She'd come out with this quirk of Charles's so unselfconsciously that I had to conclude she herself hadn't made the connection between Charles's horror of blood and his now-certain innocence. She'd been thinking of some other exculpating fact earlier, something she wanted to keep secret. Of course, the result was the same; Barbara and I could scratch Charles from our list. That left three, and one of those three was Don. The odds that he was the rapist had just leaped appreciably.

As Mimi and I cleared the table, I tried to keep my mind blank. I was able to join in the conversation just enough to keep my preoccupation under wraps. But after an hour, when we were all in the living room and Elaine was carrying in coffee and dessert, an awful line of logic insisted on screaming out in my mind.

Mimi had thought—briefly, and for whatever reason—that Charles might be the rapist. So she wouldn't see him. Now Mimi would see Charles. So he wasn't the rapist; Mimi said she *knew* he wasn't guilty.

How could Mimi know he wasn't the rapist?

She knew who *was*.

But why would she keep silent about it? Who on earth would Mimi protect from such a charge?

Her father, Don.

THE WHOLE ROOM BLURRED BEFORE I CAUGHT myself. I felt sweat break out on the palms of my hands. I set down my coffee cup with a loud chink. Elaine glanced at me reprovingly before she resumed her conversation with Mimi. She didn't know how lucky she was; I'd almost dumped both cup and coffee on the carpet. I grabbed control of myself with a tremendous effort. I shot a quick look at Don, sitting on a love seat beside Mimi, opposite me.

I was thinking, quickly and desperately. I was probing the raw gash, trying to remember. Trying to dig out fragments so the wound could be closed. What could I remember? I'd told the police I didn't know anything about my attacker. I hadn't seen him. But I had to be able to remember something, something else, something that might eliminate Don. Okay. Calm, now. Calm.

I remembered. He'd been heavier and shorter than, say, Cully; but that category included many men besides Cully's father.

He hadn't really been very strong. Otherwise, the damage inflicted would have been worse, far worse. I touched my face; I remembered. Don was hardly in good shape, and he must be at least fifty-five, probably older.

No beard on the attacker. None of the men on our list had one.

I had to yank myself out of the stream of my memory. Cully was eyeing me in a dubious way, his dark eyebrows humped together. I found I was on the verge of bursting into a laugh that would have been very unpleasant to hear; I'd wildly imagined asking Don to lie on top of me to see if it felt familiar. I mashed that laughter into a smile and offered it to Cully. He looked startled, as well he might; it must have been ghastly.

The worst thing about these few minutes of horror was that they passed in Elaine's living room. Everything in the room was civilized, conventional, expensive. The man who fit into this room simply couldn't do such a thing.

In a kind of suspended animation, I turned to Cully and asked him to give me some details about the party we'd been asked to for the night before Thanksgiving.

"One of the psych professors is throwing it," he said,

relief evident in his voice. He was grateful to me for apparently snapping out of a bad mood. "He lives just three blocks away from Mimi's. It's a costume party."

"What? Right after Halloween?"

"It was going to be on Halloween, but he caught the flu or something."

"What on earth can we go as?" It was wonderful to work out this little problem. I had managed once again. I was on top of this situation. I could do it. Maybe Cully's father had raped me and killed Alicia, and I was trying to think of a costume to wear to a party. Hell, I could do anything.

"I think you ought to go as either the Sugar Plum Fairy or Wonder Woman," Cully said. It was such an amazing thing for Cully to say, and the smile he gave me was so crinkled and sweet, that I almost kissed him.

"Grandmother's trunks are still in the attic, and heaven knows what's in them," Mimi called from across the room.

It dawned on Elaine that Cully and I were going to a party together, that I was his date. Her eyes narrowed in irritation and jumped sharply from her son to me and back again. Cully caught the look, casually took my hand, and with a bland face continued the discussion of what was likely to be unearthed in the attic.

I shuddered to think.

I GOT THROUGH THE REST OF THE EVENING. IT was so unreal to think that a person I knew and loved could have raped me that I couldn't accept it either emotionally or intellectually.

I shot secret looks at Don every now and then, and on the outside he was just as nice as always. His face was just as amiable, his bald patch just as shiny. His conversation was certainly just as bland. As he discussed the vital need for a new traffic light at one of Knolls's intersections, I couldn't remotely imagine that mouth uttering the foul words I remembered.

I was more confused than I had ever been in my life.

I will never know how I did it. I don't think all of me was in my body that night. I think part of me just got up and left. What remained handled it. I did get through the rest of the evening.

Chapter 12

WHAT COULD I TELL BARBARA? I DIDN'T THINK I'd see her until Monday. She had a date with her fellow professor, J. R. Smith, on Saturday. She really was going to learn how to play poker. Cully and I were going to a nearby state park on Sunday, to shuffle through the falling leaves and have a change of scene.

I surprised Cully with the enthusiasm of my leaf shuffling. I bounded, I sang, I talked about my classes, I told him I thought my mother was improving. I was a one-woman band all day. Cully was obviously a little puzzled by my frenetic mood, but he tried gamely to enter in. I even tried to lose myself in passion; and for an amazing hour among the leaves I succeeded.

I told myself over and over that Don was leaving town Monday night, for a whole week. If nothing happened before he left, I'd have a week to think, a week to decide what I must do and who I should keep faith with—Mimi or Barbara.

I lay awake most of Sunday night, waiting. Those hours of torment were the penalty for my indecisiveness. Every second Monday morning, as I sat through my classes or walked down the halls, I was terrified that someone would come up to me and begin, "Oh, Nickie, did you hear about the girl last night . . ."

By midmorning, when Barbara met me in the student center to tell me Theo was type O like Don and Detective Tendall, it hardly seemed to matter. I was glad she was in a hurry to get to a conference with a student. To preserve at least a partial faith, I told her about Charles's weak head for blood. But I didn't mention Don.

At three o'clock I knew the Houghtons' flight had taken off from the Memphis airport. I was sitting in the library snapping the point off my pencil and sharpening it again, to the discomfort of the students around me. Their faces became even more guarded when I shut my eyes and said a brief and silent thanksgiving.

Now I had time.

That night, I buried myself in the paper due that week, and in studying for one remaining test. I finished the paper. Cully laughed at my reading glasses and typed my paper for me while I studied.

"Your handwriting is terrible, but your paper is very good," he told me, and I felt myself turn pink with pleasure. I dived back into my books, as much to dodge thinking as to make a good grade.

I TRUDGED HOME AFTER TUESDAY'S TEST, MY EYES watering in the sharp wind, and found Detective Markowitz waiting on the front steps. It was almost as if I'd conjured him up. With the test out of the way, my mind had been running around and around my dilemma.

"You're looking better," he said approvingly. "How you feel, darlin'?"

"I feel a lot better, too," I lied. It would have been the truth a few days ago. I smiled at him. He still looked tired and world-weary, but there was an air of cheer about him that I enjoyed. It was quite a change.

"I swear, I had no idea you was such a beauty," he testified as I unlocked the front door. I told him to come on in.

After he refused coffee or cola, I perched on the couch and asked him what I could do for him. "Something new?" I said hopefully.

"Well, not much, but something," he said. I had known there was a reason for that cheer.

"Fact is, we've eliminated a mighty lot of people. Now, you might not think that's much," he said as he saw my face fall, "but in police work, that's a lot. It's not like in the books. The sooner we get suspects out of the way, false suspects, the sooner we can get at the real one. And I've worked so hard and so long on these cases that I just decided I'd be happy about that."

Even as he told me this, his little manufactured happiness vanished. "I've got a daughter myself, you know," he said quietly. "We're doing everything we possibly can, honey. So I decided to drop by, again; I know it's hard on you, having to think about it—"

What else had I been doing?

"—but I thought I'd ask, one more time, if there was anything, *any tiny thing,* you've recalled since we last talked to you. The last time I saw you, it was still just a week after. I thought maybe you might have thought of something by now, now you've had time to calm a little."

"Well," I said hesitantly.

He pounced. "Something?"

I knew I was going to let him down. "This is going to sound stupid," I began. "I don't remember anything specific, but I do know there's something to remember. It hasn't come to me yet, though."

"I see," he said doubtfully.

"There's an impression I got," I blundered on. "But it won't come to mind yet. I told you this was going to sound stupid."

"No, no," he said politely. "Call me, any hour, any day. I'm in the book. If you remember. Now, as long as I'm here, would you feel like going over the thing with me again?"

There was nothing I felt less like doing. But of course I said I would.

"I couldn't tell how tall, because he was bending over the bed," I started out. "But not extremely tall, I think." I looked at my feet to concentrate better. Markowitz's brown eyes were too eager. He was on edge and desperate to get something definite out of me. I didn't have anything to give him.

"He was pretty heavy," I said. I bit my lip. "He was white. He didn't sound very young. Not a kid's voice." I rummaged through my memory. I had thought my film was so exact, but it had been skipping things lately, thank God. "Nothing else," I said finally. "I just can't form any other conclusions. It was so dark, and with the pillow over my face . . ."

"Sure, sure," Markowitz said hastily. He didn't want me crying on him. He reached up to check his Jerry Lee Lewis hairdo. It was a weary gesture.

Then I had it.

"He was *bald!*" I shouted.

The detective's head snapped up. His brown eyes glittered from that blank face. "What?" he said intently.

"He was bald," I said more slowly. I had it now; I remembered. That nagging feeling, like an itch beneath a cast, was gone.

Markowitz looked as though he wanted to turn me upside down and shake the information loose. "How do you know?"

"My arms . . . when he . . ." I took a deep breath to brace myself. "When he lay on top of me, my arms were crossed over my bosom, and the top of his head brushed them, and I felt scalp, not hair."

The detective actually grabbed my arm. "Are you sure?" His voice was little more than a whisper.

"Yes."

Markowitz leapt to his feet. Excitement was jolting through him like an amphetamine. He walked to a window, ran a hand over his hair again, put both hands in his pockets, took them out. His hair was so carefully waved that it looked like a toupee. I wondered suddenly if his partner Tendall did indeed wear a toupee. That thick gray hair, so carefully styled . . .

"How bald?" He swung to face me.

"What?"

"Completely bald? Or just a little hair combed across the scalp? Or bald on top, with hair around the sides of his head?"

I tried to make the memory more specific. I closed my eyes. I actually crossed my arms over my breasts.

"I don't know. I can't remember any more than that," I said finally.

Markowitz accepted my word, to my surprise. It seemed he was so excited at finally having a real clue that he could barely wait to get back to the police station to tell his partner Tendall. And he was proud, I could tell. He'd come back to see me that one additional time, without real hope, just because he was a good cop, and a desperate cop. I didn't tell him that if he hadn't had the habit of running his hand over his hair, I never would have remembered.

Markowitz said goodbye hastily and absently. From the front window, I watched him actually do a little dance step before he got into his car. Then he turned and waved.

I walked back to the bedroom and threw myself down on the bed. Now I understood why I'd felt so oddly uneasy around Don and Charles. That evening at Don and Elaine's, when I'd seen the lamp shining on Don's bald head, I'd remembered there was something *to* remember. Charles's hair was clearly thinning. He combed long strands across, but tanned scalp shone through. Thank God, Cully still had lots of hair.

But when I thought about it, I realized I'd met a lot of men in some stage of baldness since I'd come back to Knolls. Barbara's friend—ex-friend—Stan. Theo. And I realized I could've saved Barbara her half-hour conversation with Jeff Simmons, now that I pictured his luxuriant blondness. I had to laugh when I visualized dignified Jeff Simmons skulking through the Houghton gardens in his three-piece suit. We had actually suspected him! I caught myself up sharp; I gave myself a slap. How could I laugh?

I could laugh. I gave myself permission. My responsibility was over. I'd done everything, every humanly possible thing, to help catch the man who'd attacked me and killed Alicia. The police wouldn't go by our list. The police wanted facts. And I'd dredged up the very last fact I had. They had the blood type. They knew about the baldness. They'd listened to us when we told them the rapist knew us.

My part in this was over, I swore. My appointed role was that of victim. I'd been the very best little victim I could. I was sick to death of being a victim. I was turning in my pain, crawling out of the bog of suspicion and doubt. I would flounder in it no longer.

I shut a long narrow drawer inside me. The corpse it held was not quite dead; but I slammed the drawer shut with my own kind of ruthlessness. Maybe it would die for lack of air.

Chapter 13

THE NEXT DAY, THE DAY OF THE PARTY, I HUMMED to myself in the bathroom all afternoon, doing things to myself I hadn't done since I moved to Knolls. Facial treatments, creams, the whole battery of makeup I'd considered never using again, all came out of boxes and tubes I'd stuck far back in my vanity.

After applying them, I felt a cool sheen slip over me, the sheen I'd worn like armor in the city. It didn't fit as well as it had. But I could still wear it. The New York Nickie had had her points. She'd had that wonderful gloss of safety most people don't even know they possess until they lose it. She hadn't been a victim.

For the first time in weeks, I consciously examined my face in the mirror. Today it seemed important; maybe the most important thing about me. I examined every pore, every wrinkle-in-the-making, as I once had done daily. I did my exercises, which had also been neglected lately. My muscles ached afterward. Cully the jogger would be proud of me.

I recalled all the warning stories I'd heard about what

happened when you dropped that daily exam and tone-up. I could hear a friend (another model) relating with horror what had happened to a comrade of ours who'd married months before; inexplicably, she had wed an upstate farmer. "In weeks, Nickie, just *weeks,* she's lost all her muscle tone," Cicely had told me in a voice filled with outrage and fear.

Loss of muscle tone; oh my goodness gracious. A fate worse than death. I snickered at the mirror and went on with my work.

Through the bathroom wall, I could hear the *thunk* of Mimi opening the oven door in the kitchen. She'd forgotten to make cornbread for the dressing and was worried about leaving it out all night to stale, since Mao and Attila had shown themselves partial to cornbread in the past.

Cully had gone to the college to catch up on his paperwork. Most of the students had left for home the day before. His secretary was at home making her own dressing. He was looking forward to the peace and quiet, he'd said, when I'd asked him if it didn't make him feel uneasy to be alone in the empty psychology building. He had looked at me rather strangely. Of course, men weren't supposed to be afraid. They didn't have to be.

I pulled my thoughts away from that dreary track. Was I going to begrudge Cully the fact that he ran no chance of getting raped?

Back to frivolity. Maybe I should turn gay. I'd known plenty of women in New York who liked their own kind, at least occasionally. But the idea had never appealed to me, even at times when I was depressed over some romance that had failed. I pictured myself waltzing into the kitchen and putting the move on Mimi, and laughed at the thought of the look on her face.

She overheard. "What's so funny?" she called from the kitchen in an aggravated voice.

"Nothing!" I'd tell her sometime when she wasn't worried about sage and poultry seasoning. I felt a little uncomfortable being invited to a party Mimi hadn't been asked to; but she had told me, almost too vehemently, that she wouldn't have gone if she'd been asked. I had raised my eyebrows.

"I've only met the guy once, and I didn't like him," she had said lamely. "And his *wife!*"

Aha. "What about her?"

"I hate her," Mimi had said to my surprise.

To answer my stare, she'd advanced the story that the woman kept a photograph of her father in his casket—on her bedside table.

How on earth did Mimi know that? Something in her face had warned me not to ask. But I'd told her about the time in New York when I'd gone out for a drink with the photographer who'd said my eyes were like opals (I'd always love him a little for that). He'd confessed to me after several Scotches that when he'd first opened shop, he'd made some money that way. "You'd be surprised," he told me earnestly, "how many people want pictures of their loved ones in their boxes." Then he'd made me swear to keep his former sideline a secret.

I mulled over that odd story as I unrolled the special pouch that held my arsenal of brushes. I decided that we all carry our dead with us. My hostess-to-be just carried hers openly and visibly.

Nickie the philosopher.

My left nostril is a fraction larger than my right. I painted it even. The work of art complete, I slithered out to the kitchen in a lounging robe I saved for great occasions, a gorgeous thin slinky thing. The big room was in a state of chaos. Mimi was determined that our Thanksgiving feast be full and traditional. She'd hauled every spice out of the rack so she could pick up what she wanted instantly. A heap of sweet potatoes was piled on the counter, and the turkey was perched to thaw in the drain rack.

Attila was prowling around the fringes of this bounty, hoping to snitch some of it. Mao was curled up on top of the microwave staring at the turkey as if it were a live bird she was stalking. Mimi was crumbling the still-steaming corn bread, a pained expression on her face. She glared at me as I opened the refrigerator.

"Now, Nick, don't get drunk tonight, you hear? You can't have a hangover tomorrow. You won't eat much if you have a hangover."

"Okay, Mimi," I said meekly. "Can I have a sandwich now?"

"Yes, ma'am," she said, and suddenly grinned. The old warmth was back. "I reckon you might find some food around here."

"What would you recommend?" I asked seriously. "The peanut butter and jelly or the leftover meat loaf?"

"Oh, boy, a meat loaf sandwich. Make me one, too, will you? Heat it up in the microwave, with cheese all over it."

I began rummaging through the refrigerator. It might take me hours to come up with the meat loaf, the shelves were so jammed. "You'd think," I muttered, "we were expecting an army instead of just us and Barbara."

"Well . . . Charles is coming."

I froze with my hand, finally, on the meat loaf. I felt the tension radiating from Mimi. She thought I was still worried about her protection of Charles, but actually I was struggling to slam a mental drawer in which a corpse had just moved and groaned. "Okay," I said, when I could. I heard her sigh behind me.

Cully hallooed from the door then, so the moment passed. I unearthed the serrated knife to slice some of my homemade bread for our sandwiches. Cully wanted one, too.

"When's Barbara coming over?" Cully asked as we sat on the benches in the breakfast nook wolfing down our food.

"Seven-thirty, eight," Mimi said indistinctly. "We're going to set up the dining table in the living room, and we're going to figure out when the turkey has to go in, and she's going to grip the bird while I reach in to get the innards out. I don't think I got him out of the freezer soon enough, to tell you the truth. I think the cavity's still frozen."

"Wear rubber gloves," Cully advised. "That's what Rachel always did."

Oh, great.

The phone rang when I was halfway to the counter to either make another sandwich or throw the meat loaf at Mimi and Cully. I picked up the receiver on our brand-new kitchen wall phone. (Mimi had gotten tired of standing in the hall to talk, and had had the old one taken out.)

"Hello? May I speak to Nickie?"

"Mother?" I felt age sit on my shoulders. I felt the stillness behind me as Cully and Mimi quit eating.

"Baby? Guess where I'm calling from!"

Oh, not the outskirts of Knolls, please no. She'd come to see me at Miss Beacham's like that, once. She didn't sound drunk. But she sounded uncertain, shaky. I felt my face settle into tense lines.

"I don't know, Mother. Where?"

"Well." I heard her take a deep breath. "I checked myself into a center for alcoholics two weeks ago."

"What?" I felt dizzy and sat on the floor with a bump, taking the telephone receiver with me. I drew my knees up. "You what?"

"Sober for two weeks," she said, and began crying.

"Oh," I said wonderingly. "Oh, Mama!" All the years sloughed off. I pounded my fist against my knee for joy. "Mama! Really? Really?"

"This is my first phone call," she said. "They don't let you make a phone call for two weeks, until they can be sure you won't plead to be taken home."

I noted the call had not been made to Jay.

"Where is he?" I didn't have to specify who "he" was.

"Gone." Her voice was very controlled. "I waited till he went out of town. I'm really kind of a coward, Nickie. I'm glad you're grown up now. Maybe you can understand. I waited till he was gone. Then I filed for divorce, and I changed all the locks on the doors, and then I packed a bag and I headed here after I called my doctor. I was so drunk I barely made it. In fact, I drove over some bushes at the entrance. But they took me."

The tears trickled down, tracking the work of hours. I

gestured frantically at Mimi and she passed me a napkin to blot them. I felt the cold linoleum of the kitchen floor bite into my rump through the thin bathrobe. The muscles in my rear were cramping. I didn't care.

"Are you there, honey?" The frail voice was scared again.

"You're wonderful," I said. "Oh, bless you, bless you."

"Hardly wonderful," said my mother, with a ghost of amusement in her voice. "Fourteen years too late. Not wonderful. And it's not over, by a long shot."

"You'll make it," I told her fiercely, trying to will my hope through the telephone line.

"For the first time, yesterday I really began to think I might," she whispered.

"You will." I paused. "Have you heard from him?"

"He can't call in," she said smugly. "I won't come to the phone."

"Yahoo! Good for you, Mama!"

"I have to go, Nickie. It's a long road out of these woods. Don't expect too much."

"You think you might be out by Christmas?"

"I don't know. I hope so. Maybe I'll feel strong enough by then."

"If you are, I'll come home," I promised. I took down her phone number and address at the center.

"That'll give me a goal—Christmas," she said, and chuckled. I hadn't heard that chuckle in so long I barely remembered she used to do it all the time.

"I love you."

"I hope so," she said. "Bye bye, Nickie."

"Bye, Mama."

We both hung up very gently.

Mimi smilingly passed me another napkin.

MY FITFUL GOOD MOOD, WHICH HAD BEEN ARTI-ficial earlier, now had some basis in fact. I almost danced as I got ready for the party. I only dance when I feel secure;

my dancing resembles nothing so much as a frog leaping from pad to pad.

"Now I know you're human," Cully remarked as I capered from the bathroom to the closet to extract my costume. I swept by him in a particularly daring maneuver and gave him a kiss on the forehead.

"Did you ever doubt it?"

"At one time," he admitted.

"Why?" I stopped cavorting and looked at him.

"Oh . . . you never admitted anything was wrong."

Well, well, well. I sat down at the foot of the bed with a thud. "Explain."

He folded his fingers together and looked at me with his lips flattened. I got a glimpse of what his patients saw. (Or did he call them "clients"?)

"You were so beautiful," he began, and I winced. It always came back to that in the end; my blessing and my curse. "You were intelligent. You did very well at school, even while your home life was falling apart. Mimi told us what was happening with your parents, eventually; but you never said anything—"

"I was ashamed," I interrupted.

"I can see that now, but at the time—I was inexperienced, too, you have to remember—it just looked like it wasn't touching you."

A very different view of one of the most anguishing periods of my life. I'd been so afraid of tainting the smooth Houghton household with my sleazy problems. Faced with the cold perfection of Elaine, who could openly discuss having an alcoholic mother? I told Cully this.

"I can understand it *now*," he emphasized. "But then, I was only a kid, too. I was busy being a mighty senior in high school, then a lowly freshman in college, and every time you came to see Mimi I would go through torment. You just seemed far too perfect for someone like me. Then you went off to New York to become exactly what you wanted to be. Brave. Beautiful and brave, smart, successful. Making a lot of money. I met and married Rachel.

Then you came to Mimi's first wedding looking like a woman from another planet, your clothes and face were so sophisticated."

"Cully, I got drunk as a skunk at that wedding."

"It was the first time I thought you might be a real human like the rest of us," he said with a grin. The pursed lips and steepled fingers were gone, and he was Cully my lover, not Cully the observer.

"Did you lust after me?"

"You bet. Wet dreams."

"Yahoo." We grinned at each other, and I licked my lips in a parody of lasciviousness. I smoothed his mustache with one forefinger. He bit the fingertip.

"I saw your face everywhere I went for years. I used to buy magazines if your face was on the cover."

"But you came to see me in New York, with Rachel," I said carefully.

"All the feelings I had for you were so indefinite, you seemed so unattainable, that it didn't seem to have any bearing on my real life, my life with Rachel."

Good. I didn't want to hear that his marriage had broken up over a fantasy, even a fantasy of me.

"Your apartment was beautiful. Your life was full of glossy people. You were on top of everything."

Of course I had wanted to seem on top of everything, because Cully and Rachel were coming. I told him that, too. He shook his head ruefully.

"When Mimi told me you were coming back here, I just couldn't believe it. I couldn't believe you had suffered any setbacks, any defeats. I let my adolescent picture of you go on and on. That never matured. The rest of me grew up, but not the part that held that image of you."

"And then . . ." I murmured. And then I got raped.

It hung in the air around us.

I pounced on Cully and nipped him on the throat. I messed up his hair, something I knew would aggravate him. "No more introspection," I commanded. "It's time to party."

* * *

CULLY MADE A GORGEOUS ROBIN HOOD. I'D found an oversized plain green shift up in the attic. Mimi vaguely recalled an aunt of hers leaving the shift behind after a visit to Celeste, and never asking for it again. Belted in, it made a fine tunic for Cully, coming down more than halfway to his knees. He had a pair of high brown boots he wore in the woods, and I made him pull on a pair of green tights of mine. Underneath his tunic, he wore a green flannel shirt. I'd made the hat, which sported a feather, from bits and pieces of green felt and an old hat of Celeste's. Cully had borrowed the bow and arrow from his friend on the police force, who practiced archery.

Naturally, Cully wanted me to dress as Maid Marian. I wondered if she had drooped around in the forest in long dresses waiting for Robin to return bragging about his exploits, or if she'd dressed up in tights, too, and aimed arrows right along with the best of the Merry Men. I finally decided that having donated my green tights to Cully's costume, it would be too much trouble to corral enough green for my own. I decided to go as a good fairy, since I'd found the perfect dress in my own closet. It was fluffy and white, scoop-necked and flouncy and romantic as hell. I'd worn it in a show and bought it on a whim afterward. It dated from a romantic revival by some designer who never made the grade.

I had spent the morning constructing my crown from cardboard and glitter and putting together a wand from a cardboard star and a fly-swatter handle, also liberally beglittered. I curled my hair furiously and fluffed it out into a blonde cloud, then painted two pink spots high on my cheekbones. I'd even unearthed some gold nail polish.

When Cully and I were ready, we presented ourselves to Mimi, who smelled strongly of sage and cranberries.

"Good fairy, please turn this frog into a prince," Mimi requested in a piping child's voice, pointing at Cully.

"Poof!" I said obligingly, in the most dulcet voice I

could manage. I waved my wand. "Young frog, you are a prince for this evening only, a limited-time offer."

"Ping," Cully responded, widening his eyes and standing up straighter to enact his transformation.

We all laughed like hell, Mimi having drunk a couple of glasses of wine while she was cooking, and Cully and I high on being in love.

Barbara came in before we left. She looked perkier than I'd seen her look for months, color in her cheeks and a little bounce in her walk. I thought she'd enjoyed learning to play poker. She was wearing boots and had a scarf wound around her neck. She warned us it was getting colder outside by the minute. "But I love it. It's like home."

"Fairy Clarabelle will waft us to the party on her magic broomstick," Cully said with a straight face.

"You better warm it up before you get on," Barbara commented.

"Think we ought to take the car?" Cully asked me. "I didn't want to, since there won't be much room for parking and it's only three blocks. But I don't want you to freeze in that thing."

I told Cully I thought I could endure three blocks' worth of cold, so we set off on foot.

ONCE GUESTS HAVE UNLACED THEMSELVES enough to put on costumes, you have the makings of a pretty uninhibited party. I decided that about two hours later as I leaned against the kitchen counter chatting with my hostess Sally (the lady who allegedly had the corpse photograph on her night table—how *had* Mimi known that?). We agreed on this matter—costumes equaling letting one's hair down—after great deliberation. I'd had one glass of wine too many, and my hostess had had about three too many. Our conversation was rather erratic.

We rambled into a heated discussion on whether men or women had originated the idea of witches. Sally thought women labeled "witches" were persecuted by men to express their general fear of women, and I thought women claimed to be witches to attain some power in a chauvinistic society. Since our conclusions were the same—witches had gotten a pretty raw deal—we ended the discussion pleased with each other.

At long last my hostess perfected her tray of sausage balls. I offered to help by carrying it into the living room; and that's how the accident occurred. The house was old, with floor furnace grates; and as I passed through the hall, my heel caught and broke in one. Miraculously, I managed to keep the tray upright even as I slid to the floor.

"Poor thing," my new friend Sally observed. "At least the sausage balls are okay."

I thought that was a callous point of view, but fortunately hadn't enough breath to tell her so.

Several gentlemen (a mouse, Hitler, and Tarzan—who must have been freezing—among them) helped me to my feet, one of them feeling me up in the process. I couldn't identify the culprit until I saw the leer on the mouse's face. I didn't know his name and couldn't recall seeing him before. With a gracious smile, I leaned forward to his ear and whispered, "You bastard." The leer disappeared in a hurry, replaced by a shocked reaction to my unladylike language.

I decided it was time to find another glass of wine and Cully. After reassuring my rescuers that I wasn't hurt, I coasted through the big old rooms looking for him. I'd last seen him in the company of a lean dark woman he'd introduced as his high school sweetheart (rather tactlessly, it seemed to me). She had giggled like a maniac and ducked her head in a way that made me positively loathe her. I'd debated opting for northern directness and telling her to buzz off, but instead had fought fire with fire and given her the sweetest smile I could construct while remarking that since those high school days were *so* long ago, she and Cully surely must have a lot to talk about. Of course, I'd removed myself immediately thereafter, and I hadn't spotted Cully since.

I didn't see him now. My vinous sense of well-being

was evaporating as my coccyx began feeling the effect of the slide to the floor. Lurching around on one heel wasn't making it feel any better. I wanted Cully to appear, fired with great concern, and beg me to tell him I wasn't damaged. He didn't. I couldn't spot Miss High School Sweetheart either. I decided after some careful thought that my attitude could best be described as "piqued."

The shoe situation had to be remedied. I considered lasting through the party by taking both shoes off, but my host and hostess had not gotten around to renovating the floors yet, and the wood looked splintery. In a spurt of independence, I decided I would walk back to Mimi's and get another pair of shoes, and then return to find Cully frantic with worry over where I'd been. A neat consolidation of motives.

"Sally, I'm just going to run home and get another pair of shoes," I informed the hostess.

She nodded vaguely and said, "Suit yourself, Mike." Crossed wires, there.

With some difficulty I found my coat, checking out a couple of bedrooms before I located the one that held all the wraps. By sheer chance I noticed Cully and the dark-haired woman weren't in any of them.

It had gotten colder outside. I didn't want to go barefoot in temperatures like these, but trying to balance on one high heel was impossible and dangerous. Someone at the party had mentioned that just north of us there was freezing rain and the rain was expected to reach Knolls in a couple of hours. This was unseasonable for the area; the Thanksgivings I remembered were chilly but sunny. Winter was paying a premature visit.

I wasn't so brave and didn't feel so smart once I had gone a block in my bare feet. They began to sting with cold. Maybe I should return to the party and wait for Cully to walk me home for the shoes, I thought uneasily. But that wouldn't make my feet any warmer. I belatedly realized I should have hunted down Cully with more determination, and sent *him* back to the house for my footwear, since his shoes were intact. I paused on the sidewalk, shivering, and almost turned back. But I'd gone nearly a block, and I knew exactly where my replacements were stored in my closet. Besides, Cully might be busy with his *sweetheart*.

I gritted my teeth and proceeded. I was half a block from Mimi's when the lights went out on the entire street. The freezing rain to the north, no doubt. "Oh hell," I said to the black night, to the silent block, to the tension that suddenly leapt from the core of my awareness. I hadn't known I was afraid. But I knew it now. I was alone in the night, and unsheltered.

Obviously I couldn't stand still. I wrapped my coat more tightly about me, clenched my teeth, and started forward. There wasn't even much light from the moon or stars; the gathering clouds of the oncoming storm were obscuring them. I could see darker shapes in the darkness. That was all.

Because of the gloom, I overshot the steps leading up to the yard. I slapped myself lightly in punishment. "Stupid Nick," I muttered. Then my bare foot met the gravel of the driveway that led around back. That might be for the better, really. If I'd gone to the front door, Mimi would have had to blunder through the length of the lightless house to let me in. The kitchen door would be easier; she was sure to be in the kitchen with Barbara. Maybe they'd already gotten the candles lit.

That was a cheering thought. But since I'd had it, I was twice as dismayed to find the kitchen windows as lifeless as the rest of the house.

I patted my way past the cars, narrowly avoided falling into the bushes flanking the back steps, and crept up them with my hands extended. I was clutching both the shoes in my left hand to leave my right free. I heard a car go by in the street. From all the whooping and hollering, I gathered that a group of teenage revelers were excited by the blackout.

I padded blindly across the porch and had the great good fortune to encounter the knob of the kitchen door on my first try. I pushed it open, wondered for a second why it wasn't locked, and stepped inside calling "Mimi!" . . . and the lights came back on.

I gaped for one long, dazzled second. Mimi was crouched by the breakfast nook and she had a screwdriver in her hand, gripping it fiercely with its business end jabbing upward. In front of her—*So ludicrous* flashed through my mind—was Theo Cochran.

He had a knife in his hand.

"Watch out!" Mimi screamed.

Confused by the sudden light and Mimi's shout, Theo had half-turned by the time I threw my shoes at him. They missed by a mile (I never could hit the side of a barn), but they provided a distraction. He dodged quite unnecessarily and then tried to decide who to attack.

Mimi settled that by a simple act of heroism. She flung herself at him.

In the middle of chaos, I frantically looked for a weapon to use in the struggle. Mimi was gripping her screwdriver in one hand and grasping his knife wrist with the other. In the shattered seconds I was frozen with shock he wounded her with a twist of the blade, and I saw blood well on her arm.

"No," I said very definitely, and grabbed the only heavy thing that came to hand: the Thanksgiving turkey, slathered with butter, resting on the counter by the sink. I grabbed the legs in their metal brace, darted across the linoleum, swung the turkey back, and brought it crashing in an arc against the side of Theo's head. On impact, the greased turkey flew out of my hands and skittered grotesquely across the floor.

Theo staggered, let go of Mimi to right himself.

She instantly stabbed him with the screwdriver, and from his grunt I could tell he was hurt, but I didn't think that blunt end would penetrate enough to wound him seriously, so I wrapped my arms around his chest from behind and bit him in the neck as hard as I could. I didn't let go even when we hit the ground. Each of my hands grasped its opposite wrist, and even the pain of falling wasn't going to loosen that hold. On the way down I caught a glimpse of a form huddled on the other side of the kitchen by the refrigerator. He's killed Barbara, I thought. I'm going to kill him . . . and then I realized that Theo was trying to stab at me backhanded and there was nothing I could do because I was pinned under him.

I bit harder, my mouth filling with salt, and he screamed but kept on trying to stab me. I caught a flashing glimpse of Mimi circling, and wondered how long it would be before he finally succeeded in gashing me. Then an extra weight and a flash of tawny fur landed on Theo's chest. He screamed louder and Attila took off for the open back door in sheer panic. Mimi seized the instant to fling herself on Theo's knife arm. I heard her grunt when she hit the floor, I released my mouthful of neck to breathe and quickly sank my teeth in again.

Over Theo's shoulder I saw Barbara stir—she wasn't dead, then—look around dazedly, and begin crawling in the direction of our struggling heap. I wanted to shout, to tell her to arm herself, but with my mouthful I couldn't, and, as it turned out, Barbara had a neater solution than a knife.

She crawled on top of Theo and pinched his nostrils shut, then put her other hand over his mouth. I heard her hiss as he bit her, I felt him writhe to get free, but I didn't loosen arms or teeth, even when the pressure of his weight on top of me—I'd felt that before—and of Barbara's body lying across my locked arms began to make me dizzy. Barbara, I thought fleetingly, we were on the right track all along. I gave up too soon.

With the respite Barbara afforded her, Mimi scrambled halfway up and knelt on Theo's knife arm, and after a few seconds he had to let the knife go. I spied Mimi's hand snaking out after it as it slid to the linoleum.

Theo wasn't struggling so vigorously, now. Barbara was making sure he didn't get any air. He was on the receiving end of death, and he must have known it.

We would have let him die, I think, if only out of fear that if any of us let go he could attack again. But Cully came in the door at that moment to find three women and a suffocating monster in a heap in the middle of the kitchen floor, the Thanksgiving turkey upended under the breakfast table.

I didn't know it, but Theo was turning a strange color by that time. I could hear the funny noises, but I wasn't sure who was making them. The weight of two bodies was rendering me semiconscious at best. I was only capable of praying desperately that some end to the situation would come soon, and of keeping my grip around Theo's body and in his neck. I didn't even know Cully was there until I heard him say, "Mimi! Mimi! You can get off now."

That didn't sink through clearly. I didn't think it was safe to relax our attack yet. I tightened my hold with all my remaining strength.

"Barbara, he's dying," I heard Cully say quietly. "Let go."

"No," said a voice I barely recognized as Barbara's.

"Mimi, call the police, if you can." But I heard Mimi already at the phone before he'd finished speaking.

"Barbara," Cully tried again, urgently. "Nickie's being crushed."

"Oh," Barbara said in a dazed voice, and at last I felt a weight shifting. "Son of a bitch," she said, and I didn't know if she meant Theo or Cully.

"Nickie, are you all right?" Cully asked in a careful voice that irritated me immensely.

I had to unclench my teeth from Theo's nasty neck to answer. "I'll tell you right now," I said viciously in a trembling voice, "I'm not letting go till the police are here."

"Nickie. He's unconscious. I think maybe he's dead, or almost."

"Good."

Mimi's face appeared in my limited field of vision. There was a smear of someone's blood on her cheek. "He really is, Nick," she told me expressionlessly. "I think it's really okay for you to get up."

I trusted Mimi's judgment more than Cully's. Mimi had no mercy either.

"How?" I asked practically.

"Oh," she said, with the slow diction of complete exhaustion. "Well. Cully's holding the knife on him," she explained carefully, "so I'll just kind of shove him off." She tried. "Nick." She bent down to me again. "You have to let go, first."

Reluctantly, painfully, I unclenched my hands, then straightened my arms. I heard a shuffling noise as Barbara came to Mimi's aid. Slowly the weight toppled off me. I felt as if my pelvis had been crushed. I drew in great draughts of air and tried to pull my knees up. My legs trembled, but I managed. I raised my hand and rubbed it across my mouth, which was completely numb. My fingers came away smeared with blood.

"You look a sight," Mimi said, and a smile twitched across her face.

"I reckon I do." I absorbed that face, then slid my eyes over to Barbara's. I made my stiff lips move upward.

"Vampire," Barbara said succinctly. She tried to answer my smile, but couldn't manage. "We were right, Nickie. We would have had him in one more week."

They were helping me up when the police came through the door like a cavalry. When they pulled off Theo's gloves and I saw the network of nearly healed scratches on his wrists, I thought of Alicia, who'd fought all alone.

Chapter 14

NONE OF US QUITE FELT UP TO EATING THE turkey, so we ended up having ham for Thanksgiving. And we held the feast in the evening instead of at noon. After being up almost all night, we had slept late.

Cully had to do most of the cooking, since Mimi, Barbara, and I were too sore; besides, Mimi's arm gash was bandaged, and so was the bite on Barbara's hand. Charles was pretty incompetent as a chef's aide. He turned up about one o'clock and made a laudable attempt to be useful, but it became obvious he'd never chopped an onion before.

Before he got there—while Barbara was still asleep in the upstairs guest bedroom and Cully was rattling pots and pans—Mimi finally explained about Charles. She had been aware all along, of course, of my bewilderment at her shift in attitude. As it turned out, she'd had some hurt and confused feelings of her own to handle.

"I really was just being hysterical that morning he came to the door," she said through stiff lips. "I infected you with it." She was curled up at the end of my bed along with Attila the Hero. "I did finally talk to him when he came by my office at the college, and we had a long show-down on the phone." I remembered that evening; I'd had to wait for her to help with the dishes.

Mimi took a deep breath. "Because of our weird behavior the morning he came by, he thought I already knew what he was going to confess to me; otherwise I guess he never would've told me . . . This is going to sound like a soap opera, Nick. Charles thought I was so upset with him not because of the tussles in the car but because I'd somehow found out he'd slept with Sally, the woman whose party you and Cully went to last night."

Oh dear, oh dear. Right after Richard's defection to the woman in Albuquerque. Mimi's pride.

"Of course I didn't know anything about it. But when he asked me to forgive him, he also told me which night he spent with Sally; it was the night Alicia was killed. So he was guilty of screwing another woman, but he wasn't guilty of something far worse. Sally's husband was on a hunting trip, and she invited Charles over—she'd dated him years ago—and things just went from there. He was mad at me when he went to see her. For various reasons."

Uh-huh. Mimi wouldn't go to bed with him. And that must have been an extremely thorough confession, because that was how Mimi knew about the picture on Sally's bedside table.

"I was hurt and disappointed. I'm still not over that. We're going to have to have a few more talks," Mimi said grimly.

"Why didn't you tell me?" I asked bluntly.

"I just couldn't. I knew you were thinking some kind of awful thought, I knew you were upset, but you know how critical you've always been of the men I've dated. I just couldn't face your saying, 'I told you so.' I knew you didn't like Charles anyway."

"You're right," I admitted. "I wouldn't have been able to keep my mouth shut on that one."

So that little mystery was cleared up; not exactly to my satisfaction, but at least to my understanding. I couldn't feel fond of Charles, but I promised myself on the spot that I'd try to like him better. He had arrived like a shot the night before when Mimi had called him, and had wanted to sleep across the door to her room to guard her! It was a good thing the police had taken Theo away before Charles arrived. I had never seen anyone more ripe for violence. Mimi had finally gotten him to go home, but with a great deal of difficulty.

"You know, Mimi," I said to change the subject, "the day Charles was over here, the day we were so scared? And we thought Theo's coming saved us?"

"We let the wolf in."

"He came to get you, Mimi."

"I thought so. I remembered that day, when I was trying to go to sleep last night."

"He had gloves on when he came in. He only took them off when I answered the door and asked him to have coffee with us in the kitchen—when he knew there were two of us here."

"But in broad daylight?"

"Right after Alicia, he must have felt pretty powerful. When he failed that day, and he saw Cully's things here—remember what a prude we thought he was?—he must have realized he had to plan better. He probably had to scramble to think of an excuse for stopping by at all. And he came up with two. The committee meeting Alicia missed, all the stuff they'd passed. And coming to tea with Sarah Chase."

Mimi nodded as I pulled myself up straighter in the bed and reshuffled the pillows behind me. She said, "Last night I also recalled Theo telling me that same morning that Sarah Chase hadn't been able to call me because their phone was out. But when we went to tea, Sarah Chase was telling Barbara she'd called her apartment Saturday morning. It was such a little thing, I can't believe I wondered about it even for a second. I was about to tell you when that Scottie ran in front of the car, and it just went out the other side of my mind."

"He almost made a big mistake that day, Mimi. I can't believe he thought he could just walk in here on the spur of the moment."

"Well, he did. We let him in, didn't we? I don't think he planned it at all. You know what I think? I think he said, 'I just got that bitch Alicia, here I am driving by Mimi Houghton's house, let's see if she's alone. I've fooled everyone so far, they'll never catch me.' He was drunk with power. That's how I see it."

"He failed. So he tried again."

"Ugh, ugh, ugh. I can't talk anymore now." Mimi, though covered in a blanket, was shivering. "I think I'm going to go climb in a hot tub and soak. Barbara'll want to bathe when she gets up, so I better get in and get out."

I slept for another hour after she left. I was only vaguely aware of Cully coming in the room, looking down at me, and pulling the covers up higher around my shoulders. His long thin fingers touched my cheek. I smiled and slept.

OUR LITTLE GROUP WAS QUIET OVER THE HAM and sweet potatoes. I think we were all preoccupied with our own thanksgivings of one kind and another, and, more prosaically, we were very hungry after the excitement.

When we'd all settled in the living room with glasses of wine in hand, Barbara said, "Well, I guess we should talk about it."

"I'd like to know," I said, "what happened before I got here last night." I hadn't heard Barbara and Mimi give their statements to the police. I'd been too busy giving my own.

Mimi pursed her lips and launched into her account. I remembered her telling the story about Heidi Edmonds the night I'd arrived in Knolls, so long ago.

"We were just fiddling around in the kitchen," she said. "We got the sack of giblets out of the turkey and put the brace back on the legs. I boiled the sweet potatoes and mashed them; Barbara put in the cinnamon and raisins and found some marshmallows. Attila was on top of the refrigerator waiting to see if he could get some turkey when we weren't looking, and Mao was asleep on the couch in the living room." Just where the little cat had been, still asleep, when the whole thing was over.

"I guess Theo was outside looking in the windows only *after* I sent Barbara upstairs to look for some Kleenex. She was sneezing—she's allergic to cats—and the box I keep down here had run out."

"So he didn't know Barbara was here," Charles said.

"No," Mimi answered. "He thought I was alone."

I felt Cully twitch beside me.

"He rang the doorbell, the kitchen doorbell, not the front. I looked through the peephole Cully put in last week, but a fat lot of good that did me. Because when I saw it was Theo, I let him in."

Alicia had let him in, too. After all, it was *Theo*. Good old bureaucratic Theo, who was actually on our list but whom we *still* didn't seriously suspect!

"He looked funny, but I didn't pay any attention at first," Mimi continued. She barely knew we were there. Her hands were still, for once, clenched in her lap. "He asked if Nickie and Cully had gone to the party. Remember?" she asked me. "He heard that when we were leaving his house that day we had tea. But he didn't hear me ask Barbara over for Wednesday night, because I asked her when we were outside in the driveway."

I wondered how it had felt to Theo, to see two of his victims and a third potential one sitting in his living room with his wife. He must have enjoyed it. I recalled his pleasure.

"Fool me; I said oh yes, that Nickie and Cully had left at least an hour and a half ago. I assumed he'd been working late at the college, like he did often, to clean up something before he and his family left for Thanksgiving. I kept waiting for him to bring up some point he wanted to talk about, but he didn't . . . I began to get uneasy then, I think. I hadn't really worried earlier, because it was still early in the evening and all the other attacks were pretty late; except for Heidi Edmonds, and she was in such an isolated place. But I did feel a little funny. I went on and turned away to pour him a glass of wine, at the kitchen counter, and he came up behind me. And grabbed me. And put the knife to my throat."

Mimi took a deep breath. Charles put his hand on hers, but she shook her head very slightly and he removed it. I put my own hand over my eyes to cover them. I felt Mimi's fear.

"Of course then I knew what he was," Mimi said, and fell silent. Cully rose to refill our glasses. When he sat down again he put his arm around me.

"Even his voice was different," Mimi said very coldly. "He whispered. He told me what he was going to do to me. It was as nasty as you can imagine."

Barbara and I could imagine. Barbara and I knew. A couple of tears wetted Barbara's face and she made no move to wipe them off.

"And he told me why," Mimi continued.

I leaned forward. I wanted to hear.

"It was because we were successful," Mimi said to me directly. Then she flicked her eyes in Barbara's direction. "Successful," she repeated.

"He said that?" Barbara asked incredulously.

"Successful," I whispered.

"That was what it boiled down to," Mimi said. "What he actually told me was that we were arrogant women who had everything in the world and needed to learn a lesson; the world would go better, he thought, if all these damned bitches learned a lesson," she said tonelessly.

"I don't understand," Barbara said.

"Because of his daughter—Nell—being so sick, do you think?" I asked. I knew I must look as dazed as the others. Charles's mouth was hanging open.

"That was probably part of it," Cully said. "And you told me his wife comes from an academically prominent family. He hasn't gone very far for someone his age—to them. Stuck as a registrar at a little southern college, with a dying daughter and a wife he knew could perceive exactly how he was situated on the ladder."

"But she loves him," Barbara protested. "You know Sarah Chase would never say anything to him about—"

"But she knew," Cully interrupted. "Even if she never said anything, he may have been convinced he knew what she was thinking."

"Oh, sweet Lucy," Charles said disgustedly.

"And the added pressure and grief of Nell in the process of dying," Cully went on. "While all of you were going on with your lives, your rich lives. Alicia was loved and prominent, Nickie is beautiful and talented, Mimi is prominent and respected and pretty. Barbara had just gotten tenure, and she was in love. And that little freshman girl, that first one . . ."

"A little one, to practice on," Charles said with more acuity than I'd given him credit for.

"Exactly—the girl who'd done everything in high school, right, Mimi? The girl who had a future in anything she chose, an achiever of the highest promise."

"But he was always so polite to everyone, the women who worked for him thought he was great," Mimi said. "I can't understand how he could . . ."

"The women who worked for him were *under* him, had no ambitions to go anywhere else or do anything else but clerk in the registrar's office until they retired," Cully explained. "It was easy to be courteous. They were never going to top him. They weren't stealing his daughter's future. And it was easy to be polite to you all, too. Look at the power he had over you, just by knowing what he'd done."

"I'll never understand it," Charles said simply. "Even if I heard him talk about it, I wouldn't understand."

"I don't want to," Barbara retorted instantly. "I don't want to even begin to comprehend a mind that sick."

"That was all speculative, anyway," Cully the psychologist said cautiously.

I'd been thinking. "Mimi, he planned to kill you too,

last night," I said out loud. "Or he wouldn't have let you see him. He must have found out he enjoyed killing women even more than seeing them walk around with his mark on them."

Mimi nodded once. Charles took her hand, and this time she didn't shrug him off.

"What happened after he grabbed you?" Charles asked when the hush became too oppressive.

"Oh." Mimi pulled herself out of a grim reverie. She looked at Barbara.

"I guess he was so involved in cursing Mimi that he didn't hear me come down the stairs," Barbara said obligingly. "And I hadn't heard the doorbell because I had my head stuck in the closet looking for Kleenex." She sneezed right after she said the word, and we all laughed weakly. "I clumped down the stairs, as usual, but he didn't hear me until I came into the kitchen. I was just saying 'Mimi, I found them' and pulling one out to blow my nose, and I looked up and saw—" Words failed her then. Only the reminiscent shock on her face told us what she had felt when she saw a trusted friend and coworker holding a knife to Mimi's throat.

Mimi picked up. "But it distracted him, I felt him jump. And I pulled away as he turned to Barbara. He went after her right away. Then the lights went out."

"Oh, shit," Cully whispered.

"Well, it gave us a second. I knew where the screwdriver was because I'd had to use it to lever the brace off the turkey's legs, like I always do," Mimi explained. "A knife would've been better, of course, but I grabbed what I could."

"I'm just lucky he didn't stab me," Barbara said thankfully. "He bumped against me just when I was turning to run out the front door to get help. And I feel like a coward, that I wasn't going to stay to help Mimi, but it was the only thing I could think of to do."

"The only smart thing to do," Mimi told her promptly, and Barbara looked relieved.

"Well, since he caught me as I was turning," Barbara

continued, "I slipped and whammed my head against the refrigerator door handle, I think, and then against the floor when I fell. Two bumps. So I was just about unconscious."

"I heard Barbara fall," Mimi said. "I thought he had stabbed her and it was all over for her. I was trying to get to the kitchen door and go out the back. See, Barbara, I was going to leave you, too. I kept remembering all those thrillers I'd read where they tell novice spies or whatever to stab from underneath, so it'll go under the ribs instead of bouncing off, so I made myself hold the screwdriver that way and was listening to find where he was—"

"And then the lights came on and I was there," I finished.

Mimi then described our epic struggle to Charles. He looked half-proud and half-horrified. He'd certainly never see Mimi in exactly the same light again.

Barbara asked, "But why did you happen to come in just then, Cully? We could have handled it by ourselves, but I guess it was good to have someone untwine us." I heard the undercurrent of resentment. I knew, then, that we had all resented Cully's arrival, his resolution of what was, for all of us, a personal struggle.

Cully looked surprisingly sheepish. As well he should, I thought, suddenly remembering Miss High School Sweetheart. With so much going on, we had not yet discussed her. Possibly we never would.

"I missed Nickie at the party. Then someone told me her shoe had broken, and I figured she must have come home to change, so . . ."

He'd really thought I'd gone off in a fit of jealousy. If he'd only been worried about the broken shoe, he'd have called the house rather than set out in pursuit.

"Does anybody know if Theo's confessed?" Charles asked.

Barbara shrugged. "I don't know if he has or if he will. They'll test samples from him along with the evidence from all of us. Something will match up, even if he doesn't confess."

"And he told me he'd killed Alicia. I guess that'll be admissible in court," Mimi said. "Though you never know. Think about it and give me a verdict, Charles . . . Listen, gentlemen, I'd like a fire. Why don't you two bring some wood in? I got a pickup load from Mr. Rainham yesterday."

After Charles and Cully had slammed the kitchen door on their way out, we three looked at each other for a long moment.

"We would have killed Theo if Cully hadn't come," I said finally.

"Yes," Barbara agreed.

Mimi stared into her glass of wine. "How do we feel about that?" she asked her chenin blanc.

Barbara extended her thin hand and waggled it to and fro. "A little of this, a little of that," she said almost casually. We smiled at each other. Mimi smothered a laugh.

"We would have had to live with it," I said consideringly.

"Look at what we have to live with now," Barbara said in a savage voice.

"Alicia," Mimi pointed out.

"Sure, Alicia," I said. "But after the first satisfaction was gone, wouldn't we have felt . . . on his level? We might have felt horrible right then, when we looked at him."

"After our blood stopped singing," Barbara murmured.

"When the rage was gone," Mimi whispered.

"It's just as well, I think," I concluded.

Barbara ventured, very hesitantly, "Do you suppose, Nickie, that Cully's going to be able to live with seeing you with your mouth all bloody?"

If we had not been sharing this moment of close communion, she would not have asked that. Mimi would never have mentioned it, under any circumstances. But in this moment it was acceptable; a valid question.

"In all fairness, I wouldn't like seeing *him* that way. I mean, it's a pretty vile sight."

The others nodded.

"I just don't know. We'll have to see. It may have been too—maenadlike—for him to handle."

"The women who ripped apart anything in their path, in a kind of holy madness, one night out of the year," Barbara reminded Mimi, who had been trying to remember.

"Oh," Mimi said, flaming up. "You mean maybe we should have sat there nice and quiet and been killed?"

"Maybe if one of us hadn't acted, if just one of us had submitted, the others would have, too," I said.

"It doesn't bear thinking about," Barbara murmured, after trying for a moment.

"No," I agreed. "We shouldn't. We won't." We would try not to, anyway.

"Sarah Chase and Nell," Mimi said. "I wonder."

"If Sarah Chase knew?"

"Oh my God, no!" Mimi protested in horror.

"That was what *I* was wondering," Barbara said calmly.

I nodded. It had crossed my mind, too. How on earth had Theo explained to Sarah Chase that she was going to have visitors for tea? There was a slim chance that Sarah Chase really had intended to invite us. In that case, maybe he'd told her he'd bumped into Mimi and me by chance, that Barbara was the only guest she'd have to call herself, but . . . Surely even the dimmest woman would smell something fishy?

"Not *consciously*," Mimi said vehemently. "She just couldn't have had all three of us over that day. She just couldn't."

I had to agree with Mimi. "But Mimi, we can't go see her or call her," I said firmly, for I knew that that was what Mimi had intended to bring up. She would see the obscenity of it in a second.

"No," she admitted. "I—no."

Charles and Cully reappeared carrying armloads of dry oak, and proceeded to build the fire with much unnecessary hustle and bustle and advice to each other. They felt the pressure of our silence as we thought our separate thoughts and each viewed her own movie. The film was getting grainy and worn, the soundtrack fading, at least on mine. Perhaps I wouldn't have to watch those scenes much longer. Mimi was gazing at the bandage on her arm; she'd had to leave the sleeve of her blouse undone to allow for its bulk.

I had put on a dress, in honor of the day and my survival. Cully had zipped it for me that morning; my arms were too sore for the job. He hadn't kissed me then, even though I'd scrubbed my mouth till it was raw, inside and out, the night before.

He bent now, as he passed the couch, and gave me a quick kiss—on the forehead. He and Charles were going out for more wood.

I rose with my empty glass in hand. I walked to Barbara, stooped over her chair, and kissed her. I went to Mimi on her couch, sat beside her, and kissed her. She held me for a minute.

Then I went to the kitchen to get some more wine.

Turn the page for a preview of
the next Harper Connelly Mystery
by Charlaine Harris

An Ice Cold Grave

Coming in October 2007
from Berkley Prime Crime Books!

"I'm the sheriff of Knott County," the lean woman said. She was leaning over the counter that divided the front of the station from the back, and she'd been chatting with the dispatcher when we entered. I've never understood how law enforcement people can stand to carry so much equipment around their hips, and this woman was bearing the full complement, too. I never like to stare long enough to identify all the items. I'd had a brief relationship with a deputy, and I should have taken a moment then to examine his cop equipment. I'd been more involved with his other equipment, I guess.

When the sheriff straightened, I saw she was a tall woman. She was in her fifties, with graying brown hair and a comfortable set of wrinkles at the corners of her eyes and mouth. She didn't look like any true believer I'd ever encountered, yet she was the one who'd emailed us.

"I'm Harper Connelly," I said. "This is my brother, Tolliver Lang."

We weren't what she'd expected, either. She gave me a scan up and down.

"You don't look like a dingbat," she said.

"You don't look like a prejudiced stereotype," I said.

The dispatcher sucked in her breath. Ah-oh.

Tolliver was behind me and slightly to my left, and I felt nothing but a calm waiting coming from him. He always had my back.

"Come into my office. We'll talk," said the tall woman. "My name is Sandra Rockwell, and I've been sheriff for one year." Sheriffs are elected in North Carolina. I didn't know how long her term was, but if she'd only been sheriff a year, she must have plenty to go. Politics might not be as urgent a consideration for Sheriff Rockwell as they would be during election year.

We were in her office by then. It wasn't very big, and it was decorated with pictures of the governor, a state flag, a U.S. flag, and some framed certificates. The only personal thing on Sheriff Rockwell's desk was one of those clear cubes you can fill with pictures. Her cube was full of shots of the same two boys. They were both brown-haired like their mother. One of them, grown, had a wife and child of his own. Nice. The other one had a hunting dog.

"You all want some coffee?" she asked as she slid into the swivel chair behind the ugly metal desk.

I looked at Tolliver, and we both shook our heads.

"Well, then." She put her hands flat on the desk. "I heard about you from a detective in Memphis. Young, her name is."

I smiled.

"You remember her, then. She's partnered with a guy named Lacey?"

I nodded.

"She seemed like a sensible person. She was no flake. And her clearance rate and reputation are impressive. That's the only reason I'm talking to you, you understand?"

"Yes, I understand."

She looked a little embarrassed. "Well, I know I'm sounding rude, and that's not my intention. But you have to understand, this is not something I'd consider doing if you didn't have a track record. I'm not one of these people who listens to that John Edward—not the politician with an *s*, but the medium—and I'm not one of these who likes to have my palm read or go to séances or even read a horoscope."

"I fully understand," I said. Maybe my voice was even dryer.

Tolliver smiled. "We get that you have reservations," he said.

She smiled back gratefully. "That's it in a nutshell. I have reservations."

"So, you must be desperate," I said.

She gave me an unfriendly look. "Yes," she admitted, since she had to. "Yes, we're desperate."

"I'm not going to back out," I said baldly. "I just want to know what I'm up against."

She seemed to relax at my frankness. "Okay, then, cards on the table," she said. She took a deep breath. "For the past five years, boys have been going missing in this county. It's up to six boys, now. When I say 'boys,' I mean in the fifteen- to eighteen-year-old range. Now, kids that age are prone to run away, and they're prone to suicide, and they're prone to have fatal car accidents. And if we'd found them, or heard from the runaways, we'd be okay with that—as okay as you can be."

We nodded.

"But these particular boys, it's just—no one can believe they would run away. And in this time, surely some hunter or bird watcher or hiker would have found a body or two if they'd killed themselves or met with some accident in the woods."

"So you're thinking that they're buried somewhere."

"Yes, that's what I'm thinking. I'm sure they're still here, somewhere."

"Then let me ask you a few things," I said. Tolliver took out his pad and pencil. The sheriff looked surprised, as if the last thing she'd ever expected had been that I would ask her questions.

"Okay, shoot," Sandra Rockwell said, after a brief pause.

"Are there bodies of water in the county?"

"Yes, there's Grunyan's Pond and Pine Landing Lake. And several streams."

"Have they been searched?"

"Yes. A couple of us dive, and we've searched as well as we can. Nothing's come to the surface, either. Both of those spots are well used, and anything that comes up and a lot of things that go down have been found, when they're there to find. And I'm sure the pond's clear. Still, it's possible that there's something in the deepest part of the lake."

The sheriff clearly believed that wasn't likely.

"What did the missing boys have in common?"

"Besides their age range? Not much, except they're gone."

"All white?"

"Oh. Yes."

"All go to the same school?"

"No. Four of them to the local high school, one of them to the junior high, one of them to the private academy, Randolph Prep."

"The past five years, you said? Do they vanish at the same time of year?"

She looked at a file on her desk, opened it. Flipped over a few pages. "No," she said. "Two in the fall, three in the spring, one in the summer."

None in the winter, when the conditions would be worst for an outdoor interment—so she was probably right. The boys were buried somewhere.

"You think the same person killed them all," I said. I was guessing, but it was a good guess.

"Yes," she said. "That's what I think."

It was my turn to take a deep breath. I'd never handled anything like this. I'd never tried to find so many people. "I don't know a lot about serial killers," I said, and the two dread words dropped into the room like unwelcome visitors. "But from what I've read and seen on television, I believe they tend to bury their victims in the same geographic conditions if not in the exact same location. Like the Green River Killer, dumping most of his victims in the river."

"That's true," she said. "Some of them prefer the same location. Then they can visit it over and over. To remember." She'd done her homework.

"How do you think I can help?"

"Tell me how you work. How do you find bodies?"

"My sister does two things," Tolliver said, launching into his familiar spiel. "She can find bodies, and she can determine the cause of death. If we have to search for a body, obviously that's going to take longer than someone taking her to the local cemetery, pointing to a grave, and wanting to know what killed the person in the grave."

The sheriff nodded. "It costs more."

"Yes," Tolliver said. There was no way to dress that up and make it prettier, so he didn't. Sheriff Rockwell didn't flinch or try to make us feel guilty about earning a living as some people did. They acted like we were ambulance chasers. This was all I could do, my sole unique ability; and I was determined to bank as much money as I could while it was still operative. Someday, as quickly as it had been given to me, it might be taken away. I imagined I would be glad; but I would also be unemployed.

"How do you decide where to look?" the sheriff asked.

"We get as much information as we can. What did you find after the disappearances?" Tolliver asked. "Any physical clues?"

The sheriff very sensibly got out a map of the county. After she spread it out over her desk, we all three rose to peer at it. "Here we are," she said. "Here's Doraville. It's the county seat. This is a poor county, rural. We're in the foothills, as you see. There's some hilly land and there's some steep land and there's a valley or two with some level acres."

We nodded. Doraville itself was a town strewn about on many levels.

"Three of them had vehicles of their own," Sheriff

Rockwell said. "We found Chester Cameron's old pickup up here, in the parking lot at the head of the hiking trail."

"He was the first one?" I asked.

"Yes, he was the first one." Her face tightened all over. "I was a deputy then. We searched all along that trail for hours and hours. It goes through some steep terrain, and we looked for signs of a fall or an animal attack. We found nothing. He'd gone missing after football practice in the middle of September. This was when Abe Madden was sheriff." She shook her head, trying to shake the bad memories out of it. "We never found anything. He came from a tough home; mom drank too much, divorced. His dad was gone and stayed gone."

She took a deep breath. "Next gone was Tyler Webb, who was sixteen. Went missing on a Saturday after swimming with friends at Grunyan's Pond, a summer afternoon. We found his car here, at the rest stop off the interstate." She pointed to the spot, which wasn't too far (as the crow flies) west of Doraville. About as far as the trailhead parking lot was from north Doraville. "Tyler's stuff was in the car; his driver's license, his towel, his T-shirt. But no one ever saw him again."

"No other fingerprints?"

"No. A few of Tyler's, a few of his friends', and that's all. None on the wheel or door handle. They were clean."

"Weren't you wondering by then?"

"I was," she said. "Sheriff Madden wasn't." She shrugged. "It was pretty easy to believe Chester had run off, but leaving his pickup behind? I didn't think so. But he had a tough time at home, he'd broken up with his girlfriend, and he wasn't doing well in school. So maybe he was a suicide and we simply hadn't found his body. We looked, God knows. Abe figured someone would come across his remains eventually. But Tyler was a whole different kettle of fish. He had a very close family, real devout boy, one of the solid kids. There just didn't seem to be any way he would run off or kill himself, or anything like that. But by then Abe wouldn't hear a word on the subject. He'd found out he had heart trouble by then, and he didn't want to upset himself."

There was a little moment of silence.

"Then?" I said.

"Then Dylan Lassiter. Dylan didn't have a car. He told his grandmother he was going to walk over three streets to see a friend, but he never got there. A ball cap that might have been his was found here." She pointed a finger to a spot on the map. "That's Shady Grove Cemetery," she said.

"Okay, a message," I said.

"Maybe, maybe the wind blew it there. Maybe it wasn't even his, though the hair looked like Dylan's. It was just a Tarheels cap. Eventually, we sent it to SBI—State Bureau of Investigation—and the DNA was a match for Dylan's. But it didn't do us much good to know that. It just meant wherever he was, he didn't have his hat."

This was certainly the chronology of a botched investigation. I was no cop and would never be one, but I thought Abe Madden had much for which to answer.

"Hunter Fenwick, a month later," Rockwell said. "Hunter was the son of a friend of mine, and he's the reason I ran for sheriff. I respected Sheriff Madden—up to a point—but I knew he was wrong about these missing boys. Hunter . . . well, his car was parked the same place Chester's pickup was found. At the trailhead. And there was a little blood inside—not enough to be able to say for sure that he couldn't have survived losing it. And his wallet was found not a half mile out of town in a ditch off this road." She pointed to a meandering county road that led northwest out of Doraville for about twenty miles before heading north and then northeast to the next town up in the mountains.

"Who next?" Tolliver asked, because the sheriff was getting lost in her own dark thoughts.

"The youngest, Aaron Robertson. Junior High. Fourteen. Too young to drive alone. He stayed at the school to shoot some hoops one afternoon after basketball practice. He always walked home. But we'd had the time change the night before, and it was dark. He never made it to his house.

His backpack was never found. No other trace of him." She pulled a sheet of opaque plastic back from a standing corkboard at one side of her desk. We looked at a row of young faces. Underneath each face was the date of the boy's disappearance. Hearing about it was hard, but seeing their faces was harder.

We all kept a moment of silence. Then Tolliver said, "The last one?"

"The last one was three months ago. Jeff McGraw. It was because of his grandmother that we called you in. Twyla didn't think we were getting anywhere, and she was right."

It galled the sheriff to say that, but she said it.

"Twyla Cotton donated a lot of money and raised some more from the families, the ones that could help. And she got some money from some people who just want this to stop, people not related to the missing boys in any way." Sandra Rockwell shook her head. "I've never seen anything like the time and energy she put into this. But Jeff was her only grandson . . ." Her attention strayed from us to the cube of pictures on her desk. Rockwell was a grandmother, too. Her gaze shifted to the last photograph in the row of faces; a boy with freckles, reddish-brown hair, a school sports jacket. Jeff McGraw had lettered in basketball and football. I was willing to bet he'd been a local hero in Doraville. I knew my southern towns.

"So you're like the frontman for this consortium of local people who've donated money to a fund to find the boys," Tolliver said. "Since the county, I'm guessing, didn't have the money."

"Yes," Sheriff Rockwell said. "We couldn't spend county money on you, or state money. Had to be private. But I wouldn't have you here unless they let me interview you. And I'm ambivalent about the whole thing."

Whoa, big words from the sheriff, in more ways than one. I'd never heard a law enforcement professional admit to being doubtful about a course of action involving me. Angry, disapproving, disgusted, yes; doubtful, no.

"I can see how you would be," I said cautiously. "I know

you've done your best, and it must be, ah, galling to be asked to call in someone like me. I'm sorry about that. But I swear I'll give it my best shot, and I swear I'm not a fraud."

"You'd better not be," Sandra Rockwell said. "And now, I've arranged for you to meet with Twyla Cotton. It only seemed right. After that, we'll pick the place you start to search."

"Okay," I said, and that was that.

TWYLA COTTON WAS A VERY HEAVY WOMAN. YOU read about fat people who walk very lightly; she wasn't one of them. She walked ponderously. She answered her door so quickly I figured she'd been standing right inside, since we'd called her to tell her we were on our way from the sheriff's department.

She was wearing jeans and a sweatshirt that read, "Number One Grandma." Her face was bare of makeup, and her short dark hair had only a few threads of gray. I put her in her late forties.

After shaking our hands, she led the way through the house. She didn't match the decor. Some designer had worked here, and the result was very pretty—lots of peaches and creams and beiges in the formal living room, dark blues and chocolate browns in the family room—but not very personal. The kitchen was Twyla's natural domain, and that was where she led us. It was full of exposed brick, stainless steel, and gleaming surfaces. It was warm and cozy after the chill gray of the morning. It was the homiest room in the house.

"I was Archie Cotton's cook," she said. She smiled at me as if she'd been reading my mind.

I'd had a white-collar upbringing for my first decade, but after that my parents had descended pretty quickly through blue collar and down below, so you could say I was a medley. It had been a case of riches to rags. Twyla Cotton had gone the better way, the rags to riches way.

"And then he married you," I said.

"Yep, we got married. Have a seat, hon," she said to Tolliver, and she pointed at a chair for me. There'd been a formal dining room, but this gleaming round table was positioned in a bay window at one end of the kitchen, and the chairs were wide, comfortable, rolling chairs. There was a newspaper and a few magazines, a little pile of bills, handy to the most convenient chair. Tolliver and I both knew not to pick that one. "Can I get you all a cup of coffee? Some coffee cake?" our hostess asked.

"I'd like some coffee if it's already made," Tolliver said.

"Me, too, please," I said. I sank into a chair and rolled up under the table.

In short order, we had mugs of coffee, spoons, napkins, and cream and sugar close to hand. It was very good coffee. The morning improved, just a bit.

"Archie had some children, already grown and gone," Twyla said. "They didn't come around as much after his wife died. He was lonely, and I'd been working for him for years. It just came natural."

"Any hard feelings from his children?" Tolliver asked.

"He gave 'em some money, quieted them down," Twyla said. "He laid it out to them about the will, and who would get what, in front of two lawyers. Got 'em to sign papers saying they wouldn't contest the will if I survived him. So I got this house and a good bit of cash, plus a lot of stock. Archie Junior and Bitsy got their fair shake. They don't exactly love me, but they don't hate me, either."

"So why did you want us here, Mrs. Cotton?"

"I've got a friend you helped a couple of years ago. Linda Barnard in Kentucky? Wanted to know what had happened to her little grandbaby, the one who was found a mile away from home, no marks on her?"

"I remember."

"So I thought about calling you in, and Sandra researched you all. Talked to some policewoman in Memphis."

"Jeff, your grandson. Is he your son's son? He's fifteen?" Tolliver asked, trying to lead Twyla to the subject we'd come to discuss. Though almost everyone we looked for turned out to be dead, Tolliver and I had learned a long time ago to refer to the missing person in the present tense. It just sounded more respectful and more optimistic.

"He was fifteen. He was the oldest son of my son Parker."

She'd had no hesitation in using the past tense. She read the question in our faces.

"I know he's dead," Twyla said, her round face rigid with grief. "He would never run away like the police say. He would never go this long without letting us hear."

"He's been gone three months?" I asked. We already knew enough about Jeff McGraw, but I felt like it would be indecent not to ask.

"Since October 20."

"No one's heard from him." I knew the answer, but I had to ask.

"No, and he had no reason to go. He was already playing varsity football, he had a little girlfriend, he and his mom and dad got along good. Parker—Parker McGraw, that was my last name before I married Archie—Parker loved that boy so much. He and Bethalynn have Carson, who's twelve. But you can't replace any child, much less your firstborn. They're all broken up."

"You understand," I began carefully, then paused to try to find some other way of saying what I needed to say. "You understand, I need some idea of where to search, or I might wander around this town forever without getting a location. The sheriff said she had an idea where we should start." America is so big. You never realize how big, until you're looking for something the size of a corpse.

"Tell me how you work," she said.

It was great to meet someone so matter-of-fact about it.

"If you have an area you think is more likely than any other, I just start walking around," I said. "It may take time. It may take a lot of time. I may never be successful."

She brushed that aside. "How will you know it's him?"

"Oh, I'll know. And I've seen his picture. The problem is, there are dead people everywhere. I have to sort through them."

She looked astonished. After a thoughtful moment, she nodded. Again, not the reaction I was used to.

"If he's in any of the areas you pick for me to search, I'll find him. If he isn't, I'm not going to lie to you—I may never find Jeff. What have you got, in terms of pinning his whereabouts down?"

"His cell phone. It was found on the Madison road. I can show you the exact spot." She showed me Jeff's picture anyway. It wasn't the same one I'd seen at the police station. It was a posed studio picture of Jeff and his whole family plus his grandmother. My heart used to break when I saw the image of them alive, cradled in the arms of their nearest and dearest. Now, I just register the features, hoping I'll see them again, even if they're just scattered bones. Because that's how I make our living.

This particular gig in Doraville felt different. Time isn't much of a factor when you're dealing with the dead. They're not going to go anywhere. It's the living who are urgent. But in this case, time was important. If the sheriff was right, we were dealing with a serial killer who might snatch another boy at any moment. His pattern didn't include winter, but who's to say his pattern wouldn't change, that he'd take advantage of this slushy time between snows; plan a final spree before a hard freeze.

I found myself hoping that if I were able to find the missing boys that something about the way they were buried, something about the location or what was buried with them, would lead to the discovery of their killer. I know better than anyone that death comes to us all. I hate the murderers of the young, because they rob the world of a life that still holds potential. This doesn't really make sense, I know; even a dissolute alcoholic seventy-five-year-old can push a woman out of the path of a speeding car and change a bit of the world forever. But the death of children always carries its own particular horror.